SDW
9118

D0525055

ILLUSIO

By Sherrilyn Kenyon

Infinity

Invincible

Infamous

Inferno

Illusion

Instinct

ILLUSION

SHERRILYN KENYON

www.atombooks.net

ATOM

First published in the United States in 2014 by St Martin's Press
First published in Great Britain in 2014 by Atom
This paperback edition published in 2015 by Atom

1 3 5 7 9 10 8 6 4 2

A CIP catalogue record for this book
is available from the British Library.

ISBN 978-1-907411-56-4

Printed and bound in Great Britain by
Clays Ltd, St Ives plc

Papers used by Atom are from well-managed forests
and other responsible sources.

MIX
Paper from
responsible sources
FSC® C104740

Atom
An imprint of
Little, Brown Book Group
100 Victoria Embankment
London EC4Y 0DY

An Hachette UK Company
www.hachette.co.uk

www.atombooks.net

In loving memory of the real
Michael Tyler Burdette. I will always miss my
precious little Bubba, and you will forever hold
a special place in my heart.

ACKNOWLEDGMENTS

As always, to my friends and family who keep me semi-sane, and who put up with my absentmindedness and long absences while I work. To my friends and family, who are spiritual warriors and who fight the good fight for all of us every day against the evil that could harm us. To my editor and the SMP team who put so much into every title—you guys really are the best ever! And last, but never least, to you, the reader, for taking another journey with me into a realm beyond the normal. Love you all!

ILLUSION

PROLOGUE

Nick? Honey? You're not really asleep, are you?"

Nick blinked his eyes open as some loud, thumping song he didn't know made his ears ring. In fact, he was surrounded by all kinds of noise. Like a party.

What the . . . ?

He lifted his head from his folded arms to find himself not in the bed he'd fallen into, but at a . . .

Prom?

Yeah, it was a fancy prom with hideous swan and star cardboard cutouts, and enough pink fabric to make him feel like he'd fallen into a Pepto-Bismol factory.

Scowling, he scanned the darkened hotel ballroom

where his classmates were partying hard to some flashy DJ on a raised dais.

How had he gotten here?

When had he come to this?

Wait, forget all of that for a minute. It'd been late fall when he'd gone to bed. . . .

Weren't proms always held in the spring?

Yeah, they were.

Crap.

How had he lost six months of his life? When had he lost them? But what floored him most were the people sitting at the round table with him. Caleb was to his right, but instead of the pretty-boy jock he was supposed to be, Caleb was a bit heavyset and wore a retainer.

At a prom?

Huh?

Retainer? Was it a costume party of some kind? After all, it was New Orleans—the only place in the world where they could turn opening a regular envelope into a grand procession. Yeah, that made more sense of what he was seeing.

Especially the usually flamboyant Simi, who was

currently wearing an understated pink frilly dress down to her ankles with a sweater buttoned up to her chin. He frowned as he followed the line of her arm to where she held Caleb's hand.

Demon . . .

Simi . . .

With Caleb?

Yeah, I'm insane and the devil's cracking icicles in his hot tub. My dad must have sucked out my brains when he died. Or maybe this is Caleb's idea of a joke? The demon did have a sick sense of humor at times.

Please, let me just be crazy. The sheer magnitude of possible and awful paranormal alternatives made a straightjacket seem like the most desirable outcome.

Casey sat beside Nick, wearing a pair of thick glasses and an outdated dress that looked like something from a 1980s John Hughes movie.

Is this a dream?

It was too real for that, and yet . . .

"Nick, you're looking kind of sick. Like you're about to hurl. Are you okay?" Casey rubbed his hand.

No. He was definitely *not* okay. He felt like someone had just sucker-punched him as his gaze locked on a short, stubby . . . geek whose eyes and dark hair were all too familiar.

No . . . it couldn't be.

"Stone?"

He beamed. "Yeah, buddy. Should I call your dad to come get you? You don't look like you should be driving."

"I can take him home."

Nick went cold at a voice he didn't want to recognize. No, no, no. There was no way *he* was here. Why would an eleven-thousand-year-old all-powerful immortal come to a high school prom?

Not like the being would be bored, given all the things out to end them.

Don't look.

Don't do it.

But like a grisly car wreck—Nick had to. His stomach tight, he was terrified of where his nightmare would take him this time.

Stop!

The moment he turned, he knew he'd died and gone to the real hell. That was the only plausible explanation he could wrap his head around. The only explanation that made sense.

Because *this* . . .

This was the freakfest of all time.

It was definitely Acheron Parthenopaeus. All five feet tall of him, with short brown hair and blue eyes.

And in a pink tux.

Nick laughed at something that was a lot scarier than it was funny. But he didn't know what else to do . . . except scream, and that might get him put in a straightjacket for real.

Maybe I have lost my mind.

Yeah, that was a little more acceptable than this current nightmare.

He swallowed hard then returned his attention to Stone. "Can I ask a weird question?"

"If you must."

Raking his hand through his hair, Nick tried to figure out why he was having this screwed-up dream. What had he eaten?

Or better yet, had something finally *eaten* him?

But for now, until he unraveled what was happening, he had no choice except to ride this . . . horror out to its conclusion.

"What's my dad's name?"

They all laughed.

Yeah, so not funny. Nick forced himself not to insult them for their ridicule. "C'mon, guys. Just play along and answer the question."

Ash snorted, then answered in a nasal tone. "You know your dad, Nick. Michael Burdette. He's an accountant who works with Caleb's father."

Caleb had a dad, too?

Sure, and fat flying fairies made Nick's tacky clothes every night and left them for him in the bathroom.

Nick arched a brow at Caleb. "And your father would be . . . ?"

Caleb scowled at him. "What is your problem, boy? You know my dad is your dad's best friend and has been since forever. Caleb *Fingerman*? Hello? Mark's my dad."

Nick started laughing and laughing. He couldn't stop. Yeah, this was all insane. He must have been hit in the head a lot harder than he thought. "Okay, joke's over, everyone. Ha. Ha. You got me."

"What joke?" Ash, Caleb, and Stone asked while the women looked at him as if *he* was the one who was nuts.

Unable to deal with it anymore, Nick rose to his feet and curled his lip. "You know, for a joke to work it actually needs to be funny, guys . . . and this is not even a little." Angry at them, he stormed off to the bathroom to splash water on his face and wake up.

Something had to get him out of this nightmare and back home.

But the moment Nick looked into the bathroom mirror, he froze in absolute horror. Not only was he in an ugly blue tuxedo that he'd *never* wear, his hair was blond, and his eyes were an average gray color.

Worse? He was a lot closer to the sink than he'd been in a really long time.

I'm short?

Ah gah! Anything but that!

His heart pounding, he checked his legs to make sure they were intact.

They were.

And yet he was only five foot eight. If that much.

No . . .

I'm six-four. Had been since his growth spurt last summer. Panic rose high as he closed his eyes and tried to summon his powers.

That only made him panic more as harsh reality cracked him in the stones. *No, no, no, non!* his mind shouted. It couldn't be.

But it was. *All* of his powers were gone. Every last one of them. He had nothing. Not even a glimmer of the scrying or clairvoyance or anything.

I'm totally without and locked in Hades.

Horrified, Nick gaped at the unfamiliar face he saw in the mirror that wasn't his. He pinched himself and shook his head. It *was* him. Somehow he'd morphed into a short blond dude.

Unable to accept it, he tried everything he could to wake up. But nothing worked. He continued to exist here in this freakworld.

It's not a dream.

Somehow *this* was real. He was real, and he was here, wherever *here* was.

Madaug walked in and sneered at him. No longer skinny and nerdy, he was the six feet four Nick should have been, and ripped. "What you looking at, Burdette? Cruising for a date?"

"Burdette?" Nick repeated, looking around for Bubba.

Madaug shoved him. "Nick Burdette? Can't you even recognize your own name?" He rolled his eyes. "Dog, boy, how dumb are you?" He went over to a urinal.

Stunned, confused, and terrified, Nick stumbled out to the prom that was filled with people he knew but didn't recognize. Reaching for something, anything to prove this wasn't happening, that he was being punk'd, he pulled his wallet out and checked his license.

It was the "new" blond him in the photo, but what hit him like a kick in the crotch was the name.

Nicholas Michael Burdette instead of Nicholas Ambrosius Gautier.

"What the Hades has happened?"

And more importantly . . . how could he undo it when he no longer had any power and his preternatural allies were now all woefully normal?

CHAPTER 1

"Nick? Boo? Get up. You're going to be late for school."

Groaning in fear of what he might find this time, Nick opened his eyes to see the navy blue curtains his mom had bought him last year when they moved into their condo on Bourbon Street. Relief flooded him.

It was just a nightmare, after all. Thank you, God!

That was his thought until he realized that the window wasn't the same. Instead of being a large single window, it was two windows with a divider between them.

Ah, crap. Not again. *Haven't I suffered enough indignities and horrors? Really?*

His heart hammering, Nick slowly swept his gaze around a room he didn't recognize.

At all.

His stomach tightened to the point he feared he'd be ill.

"Nick?" His mom knocked lightly before she pushed open the door to smile at him. "So you are up, sleepy-head. Hurry now, or else you'll get another tardy."

Even more unsettled than before, Nick gaped at the sight of her in an expensive dark blue business suit with her blond hair cut short to frame her beautiful face. That definitely wasn't her waitress uniform.

"Mom?"

Scowling, she moved to stand by the bed and placed her hand to his forehead. "Are you all right? You look pale."

Stunned, he couldn't speak as he stared at a stranger in his mother's body.

"Cherise? It's London calling. They need to speak to you. Said it can't wait."

His eyes widened at the sound of that familiar deep, thick Tennessee Southern drawl. Bubba? What the heck was Bubba doing in his house at seven thirty in the morning? It'd been bad enough when Nick had come home from the prom and found him here. But that he'd attributed to a date.

No, wait. That wasn't right. Someone had told him at the prom that Bubba was his father now. Caleb?

For some reason, he couldn't remember.

And why in the world would someone in London call his mom?

Maybe London's a name?

No. Not possible. This was bad bad. His mom didn't know anyone named London. . . .

"I'll be right there, Michael." She squeezed Nick's cheek. "You don't have a fever. Did you stay up too late?"

Honestly? He feared some kind of terminal brain damage. How hard had that demon slammed him on the ground while they fought to get his mom back?

His door opened again to show "Bubba" in a black Armani suit. Nick only knew that designer brand because they were the ones his immortal boss, Kyrian, favored and Nick had had a seizure the first time he'd gone to pick one up and had seen the cost of it.

Who wore that stuff and why?

Huge as ever, Bubba had abandoned his beard for smooth cheeks and wore a short, stylish cut. Yeah, this definitely wasn't the burly redneck who hunted zombies in the bayou with his lunatic best friend. One who was paranoid as all get out, and armed to a level that the ATF had him on their watch list.

As if he hadn't morphed into some creepy businessman, Bubba came in and handed a cordless phone to his mom.

Removing her expensive earring, she cupped her hand over the mouthpiece and whispered to Bubba. "I think our Boo is sick. See what you think." She stepped out of the room to deal with her call.

Bubba knelt his gigantic form by the bed and brushed the hair back from Nick's forehead. "You all right, buddy?" Now there was a loving tone Bubba had never used with him before. That was even more terrifying than having a Charonte demon try to eat him.

Completely dumbfounded by it all, Nick dropped his gaze to the huge football championship ring on Bubba's hand. The diamonds on the front formed a pattern reminiscent of a fleur-de-lis. They were framed by the words "Forty" on one side and "Niners" on the other. The name "Burdette" was on the "Forty" side and "Super Bowl XXIV 55-10" on the "Niners" side. Gasping, he fingered the ring as he remembered Bubba's mama telling him how Bubba could have gone pro after college, but had decided to stay home with his wife and son instead. "This looks so real."

Bubba snorted. "It is real, you know that." He duplicated Nick's scowl. "What's going on with you, Squirt? You have a test you're trying to avoid?"

"No. I . . . uh . . . yeah, no, I'm fine. Not a morning person."

Laughing, Bubba stood up and pulled the covers off Nick. "Come on. Mom made pancakes for breakfast and they're getting cold." He left the room.

Still disoriented and confused, Nick rolled out of bed. This was so screwed up. Raking his hand through his hair, he gaped at the photo on his desk of a sweaty Bubba in a 49ers uniform holding him as a toddler, dressed in a matching 49ers jersey with BURDETTE on the back. At least Nick thought it was him. The face and blond hair belonged to the stranger he kept seeing in the mirror. It was a picture from a newspaper where the 49ers had won the Super Bowl, January 28, 1990.

What the heck?

In 1990, Nick would have been six. The "Nick" in the photo couldn't be more than three or four.

"I'm in another coma." At least *that* made sense to his scrambled mind.

Yeah, he could definitely go with that. Instead of being sent to the Nether Realm, he was trapped here, wherever *here* was. Caleb or Kody would wake him up at any moment and everything would be back to normal. He just had to make sure he didn't get sucked into a hell realm and eaten by a demon or zombie until they figured this out and performed another rescue mission.

C'mon guys, hurry. He wasn't sure how long his sanity would hold.

Cringing at what he saw in the bathroom mirror, he curled his lip. Gah, it was so strange to see someone else peering back at him. While he'd never been vain, he missed the way he used to look. The dark hair.

And height. He really missed being tall. Short sucked. How did short guys stand it?

Give me growing pains any day over this.

Turning on the shower, he took a moment to replay the last events he remembered through his mind. He'd been in *Le Monde au Delà du Voile*—the world behind the veil—where his mother had been taken after being kidnapped by demons. He, along with Kody and Caleb, had fought off the huge demonic werewolf Zavid and demons to get her and his father out. His dad had died in the fighting and he'd given Nick all of his Malachai powers. Powers Caleb and Kody had bound up tight until Nick could learn to use them, and to better protect him from the supernatural predators that wanted to kill him and take those powers for themselves.

Nick froze as another fear went through him. His powers were forever malfunctioning. Could the binding potion from last night be the reason for all of this? Had it backfired and changed everything?

Made sense. He'd once turned his friend Madaug into a goat by mistake. Maybe the potion last night had turned Madaug into a douche. . . .

And me into a short loser.

As he left the shower, he winced at his reflection. "And I thought I was skinny before. . . ."

Dog, he looked awful. His arms were so frail, he was surprised he didn't snap them off reaching for the towel. Not the image he wanted for the rest of his life. Toweling his now-blond hair, he tried not to think about it as he dressed and headed downstairs. The only good thing about this weird life was the lack of tacky Hawaiian shirts in his closet. It appeared his mom had finally let go of her *Magnum, P.I.* fetish and gone shopping somewhere other than Goodwill.

He paused on the stairs to gape at the photos of him, his mom, and Bubba from Nick's birth to high school. *Dang, is there not one incarnation of my life in any alternate universe where my mom didn't take a photo of me naked in the bathtub with a rubber duck? Really?* He didn't know what was more shocking, those weird non-doctored photos or the massive size of this humongous house.

For that matter, it took him several minutes just to find the kitchen. *This is worse than trying to navigate*

Kyrian's mansion. At least there, he had Rosa to ask for directions whenever he got lost.

Eyes wide, Nick hesitated in the doorway as he saw Bubba at the table, reading *The Wall Street Journal* while his mom cleaned up the griddle that was part of their massive gas stove. That thing alone looked like something out of an alien movie.

He'd never seen a more normal morning scene in his life. And that scared the bejeezus out of him.

She glanced over to him and smiled. "There's my favorite Boo. You feeling better, baby?"

Hardly . . .

"Sure, Ma."

Bubba checked his watch. "You better grab it to go. I don't want to have to talk to Mr. Hutchins again about your tardies."

Nick scowled at the unfamiliar name. "Mr. Hutchins?"

"Principal." Bubba folded the paper up and placed it on the table.

Nick was even more confused than before. "When did St. Richard's get another principal? What happened to Mr. Head?" Did zombies eat him, too?

"Who's Mr. Head?" his mom asked.

Nick stopped while he was way behind. At least until he caught sight of the date on the newspaper by Bubba's hand. His heart stopped. No flippin' way. It had to be wrong. "April 22, 2002? Is this a fake paper?"

Bubba frowned at him. "Maybe we should take you to a doctor."

That was all he needed. A visit to a psych ward. "No, I'm fine. Really."

Discreetly, Nick pulled out his license and checked his date of birth. His stomach hit the ground. If that was right, he was still sixteen, but that wasn't the right birth year for *him*.

Everything here was wrong.

How is this possible? How?

"I better get to school," Nick breathed. "Where's my backpack?"

His mom ruffled his hair. "I think you left it in your car."

"The Jag?"

Bubba burst out laughing. "You wish. I'm not letting you drive the Jag until you're eighteen, buddy. It's in your Jeep."

Okay, go with it. Don't react.

All is right in my world.

Yeah, right. Nothing about any of this was right or normal. Which, given his royally screwed-up life, said a lot. He wanted to scream until it went back to the way it was supposed to be.

His mom brought the keys to him and held her hand to his forehead again. "Are you sure you're all right?"

Better a lie than a straightjacket. "Fine."

"Michael . . . I'm thinking we might need to take him to a doctor."

"Sweetheart, you've got to quit babying him so. He's a man with a job. He says he's fine. He's fine."

Nick arched a brow at that. Could he still be working for Kyrian or Liza in this place? If Kyrian was around, he might be able to help. Surely a two-thousand-year-old immortal warrior who'd sold his soul to a goddess would know something about alternate realities. For that matter, Nick might be able to borrow Kyrian's ring and summon the Greek goddess Artemis himself and get some long overdue answers.

His mother bit her bottom lip as she brushed her hand through Nick's hair. "He's still my baby."

Grateful that hadn't changed, Nick gave her a quick hug before he headed for the front of the house.

Bubba cleared his throat. "Where are you going, son?"

"The curb."

"Why? Your Jeep's in the garage."

They had a garage?

Nick looked up at the ornate crown molding in this expensive house. Of course they had a garage. . . .

"Oh. Okay." He headed in the opposite direction.

With a slight hesitation, he opened the door that he assumed was the garage only to find himself in the pantry.

Crap.

"Um . . . grabbing some Pop-Tarts for the road," Nick said, covering his mistake. Still, they both stared at him as if he'd escaped Arkham Asylum. Offering them a fake smile, he grabbed the pastries, crossed himself, and hoped he got the next door correct.

Nope. Bathroom.

With a pain-filled groan at his rampant stupidity, Nick pretended to use it before he tried again. At least there were only two more doors to go.

Fifty-fifty chance.

Thankfully, third time was the charm. He let out a relieved breath as he stepped down and saw a red Jeep, black SUV, and silver Jaguar in the three-car garage. Man, that was so wrong. That Jag was the same car Acheron had given him when he'd brought Nick's license over to their condo.

I want the life back where I get to drive that *without Bubba flipping out on me.*

Then again . . .

This *was* a normal life. *Really* normal, like other people's lives. No one was trying to kill him, or eat him. He didn't have a principal who thought he was the biggest loser on the planet. Half the football team wasn't turning into zombies or werewolves. There was no psycho-demon coach threatening him if he didn't help kill his fellow teammates. Bubba and Mark weren't cattle-prod-wielding lunatics.

You know, this has possibilities. It might not be bad to

be normal for a while. Weird and poor hadn't worked out that well for him. Rich and well dressed might be another story.

Feeling better about it all, Nick decided he'd stop complaining about everything and just try this life on for a while. It might suit him.

After climbing into his Jeep, he made his way to school, where no one stared at him as if he'd just run over their dog. In fact, it was disturbing how little attention he garnered. No one seemed to care at all that he was here.

I could get used to this.

"Hey, Nick."

It took him a second to realize it was Caleb . . . Fingerman, not Malphas, who was walking up to him in the hallway.

"Hi, Caleb."

"Feeling any better?"

He scowled at Caleb's question. "Pardon?"

"I called to check on you, but your dad said you didn't feel well. That you went to bed as soon as you got home, without saying a word to anyone."

Yes, he had. After stumbling through the mansion

and finding his room, he'd been hoping it was all a bad dream and that he'd wake up at home.

Bust on that thought.

"Yeah. I think it was just a bug." Nick headed for his locker. As he tried to open it, the larger and snottier Madaug grabbed him and snatched him back.

"What are you doing, buttmunch? You trying to put a love letter in my locker or something?"

Nick shrugged his hold off. "I was going to my locker."

Madaug shoved him across the hall. "Yours is over there, doof. How many paint chips did you eat for breakfast?"

Scowling, Nick met Caleb's concerned gaze.

"Are you sure you're okay?"

Nick returned his backpack to his shoulder. "Can you keep a secret?"

"Always."

"I think I have amnesia."

Caleb's eyes widened. "From what?"

"Being slammed into lockers by dung-sniffing Neanderthals." Nick passed an evil glare at Madaug as

he walked past them. "I can't seem to remember anything. Like, where's my first class?"

"Did you tell your parents?"

Nick shook his head. "You know how my mom is.
I don't want to go to the Mayo Clinic for a hangnail.
I feel fine. I just can't remember anything."

"That's not fine, Nick. That's a big problem."

Yes, it was. But not for the reasons Caleb was thinking. "Please don't tell anyone, Caleb."

"All right. I'll help, but if it doesn't get better, you
really need to have it checked out."

"I will."

Caleb showed him to his locker and then opened
it after Nick couldn't. "The combo is your dad's jersey
number, your mom's birth year, and the year your dad's
team won the Super Bowl."

He arched a brow at Caleb's dissertation. "How do
you know that?"

Caleb shrugged. "We've been best friends since
birth. There's nothing about you I don't know."

Yeah, right. He didn't know that Nick didn't belong here, and that in another life Caleb was a badass

demigod demonspawn, and Nick was his half-breed demonkyn charge who was wanted by most anything not human-born.

Don't think about it. . . .

Grabbing his chem book, Nick stood up, shut his locker, then clicked his heels together three times.

Caleb gave him a strange look. "What are you doing?"

Nick sighed heavily. "Seeing if what worked for Dorothy and witches worked for demonspawn, too."

He scowled. "Dorothy? Demonspawn? What in the name of sanity are you talking about?"

"Nothing." Nick scanned the hall as he tucked his book into his backpack. "So where's Kody?"

"Kody who?"

"Kennedy. My girlfriend . . . sort of." At least she was whenever she wasn't trying to kill or confuse him.

"Did you forget that, too? Casey's your girlfriend."

So it'd seemed at the prom, but given Casey's bipolar *affaires de couer,* Nick wasn't eager to renew their "friendship." Honestly, he wanted to stay away from her for a while.

Just to be safe.

"Yeah, but where's Kody?"

Caleb continued to stare at him as if he'd grown another head. "Where does she go to school?"

Was he serious? "Here. With us."

He shook his head. "We don't have a Kody in this school, Nick."

That sick, awful feeling returned to his stomach. No Kody? How was that possible? If she existed in his realm, wouldn't she have to be here, too?

And if she was gone from here was that a good thing, or a really bad one?

"Hey, guys! Guess what I did?"

Nick cringed at the new incarnation of Acheron as he joined them. He still couldn't get used to or accept this person as his friend. His Ash was not normal in any sense of the word. He was the Goth king, Acheron, towering over Nick and the rest of the world with his massive seven feet of augmented height. An eleven-thousand-year-old warrior, Acheron was the epitome of lethal, in-your-face badass.

And with that thought, Nick felt that familiar weird fissure of preternatural power emanating in the air between them.

It was definitely Acheron's essence.

But as soon as he felt it, it was gone and he was back in this "normal" realm.

"Nick?" Ash put his hand on his shoulder to steady him. "You all right?"

No. His head swam viciously, and for a moment, he thought he might collapse. Everything around him was wobbling, like he was watching the world through water. Pain radiated through his entire being and settled hard in the pit of his stomach. He looked down at his hand that no longer appeared human at all. His skin bubbled then turned translucent.

Terrified of someone else seeing it, he clenched his fist tight and hid it under his shirttail. *Great. All I need is to turn into a human jellyfish right in front of everyone.*

That would not be a fun explanation to have to make. He'd rather back over his mom's favorite houseplant.

And still that wobbling persisted. Something was seriously wrong with him, and he needed to find real help. Someone who could tell him what was going on and which reality was his. . . .

This world? Or the one he thought he knew?

What if everything in my life until now has been a dream? Or worse. What if it wasn't?

Licking his lips, Nick met Ash's befuddled stare. "I, um . . . feel sick. I . . . I need to head out. See that doctor you told me about." He handed his backpack to Caleb then started for the door.

"You can't leave campus!" Caleb hissed.

Nick snorted at Caleb's panic. "Stop me." He opened the door and went straight for the street. Yeah, he might get into trouble later, but right now he didn't care. Forget this normal crap. He had to have answers.

From someone.

Sprinting over to Royal, he went to Bubba's store, the Triple B. But instead of the computer and gun store Bubba owned, it was now a beauty salon. . . .

Everything in it was pink and white. Girly. Bubba would die to see this. His precious sanctum had been defiled by rollers and hand lotions. Hairpieces.

Celebrity gossip rags, instead of zombie survival classes.

There was no sign of the store where Nick had spent the last few years learning about computers, lunatic conspiracy theories, and pending government-sanctioned zombie attacks. How to protect himself from the undead, undesirables, and unknown. Strange, but he really missed *that* Bubba and Mark. Heck, he even missed the stench of Mark's duck-urine zombie-deterrent deodorant.

Grief-stricken and disoriented, Nick headed down the street to where Liza's doll store had been in business since long before his birth. Just like Bubba's, it was gone. Instead of glass shelves filled with handmade porcelain and vinyl dolls—some that doubled as stabbing weapons—it was another ubiquitous antique store.

This isn't right. He wanted to cry at the absence of the people he knew and cared about. Crazy and eccentric though they were, they were his family. He couldn't stand the thought of not seeing them again.

What had happened to Ms. Liza?

His senses reeling, Nick made his way to Canal to grab a streetcar so that he could head over to Kyrian's house in the Garden District. Bubba had said Nick had a job.

Maybe, just maybe, he still worked for Kyrian.

Maybe this part of his life hadn't changed. *Please give me something to hold on to.* Desperately, he clung to that hope. Something had to make sense. Something had to be the same.

Right?

Stepping off the streetcar, Nick wasn't sure what to expect, especially after all he'd seen so far. But if Kyrian was still here in this reality, he'd have to be a Dark-Hunter . . . wouldn't he?

Just don't be an attorney. Or something equally banal. Not like what had been done to Acheron. Nick wasn't sure he could handle *that* kind of shock again.

He slowed as he walked past a faded blue antebellum mansion. The windows were open and someone was playing a piano. Even though he was Catholic, he knew the popular Southern Baptist hymn that was often a favorite among the street musicians who sang in the Quarter. It was one Tyree's grandma would often hum whenever she shelled beans on her front porch when he was a kid.

And when the unknown older woman's voice began the strains of "Will the Circle Be Unbroken," a chill went straight down his spine.

There's a better home a'waiting . . .
In the sky, Lord, in the sky.

Back in Nick's world, the demonspawn version of Caleb had told him to listen to the signs that the universe sent him. They were warnings and guides.

Could this be one of them?

Did it mean that *this* was his new home and that he'd be stuck here forever?

Too scared to contemplate what it could mean for him, he crossed the street and made his way to Kyrian's. It wasn't until he reached the driveway that he remembered he hadn't had to take the streetcar, after all. He could have just driven his Jeep over. But then he'd done without a license all this time . . . it was hard to remember he didn't have to walk anymore.

And maybe that was a sign, too. His life, and his body, were changing faster than he could keep track of.

Nick paused halfway up the driveway as he realized another fact. There was no locked gate to prevent someone from entering the property. That didn't bode well. Kyrian wouldn't be so lackadaisical. Not with his safety, and definitely not with all the things that hunted him.

Crap.

Cold and fearful of what he'd find, Nick climbed the white stairs and approached the familiar door. *Please let Rosa answer . . . please.*

Tears misted in his eyes as every instinct told him to run. To not discover what was on the other side of that portal.

But he had to know. One way or another. And Gautiers weren't cowards in any sense of that word. Whatever fate threw at them, they faced it with a straight spine, and full on.

Prepared for the worst, Nick forced himself to knock.

An older woman in some kind of purple designer jumpsuit, holding a small gold Pomeranian, answered it. "Yes?"

"Um . . ." Nick swallowed hard, hoping this was Ms. Rosa's alternate form in this world.

Acheron and Caleb were now geeks. Madaug was cool.

It could happen to Rosa, too.

"Is Mr. Hunter home?"

She frowned. "I'm sorry. There's no one here by that name."

Her words hit him like a fist as he felt his hope deflate. He hadn't realized until then that he'd been holding his breath, praying to see some semblance of his old life in front of him.

Dang it all.

"Sorry I disturbed you, ma'am. I must have been given the wrong address." Feeling even sicker than before, Nick turned around. He'd just reached the steps when the woman's voice stopped him.

"Now that you mention it . . . I do believe we purchased this home from someone named Hunter."

Hopeful, he looked back at her. "Kyrian?"

"Yes! That was it. I remember 'cause it was *so* unusual."

Kyrian *had* lived here. That was a good sign. "Do you know where he went?"

Grief darkened her eyes as she stroked the dog's head. "Up to Jesus, baby. Sorry. We purchased the house as part of an estate sale after that poor man was

murdered down in the Quarter . . . but that was . . .
goodness . . . twenty-five, thirty years ago. Long before you were born. How do you know him?"

Nick blinked back the tears that suddenly stung
his throat. "He was family to me."

"Oh honey, I'm so sorry. Do I need to call your
mama for you? Or someone else? Are you all right?"

Nick nodded. "Yes, ma'am. I'm fine. My mama
don't need to know I was here. Sorry I disturbed you."
Completely dazed, he headed back to the street as her
words sank into his heart with talons.

Kyrian dead.

Did that mean that Kyrian had been a Dark-
Hunter? That he'd been killed in action while trying
to protect humans? Or had he been normal and living
in this time period, too?

Gah, trying to unravel this made his head feel like
it was going to explode.

I am too young for this. He should be at home playing ungodly amounts of Nintendo. Hanging out with
his friends, talking about girls and manga. Or doing
whatever it was that normal kids did.

"Ow! Hey! Hello? I'm standing here."

He jumped at the outraged cry as he realized he'd been so lost in thought that he'd accidentally bumped into someone on the street corner. "Sorry." He looked up into a familiar pair of blue eyes and a face he knew real well, even though the hair was brown and a frizzy mess of curls instead of the dyed black he was used to on her. "Tabitha?"

With an exasperated sound, she rolled her eyes. "Please tell me you're not one of Tabby's zoo crew. Though to be honest, they don't usually get us confused." She held her hand out to him. "I'm her sister Selena. You are?"

"Nick." He shook her hand as hope sprung up new again inside him. *Please, God. Give me this one bit . . .* "Tabby still stalking the undead?"

"Oh God . . . you really *do* know her."

Laughing in relief at something familiar, he noted Selena's unorthodox appearance. She had on an embroidered purple skirt and white tank top with a fringed brown leather jacket. Not to mention the purple and pink Tarot Card Reader price list poster tucked under her arm. "You're psychic?"

She arched a brow at him. "Obviously, *you're* not. Observant either, for that matter. Strike two for you."

For once, he ignored her sarcasm. He was too grateful to have someone "normal" and familiar around him. And right now, getting some real answers was much more important than firing back an equally nasty retort. "Do you believe in past lives and alternate universes and stuff?"

"Of course I do. It pays my rent."

She was making it harder and harder to hold his smart aleck in. "No, I'm serious."

Selena pinned him with a stern frown. "So am I. I'm not one of the fakes on the street. I honestly believe in what I do. I know for a fact that it's all real."

"Then could you help me?"

"Help you what?"

"Find my way home."

CHAPTER 2

Pursing her lips in sympathy, Selena patted Nick on his shoulder. "Sure, kid. Where do you live?"

Nick shook his head. "Not like that. You said you believe in alternate realities, right?"

"Yeah."

He braced himself to sound like the absolute flaming moron lunatic he was. *Just don't call the cops on me.* He had no desire to repeat *that* nightmare. "I'm not from *here*, okay? I went to sleep in my world or dimension or whatever it's called, and I woke up here in this one. And no offense, this one is . . ." He bit back the word *weird*, because it wasn't weird. It was normal. But for him, normal was the strangest kind of weird imaginable. "I don't belong here and I want to go home. Please help me return to my world."

She took a step back. Not that he blamed her. If someone had said that to him, he'd have been running for safety in the opposite direction after the third word out of their mouth. Said a lot for her that she was only staring at him.

Nick started to close the gap between them, then stopped himself. If he did that, she might bolt. "Look. I know I sound crazy, okay? But in my world, your sister Tabitha has a boyfriend named Eric St. James. She graduated from St. Mary's, and your aunt Ana owns a Voodoo shop named Erzulie's on the corner of Royal and St. Ann. Your sister, Tiyana, who's named after her, works there, too." He clapped his hands as he remembered another detail he hoped was still right. "And Tabitha has a twin named Amanda, and um . . . what's her name . . . your other sister's a midwife who did an internship with a woman named Menyara Chartier—my godmother. And your aunt Kalila, who isn't really your aunt, but your mom's best friend from childhood, does the Haunted History vampire and Voodoo tours in the Quarter. I've handed out flyers for her and Sid. And you have another blood-related aunt who owns Pandora's Box on Bourbon Street. Tabitha works there sometimes, and in your aunt Zenobia's jewelry store on Royal."

Selena burst out laughing then sobered. "Wait a minute . . . you're really not lying. You believe everything you just said to me."

"It's the truth . . . at least it is where I come from."

She reached out and cupped his cheek before she pulled him against her and held him close. Nick wasn't sure why she was sexually harassing him, but he didn't fight her hug. Instead, he held his breath, praying she believed him.

After several really long, uncomfortable minutes, she let him go. Stroking his cheek in a motherly fashion, she nodded. "All right. We need to find out about your home and see about returning you to it."

Really? That was it? He'd expected a little more fanfare or argument. "You believe me?"

She shrugged. "Honestly? I'm not sure. But you're either one heck of a stalker to know all those names of my family members or . . . Tell you what, let me drop my stuff off with my friend who has a stand in the Square that's right beside mine. Walk with me and—"

Nick interrupted her as everything fell into place for him. "You're Madame Selene, aren't you? I've seen your stand a million times as I walked past it in the Square, but I never realized you were Tabitha's *sister* Selena." Partly because he never really looked at any of the psychics there.

As far back as he could remember, his mother had always been adamantly opposed to them as fakes and frauds, and since he'd learned what he really was, he'd been too afraid to go near them in case they weren't all charlatans. With the paranormal price on his head, it paid to be cautious. Last thing he needed was a psychic trying to collect his bounty like everyone else.

Or worse, his Malachai powers.

But this one . . . her elaborate stand was hard to miss, even from a distance. "You're the psychic who has the card table right outside the Visitor's Center next to that artist woman who has all those pastels of landmarks . . . Sunshine Artworks."

She appeared impressed. "Who's your mama, boy?"

"Cherise Gautier." He smacked himself on the

forehead as he remembered she was different now. "In *my* time. Here, she's Cherise Burdette née Gautier."

Gaping, Selena laughed. "Triple Threat Burdette? The huge football player's wife?"

Triple Threat . . . yeah, that definitely described the man Nick knew so well. Much more apropos than the Triple B Bubba used in his realm. "You know Bubba?"

"I know Cherise and Michael both. Cherise and I used to work at the Café Pontalba together when we were in college. It's how they met. Michael was in town for a game. But I haven't talked to her in years."

"Yeah, well, I talked to her this morning, and if she hears one word of this, she'll have me committed."

Selena laughed. "Boy, any sane person would have you committed. You're so lucky I'm nuts and that I accept the impossible as everyday fact." She looped her arm through his and pulled him in the direction of the streetcar.

As they walked, there was something about her that confused him even more than waking up in this bizarre place. "Why are you exactly the same when no one else is?"

"I wouldn't say *no one*. Tabitha doesn't sound like

she's all that different. Tiyana, either. My theory would be that some of us are just too dang stubborn to be anyone else. Our personalities are so strong or intense that no matter where you put us, we'd still be us. Or you could say that the universe wills it so. Does it really matter?"

"Does to me, especially right now."

"Why?"

" 'Cause some of the changes of the people I know don't make any kind of sense, especially given what you just said. Trust me, no one has a stronger personality than they do." He stopped short of mentioning that Caleb and Simi were demons in his world or that Acheron was an immortal . . . something with a great deal of power. How could they be those things in his world and be typical humans here, while Selena and possibly Tabitha were the same in both places?

Just didn't make sense to him at all.

Selena patted his arm. "Well, don't worry about it. We're going to fix your situation and find out what's really happening."

He caught the underlying note in her voice that sent a shiver down his spine. "What do you mean?"

"Well, if you're here and this isn't where you're supposed to be, and yet there was another Nick living here before you arrived, it begs the question of where that other Nick went, doesn't it?"

Ah, dang. He hadn't even thought of that. His newly spawned ulcer burned at the mere thought. "Are you telling me there's some dude in my skin at home?"

"That would be my assumption."

Great. Just flippin' great. That was all he needed. Someone else screwing up his screwed-up life. Like he didn't do that enough on his own. But worse . . . the other Nick, if he was from this world, wouldn't know he was part demon, nor would he have the skills to fight those who wanted to enslave him.

Or kill him.

And that was just his mother and girlfriend. Never mind all the real threats to his life.

"You've got to get me back there. That Nick . . . he could mess up everything. Bad bad."

He could unlock Nick's Malachai powers and unravel the entire universe.

His gut knotting even harder, he allowed Selena

to escort him to her red Mustang, then drive him back to the Quarter. But instead of going to her stand like she'd said, she veered off to the corner of Royal and St. Ann's, where Erzulie's Authentic Voodoo was located.

Nick frowned at the pink building that was impossible to miss in both worlds. "Your aunt still owns this?"

Selena parked the car. "Sort of. Tabby and Tia are technically the owners now. They're making payments to her for it."

"What about Pandora's Box?"

She turned off the car and unbuckled her belt. "That hasn't been part of our family since our aunt was murdered in her store ten years ago."

Nick let out a sympathetic sigh. "Sorry."

"Thanks." She got out.

Before joining her, Nick took a moment to absorb what she'd said and lay it down with what Ambrose had told him about Nick's future. None of it made sense. Why would some things here be so altered while others weren't?

Totally twisted.

For now, though, he'd go with it. Not like he had any other choice.

He got out of the car and waited on the curb while Selena locked the doors. As they walked around the corner and neared the shop entrance, a weird sense of déjà vu hit him. Hard.

One of the last things they'd done before he'd been sucked out of his realm was to come here and buy the items Caleb needed for the binding spell they'd used on Nick's powers.

The minute Nick had entered that store, all heck had broken out into the longest night of his life. Now, it seemed like a lifetime ago.

How could so much happen in such a short span of time? But then that was life.

The hits just keep on coming. . . .

Selena led the way into the neat pink and purple store that was identical to the one from his world. Right down to the green shutters and dark shelving that held Voodoo dolls, spells, oils, perfumes, soaps, wangas, and all manner of things.

"Hey, Tab!" Selena shouted so loud, it made Nick jump. She frowned at his reaction. "You ought to see a doc about that nervous disorder, buddy. Reflexes like that, you must have been a cat in a former life. Congrats on evolving."

He didn't respond as he eyed the large Voodoo altar on his left that had been set up for the goddess Erzulie the store had been named for. Last night, Selena's aunt had threatened his body parts if he touched it or any of the offerings that lined it and the floor around it.

Tabitha most likely wouldn't give a warning shot. She'd just geld him.

And speak of the devil, she came out of the back room. Only she was much more sedate. Gone was the Queen of the Damned-and-Emo and in her place was a woman in a muted blue sweater and jeans.

She brushed a hand through her dark auburn hair. "Tabby isn't here. She and Tia ran off to the rock shop for some new shipment they"—she made air quotes with her fingers—"had to see." She rolled her eyes. "It's another box of rocks. Really. What is it with you whackadoodles?"

"You must be Amanda," Nick said without thinking.

She narrowed a suspicious gaze on him. "Yeah. And you are . . . ?"

"Friend of the whackadoodles," Selena answered before he could speak. "Ignore the kid in front of the altar."

"Not a problem. I've got plenty of work to do in back. I'm teaching myself to make a Voodoo doll of Tabby I can stab with pins."

Selena scoffed at her. "That won't work."

"Won't stop me from trying. I obviously adore futility, as I've struggled to talk sanity into the lot of you for almost thirty years now." Amanda returned to the back room. "Don't touch anything and get cursed while I'm not out front to stop you."

Strangely amused by Tabitha's twin, Nick met Selena's perturbed grimace. "What now?"

She didn't answer as she began pulling things off the shelves and placing them in a small wicker basket that she'd picked up from the stack of them by the register.

"Are you making a potion?"

Selena held a wrapped package up to smell it before she added it to her stash. "No, I'm out of soap and perfume at home. My aunt makes sure that only the best ingredients go into hers and they're all natural."

Ah . . .

Nick glanced to the door and windows, and remembered Mark and Bubba fighting demons and a Hel Hound from the night before. Gah, it was so strange to be here where no one knew his real life. Knew what he'd been through.

Maybe I am crazy. Maybe *this* was his real life and the other a delusion. Kind of like *The Wizard of Oz.* Maybe the demon Caleb was just a manifestation of the boy he'd grown up with and Nick's subconscious had demonized him for eating a slice of Nick's pizza or something.

Could happen.

Certainly made a lot more sense than Nick had jumped realities for no reason while he slept.

What is reality, anyway? Really? Was it what he knew or what he *thought* he knew?

Man, a guy could seriously lose his mind attempting to make sense of it all. Closing his eyes, he tried one more time to tap any of the powers the Grim Reaper had taught him.

Nada.

Not even a burp or hiccup.

He was as powerless as the day he'd been born.

Irritated, Nick moved to the counter, where there was a small display of pendulums. They weren't that different from the one he had that Grim had taught him to use. Without thinking, he reached for the one made of jet. It should protect him from whatever evil was messing with him.

But the moment he touched it, it shattered into a million pieces. With a Cajun curse, he jumped back to see the blood on his index finger.

Facing him, Selena gaped. "What are you?"

Before he could answer, his chest began burning like someone had set his clothes on fire. Clutching his heart, Nick fell to his knees. Dog, it hurt. Bad.

His breathing ragged, he tried to center himself. To bury the pain so that he could function. But just like earlier at school, he couldn't. It felt like something was trying to suck him out of here.

Or take him over.

Worse, his hands turned translucent again.

"Nick!"

He heard Selena, yet he had no way of answering her. Words wouldn't form, no matter what he tried. Someone laughed inside his head. Only it was more like a roar.

With the speed of rapid-fire arrows, images flashed in his mind. He saw his own past and a past he didn't know at all. Bubba was the same lunatic he knew and at the same time he was the man who was his father here. In another place and time, he was a scarred commando in the jungle, fighting zombies and other things Nick couldn't identify. He saw his mother dying, over and over, in world after world.

His own future self on a demonic rampage . . .

Flames leapt around him as he flew through a destroyed New Orleans landscape that was littered with bodies and twisted remains of cars and military transports and weapons.

Sicut erat in principio, et nunc, et semper, et in saecula saeculorum. . . . Kody's voice filled his head. *As it was in the beginning, it is now and will be to the ages of ages.* Closing his eyes, he allowed her gentleness to give him something he could focus on.

Pax tecum, little brother. Ash's voice joined hers in his mind.

And then a third soothing voice joined theirs. *Speak your name, demonspawn, and I will give you what you want most. Peace will be yours. Forever.*

Nick scowled. Speak his name? That made no sense. Why was the voice in his head if it didn't know him?

I am crazy.

"Nick!"

Swallowing hard, he looked up into Selena's panicked eyes and saw what was to come for him in his world. "You summoned Julian of Macedon for Grace on her birthday. She set him free. And Kyrian . . ." *In six months from now, he's supposed to meet Amanda.* Nick could see it all so clearly.

That was why Ambrose—Nick's future self—had told him to stay clear of Amanda and Tabitha. Ambrose knew exactly what was to come for them, and by messing with the timeline, Nick could stop Kyrian from finding happiness and breaking free of his pact with Artemis.

Nick could stop Kyrian's destiny and thereby alter everything.

One life touched thousands. For the first time, Nick truly saw the vastness of it all and fully understood.

Every man is born as many and dies as one. With every choice made, a part of the future died and an opportunity was lost. You narrowed your options and steered yourself down the path of your life.

A path that led Nick straight to a fate he didn't want. He'd been born to end the world. . . .

To destroy everything he loved and valued.

Defy your destiny!

"Nick!"

Darkness surrounded him. It breathed into him and pressed against his chest until he feared he was dying. He couldn't get it to turn him loose. It was here and all it wanted was his life. His powers.

His immortal soul.

Nick shook his head as he struggled for consciousness. But he was losing this battle.

He was losing himself.

Give. Me. Your. Name!

CHAPTER 3

Houston, we got us a serious problem. All our thrusters are blown and we're about to combust into a fiery mess."

Unamused by Caleb's dire tone, Kody paused in her dressing to switch the phone to her other ear. "What demon inhalant have you discovered now? And who you got crying in the background? Is that Nick? Caleb, what have you done now?"

"Yeah, that be the very problem I'm calling about, and yes, that be your boy you're hearing. Only the crybaby is not *our* Nick."

She held her breath at Caleb's words. "My patience is out. Speak a language I understand."

"Fine. Nick ain't Nick. The Nick you hear woke up

this morning, screaming for his mom and—get this—his father, and saying that he's not in the right place or time. He doesn't know me. Or Zavid. He's never seen Nick's room before, and you don't want to know what he did when he saw himself in the mirror and saw a face that is not the one he's used to seeing. Just be glad you were at home, though to be honest, I'm surprised you didn't hear his supersonic schoolgirl scream all the way over there."

Cold terror gripped her. Without hanging up, she teleported from her house to Nick's bedroom, where she found him curled into a ball on his bed. Shirtless, he wore only a pair of dark blue flannel boxers.

Kody knew that long, ripped body that jutted out from under the dark blue comforter where he'd buried his head. But the whiny tone was one she'd *never* heard from Nick before.

With hair as dark as his alternate raven form, Caleb hung up the phone at her appearance. He gestured toward the bed, where Nick had his arms wrapped firmly around his head while he sobbed in agony. "Want to take it from here? He don't know me and he don't want to see or talk to me."

Then he definitely wouldn't know her. Still, she felt compelled to try. "Nick?"

Still whimpering, he lowered the comforter from his face. His lips quivered. "Do you know me?"

No, she didn't. She saw a stranger in those bright blue eyes. Horrified over this discovery, she narrowed her gaze on Zavid, who sat shirtless and barefoot in a corner on the floor. The newest member of their crew, he was a demon Nick had saved last night from a brutal death sentence. His hair was as black as Caleb's, and like Caleb and Nick, he was incredibly handsome with the unearthly beauty that always clung to preternatural creatures. "What did you do?"

Zavid curled his lips at her. "Sure, blame the Hel Hound. Like I did this. What is it with you two?"

She glared at Zavid and dared him to lie. "I didn't do this. I know Caleb didn't do it. Only other creature in this room with those kind of powers happens to be you, buster. What did you do?"

Zavid pointed to Caleb with his middle finger. "Ask your other boyfriend. That daeve demon troll bound my powers last night while I slept. There's no way I could have done anything to anyone. I'm so weak right now, I can't even shapeshift."

Caleb snorted. "Don't cut your eyes at me, punkin. The daeve didn't do this." Folding his arms over his chest, he met Kody's gaze. "Whatever happened in this room while I was asleep on the couch outside, swapped out Nick's soul and drained Z. Had nothing to do with me."

"Are *you* drained?" she asked Caleb.

He shook his head. "For some reason, probably self-preservation, fear, and intelligence on their part, whoever did this left me alone."

Scowling, Kody tried to make sense of their situation. But nothing added up. It wasn't possible for something to have gotten in here and done this. The Egyptian goddess Ma'at had sealed this house with sacred emblems that kept it safe from any preternatural attack.

No one could get near Nick inside his home. Not without an express invitation that none of them were dumb enough to issue.

It baffled Kody. "And nothing set off Ma'at's alarms?"

Caleb shook his head slowly. "Any ideas what could break in here, under the noses of three demons, the protection of a goddess, and do this?"

No. She had no idea. Kneeling on the bed, she cupped Nick's terrified face in her hands. "Look at me."

He obeyed, even though he continued to tremble and sob in a way their Nick never would.

It broke her heart to see the handsome face she knew so well, and not see recognition in those beautiful blue eyes. Her Nick was powerful and defiant in everything he did. Cocksure and sweet. The boy on this bed held none of the charisma or courage of her boyfriend and enemy.

Kody bit her lip as she used her powers to scan him.

To her horror, he was completely human. Not a drop of Malachai power or Nick's true soul remained inside his body. That wouldn't necessarily be a bad thing, except for the fact that he still had Malachai blood running through those veins. Even without the powers, the blood carried its own special properties that made Nick a very attractive trophy for those who wanted to use his blood for nefarious activities.

For that matter, his heart, eyes, or any Malachai organ, bones, and skull were even more prized by those who practiced the darkest magick.

A Malachai was the rarest and strongest of all demonkyn. Alive, they were lethal and hunted. Dead, they were priceless. It was one of the reasons a Malachai usually used the last of his powers to combust himself as he died. That ensured that no other creature could use any part of the Malachai to go after his son. To make sure nothing could ever enslave him once he was dead.

The Malachai was the most loathed and pursued creature in existence. He lived a life fraught with enemies, danger, and battle.

And this boy in front of her was in no way a fighter or a survivor.

He was Kibble. And Nick's enemies would tear this kid apart.

Scared for them all, she met Caleb's furious glower. "Could this have been done by whomever or whatever kidnapped his parents last night?"

Nick gasped. "My parents were kidnapped?"

She patted his cheeks. "No, Nick. Not *your* parents."

"I don't understand." He panicked even more. As soon as he pulled away from her and cringed against the wall, a blast shot past her, into him. One that sent Nick sprawling unconscious, onto the floor.

Gaping, she arched a brow at Zavid as he lowered his hand.

With a loud snort, he rolled his eyes at her. "Oh, like you didn't want to knock him unconscious. He's been whining like a brat for the last hour. I couldn't take it anymore. Instead of looking offended, you should be glad I didn't kill him for the headache he's given me."

Kody scoffed at the idle threat. Because of the laws that governed demons, Zavid couldn't harm his master. Not without causing himself an unbelievable level of agony for the rest of eternity. "You can't kill him."

"You seriously underestimate my threshold for pain."

She felt a heavy desire to strangle him and test that boast. "I thought you said your powers were drained."

"They're slowly coming back. Shall we see if I have enough yet for another blast?"

"Stop," Caleb growled. "Both of you. We don't have time to fight among ourselves. We have to figure out why someone separated Nick's body from his soul and who that creature is. Because, let's face it, they didn't do this for us. Or to make our lives easier."

He'd barely finished that sentence before the room went completely dark, as if someone had flipped the switch on the sun and washed the earth in night shadows.

Kody cursed as a new fear wrapped itself around her heart. "Please, someone tell me that's not an eclipse."

Caleb was the first one to the window. "I'm not saying it's an eclipse. But this round moonlike object is completely covering the sun. And it's really windy outside."

Of course it was. Kody groaned in agony of the portents.

Still sitting on the floor, Zavid rubbed his hand against his chin. "Does this have any significance?"

Sighing, she gave him a pained glare. "Not to anyone other than all sentient life forms on this planet . . . Never thought I'd envy a cockroach."

Zavid rose slowly to his feet and went into a predator's crouch. He turned a small circle in the room. "Do you feel that?"

Both she and Caleb nodded. There was no mistaking it. The very air grew heavy, thick. Like the hottest summer on the sun. Thunder clapped so hard, it shook the building and rattled the windows an instant before a heavy blood rain poured down outside, drenching the sidewalks with red water that ran like blood through the street. The winds outside howled with the sound of a dragon's cry.

"Well," Caleb said slowly. "We can look on the bright side."

She couldn't wait to hear this. "And that is?"

"Modern man will think it's from a meteorite or some other natural phenomenon. At least no one will be screaming and running for the mountains."

"Yeah, but they should."

Zavid scowled at them. "What do you two know that I don't?"

Kody glanced to the unconscious Nick before she answered. "Ever heard the term 'ušumgallu'?"

"The great snake? Yeah? What about it?"

"The door on its prison is now open for business and they're being summoned together." Caleb jerked his chin toward the window. "That piercing screech torturing us? That's the sound of the Šarru-Dara." That was one of the seven demon generals who made up the ušumgallu. Each one was deadly on his own, but when the seven came together, they were invincible.

Not even the gods could stop them.

"The Blood King?" Zavid laughed nervously. "That's not possible. Only the Malachai can summon together the ušumgallu and unleash his generals to attack."

"Yeah, I know," Caleb said, his voice laden with sarcasm. "But Nick's father was killed in battle last night. Whenever the elder Malachai dies, his generals are summoned together from their prisons for one task . . . to end the world."

"What?" Zavid breathed in disbelief. "Are you serious?"

Kody gave a subtle nod. "After the death of his wife and unborn child, the first Malachai arranged this as the final 'up yours' to the gods to ensure that if they broke their word and killed him, he'd take the world with him. Only his son, a full-fledged Malachai, can command the combined forces of the ušumgallu and send them back into their holes."

Zavid went pale. "And if we don't have a Malachai to stop them?"

Kody rubbed her hand over her face as she contemplated *that* nightmare. "The six demon generals will join forces and summon together their armies. Then they will cast down all the orders of this earth and rain hell itself upon all sentient beings for eternity. And no one, not even the gods, will be able to stop them."

Caleb flashed a taunting grin at the Hel Hound. "Doesn't it make you all warm and fuzzy? Just think what they're going to do to us for fun and prizes."

Zavid cursed under his breath. "We have to find the real Nick and stop this." He looked at Kody. "How long do we have?"

"Till the new moon . . . roughly three days. At that time, the ušumgallu will unite and come into their own."

Caleb let out a sound of disgust. "Even if we unbind Nick's powers, there's no way he can learn to control them in seventy-two hours."

Kody refused to be daunted. She'd faced much worse odds . . . of course, she hadn't really survived those, but still . . . They had no choice except to succeed. "Then we have to stop them before they're freed and can summon their armies."

"Where do we start?" Zavid asked.

"Absolutely no clue." Kody glanced over at the unconscious Nick on the floor before she met Caleb's gaze. "Did you happen to find out anything useful from our new friend before Cujo blasted him?"

"He's from 2002 and as near as I could ascertain, he lives here in New Orleans and attends St. Richard's."

Her jaw dropped. "2002? Is he the same age as our Nick or older?"

Caleb used his powers to put Nick back into bed, then he buried Nick under the comforter. "He's sixteen in *his* year, but apparently his reality is very different from our Nick's. Unlike our favorite pain in the neck, this one is completely normal. As are his parents."

Which made sense. While there were multiple dimensions and alternate realities, they were all bound by the laws of the Source. And those laws stipulated that only one Malachai could exist at one time, period, which was what had made her job so hard. Tracking down the one through time wasn't easily done. Especially when he'd been hidden as carefully as Nick had.

Caleb sighed in disgust. "I don't know about the two of you, but time travel isn't one of my powers." He looked at Zavid, who sank back to the floor.

The Hel Hound leaned his head back against the wall. "Same here. That is a very special and extremely guarded power. Only a tiny handful of species are allowed it. And Aamons aren't one of them."

Because the repercussions were dire. One misstep in time and the entire fabric of the universe could unravel. Even the gods tended to avoid time travel, and woe to any who willfully tampered with the time sequence. It was the most forbidden of all actions.

And the most heavily punished.

As with all things, any action taken caused an equal and opposite reaction. It was why she hadn't killed Nick yet, even though she had every right to and had been ordered to see him dead. Why she was so careful about tampering with the lives around her. Hers was a sacred calling and it wasn't one she took lightly.

Caleb narrowed his gaze on her. "What about you?"

"What about me, what?"

"Can you time travel?"

She intentionally didn't answer his question. Instead, she turned her attention to Zavid. "What about your sister? She was working with Grim to bring Nick to him. Could she be behind this?"

By the shocked expression on Zavid's face, she could tell he'd had no idea his sister had taken part in setting Nick up. The pain and grief in his bright lavender eyes seared her and made her ache that she'd caused him such bitter agony. It was a pain she was all too acquainted with.

His breathing ragged, Zavid shook his head. When he spoke, his voice was thick with raw, unshed tears. "My sister's dead. She died a long time ago."

Caleb's eyes shone with his own sympathy for the Hel Hound. Like them, he'd lost everything that mattered to him, and it was hard to make it through the day, knowing you'd never see your loved ones again. "Grim must have resurrected her for some reason."

His jaw slack, Zavid snapped his attention to Caleb. "You saw her?" There was so much agonized hope in those words that it brought tears to Kody's eyes.

"I did. She was trying to free you from Hel."

A single tear slid down his handsome cheek before he angrily wiped it away. "My sister was everything to me."

Kody had to look away as unwanted memories flooded her with pain. She knew that tone of voice. Had heard it from her own overprotective brothers on more than one occasion. "She was younger?"

He nodded then wrapped his arms around himself as if he had a sudden chill. "I swore to my parents when they were killed that I'd never allow any harm to come to her." He swallowed hard. "I failed them all."

Caleb stepped closer to him with a pose that said he wanted blood from the ones who'd harmed a woman. A throwback to the day he'd lost the only woman he'd ever loved to the hands of his enemies. "What happened?"

A furious tic started in Zavid's sculpted jaw. "She fell in love with an idiot, and when he ran afoul of Hel, she sold herself to the goddess to save him from his stupidity. Needless to say, it didn't work out for either of them."

Kody winced as she realized what had happened to the poor Aamon demon on the floor. "You went in her stead?"

He nodded. "I knew what slavery meant for our kind. I couldn't let my sister do that. I knew she'd never survive it."

And given the scars on his body, he was right. Nick had told her that the Norse gods had used Zavid for gladiatorial matches where they'd bled him to the brink of death. That they had dehumanized him to the point that he hadn't even remembered his own name when Nick had met him.

They had called Zavid "Beast," and a beast was what he'd become. All he'd known. Only Nick had seen through the feral hatred to the heart of the man.

Nick, alone, had saved Zavid when anyone else would have put their head down and kept going, leaving the Hel Hound to die. Especially after the way Zavid had attacked Nick and Caleb.

And her.

"How did your sister die?" Caleb asked quietly.

Zavid swallowed hard before he answered. "Zarelda tried to free me from the goddess."

In that moment, Kody finally saw the true heart inside Zavid that had called out to Nick. The Malachai was always able to see straight through someone's façade. To know their weaknesses so that he could destroy them more easily. Up until Nick, every Malachai had used that knowledge to hurt and to wound.

To kill.

Nick used it only for good.

There were so many reasons she didn't want to kill Nick, even though she had every right to demand his head on a platter. Even though she was under orders to do so . . .

Trying not to think about that or her past, she met Caleb's frown. "You think Zarelda might know something about Grim's plan?"

"No. But she might know something useful." Caleb shifted his gaze to Zavid. "You're the only one of us who can summon her."

He laughed bitterly. "No. I can't. Hel stripped that power from me as punishment after Zarelda tried to release me. I have no telepathy whatsoever. Haven't had it for centuries."

That closed that door effectively. Running out of ideas, Kody turned back to Caleb. "Know any necromancers?"

Caleb gave her a wry grin. "Actually, I do. Talon can commune with the dead."

"The Dark-Hunter?" Kody asked to make sure they were traveling along the same idea path.

"You know anyone better?"

Yes, but she'd purposely avoided Acheron. For many reasons. "How's Talon going to react if we show up at his cabin in the middle of the day? As far as he knows, we're human kids who hang out with Nick."

"Point taken." Caleb growled. "I'm out of ideas, then."

That left her with only one other option and it was

the closest thing to Acheron she dared approach with something like this—Acheron's demon daughter. "Let me see if I can contact Simi."

Caleb laughed. "Good luck with that."

"Don't scoff, oh ye who has no better idea."

He held his hands up in surrender. "Fine. Call me if she starts to eat you. Maybe I can stop her."

From anyone else that might sound odd, but since Simi was a Charonte demon with a ferocious appetite, it *was* a possibility. "I think I'll be all right. Just don't let Cherise find out she has two unexpected house guests and that her baby boy isn't her baby boy."

Caleb visibly cringed. "On second thought, I'd rather go with you and take my chances with Simi."

"Sorry, slugger. Cherise at least knows you. We can't risk her running into the other two on her own."

"Fine, but the next time something puts you on its menu, I *will* remember this."

"Yeah, yeah." Smiling, Kody flashed herself back to her house.

Her smile died the moment she saw the large recurve bow on her wall, over her bed. It was so hard to be with Simi when Kody knew what would one day become of them all. It was an ending they kept speeding toward, and one way or another, Kody had to derail it.

And while Simi knew Kody wasn't human, she had yet to guess the truth of who and what she really was.

And why she was here.

Most of all, Simi had yet to realize that they were related. Every time Kody saw the demon, she wanted to hug her. To crawl into Simi's lap like she used to do when she was little and have Simi rock her and tell her that the Simi wouldn't let anything bad happen to her. That she was the Simi's precious akra-belle.

But those days were long gone.

And there was much more at stake than just Kody and her family.

"Simi?" Kody called, reaching out with the power she'd been taught as a toddler. Like her uncle, she had the ability to summon any Charonte, from any realm. She could even control them, but she wasn't into that any more than her uncle had been. She didn't believe in taking away anyone's free will. Not for any reason.

Within a few seconds, Simi appeared before her, yawning so wide she exposed her fangs. Her black and red hair was rumpled around her small horns and as she stretched, her wings expanded.

"Were you napping?"

Simi shook herself and rose to tower over Kody. "No, silly semi-human. The Simi was sleeping. I know it daylight here, but in Similand, it the middle of the night and I was barbecuing dream sheep in my sleep." Simi cocked her head as she took note of her surroundings. "Where's Akri-Nick?"

Kody bit her lip. "We have a bit of a problem with that."

"You done broke up again? No, Akra-Kody. Say it ain't so."

"It ain't so."

Simi formed a small O with her lips as she considered the alternatives. "You lose him? Where was he when he got lost? You know, you gots to be careful with them boy-people. They wander off and do all kinds of strange things. Akri once accidentally wandered off and left the Simi alone in a whole field of moo-moos and forgot to tell the Simi that they weren't to be eaten. They's good, but off menu. Made that old Poseidon god very angry."

Kody laughed. "I didn't lose him like that, Simi."

"Oh. Then what'd you do?"

"I left him to sleep, but I think while he was sleeping he was sucked into another dimension and into the future, and someone else is now here, in his body. Can you time travel?"

Simi sucked her breath in sharply. "Akra-Kody, that's a bad bad idea."

"But can you do it?"

"The Simi can do lots of things, and as Akri say, just because you can, doesn't mean you should. But in this case . . . not without Akri, and he won't never let the Simi do that. He'd sooner give the Simi people to eat."

Kody sighed as she realized she'd have to go this alone. Not like that was any different than what her existence had been, but still . . .

She'd hoped to have some form of backup when she went into the unknown. "Then I'll have to do it myself."

"Alone? What? Why would you want to go and do that?"

"I have no choice, Simi. It has to be done. Nick can't stay unprotected."

"How you find him when you don't know where it is you lost him?"

"I have a general idea where he is. Kind of."

Simi quirked an eyebrow at that. "What if he moves? Boys tend to do that. A lot. They not real stationary creatures, especially when they young and virile."

Kody laughed in spite of her fear. Simi had a valid point. "Without his powers . . . I don't know if anyone can find him. We have nothing to use to pinpoint him with. But I have to try."

Pursing her lips, Simi tapped her forefinger against them. "Why don't Akra-Kody go ask Menyara? She always knows where Akri-Nick is."

Honestly? Because Menyara was the one being who had the powers to see through Kody's guise. To recognize her. Even though Kody was shielded, Menyara was also the Egyptian goddess Ma'at. And as such, her powers were infinite.

Since the day she had been sent to stop Nick, Kody had been very careful to fly below Mennie's radar. To never look her in the eye for fear that her great-aunt would see Kody's mother in her. Sense the bloodline they shared.

But as she heard the storms outside picking up strength as the darkest powers gathered, she knew Simi was right. They didn't have time to play around and avoid uncomfortable situations. She had to go see her great-aunt and face the past.

Her vision swam as tears gathered in her throat to choke her.

"Is Akra-Kody okay?"

No. She hadn't been fine in a long, long time. But she didn't want to share that. Not even with Simi. Thanks to the Malachai, she was alone in this world, and stronger than any being should ever have to be.

"I'm fine, Simi. I'll go ask her like you suggested." As she started to flash away, Simi took her hand and squeezed it so that she could teleport with Kody. As much as she wanted Simi with her, she knew better. What she'd need to say to Menyara, Simi couldn't overhear. If the demon ever learned who and what Nekoda really was, it could cause unbelievable damage to the time sequence.

Kody patted her hand. "I need to do this alone, Sim. Is that all right?"

Smiling, Simi nodded. "The Simi wait here then." Without a second thought, Simi headed to Kody's bed to lie down with her feet running up the wall. Simi's toes almost reached the bow Kody had received from her mother.

Kody laughed as she remembered being a small child and sleeping the same way. It had driven her parents to distraction.

Are you a Charonte simi, too?

Yes! she'd always answered back, proud to sleep like her favorite aunt. Many times, she'd napped on Simi's stomach with her legs propped on top of Simi's, while Simi kept her arms wrapped so tightly around Kody that it had been hard to breathe. Even so, Kody had never complained. Every child should be enveloped in such love. And so long as Simi held her like that, she'd known that nothing and no one could ever harm her.

Not without Simi eating them whole for it.

And both Simi and her husband had died while protecting Kody from the Malachai. Even now, Kody could see the horror of that night in her mind. She'd barely been school age when the Malachai's army had found their hiding place. Simi and her husband had stayed behind to hold the Malachai back while Kody's brother had run with her into the night.

Ari had used his own powers to shield her from their demonic pursuers. "I will keep you safe, Belami. Always. Nothing's going to hurt you so long as I live."

And just like Simi and her husband, Ari had fallen to the Malachai. Everyone Kody loved had been destroyed by the beast Nick was destined to become.

How can I fight for him?

You have no choice. Only Nick can defeat the ušumgallu. She had to save him. He was the only hope they had.

The time sequence couldn't stop here. It had to go forward. Too many lives depended on her, as well as the fate of the entire world.

Determined, she flashed herself to the front porch of Menyara's small duplex condo that Menyara had once shared with Nick and his mother.

Kody took a moment to compose herself. Because Menyara was her blood family, it was always hard for her to be around Menyara and not betray herself. Every time Kody saw the petite primal goddess, she wanted to throw herself into her arms and cry. To tell Menyara who she was and what was to come.

But she couldn't, not without destroying everything.

With a ragged breath, Kody knocked on the door and braced herself to meet her aunt.

Dressed in a light yellow cotton dress, Menyara opened the door and arched a brow at her. Today, she had her sisterlocks curled about her beautiful face.

Kody ached to bury her hand in them like she'd done as a child. Back then, whenever Menyara visited, she'd rock Kody and sing ancient Egyptian lullabies to her. Kody would twist her fingers in Menyara's hair and bury her face in the rose-and-hyacinth-scented strands until she fell asleep, nestled in Mennie's warmth.

How she loved this woman.

Menyara smiled at her. "Miss Kody, to what do I owe this honor?"

Kody opened her mouth to tell her what had happened to Nick, but no sound would come out.

Suddenly, she couldn't breathe at all. Her throat tightened as if someone was choking her. Tears gathered in her eyes.

Then everything went dark.

CHAPTER 4

Nick came awake to the sight of Amanda and Tabitha standing over him. His cheeks stung as if someone, probably Tabitha, had slapped him a few times in an attempt to revive him.

Amanda let out a relieved breath.

Tabitha snorted. "We're in luck, T. He's not dead . . . yet. We didn't kill him. Hallelujah! We don't have to call the lawyers or hide another body."

Another?

Scared of that thought, Nick scowled at the familiar raven-haired Goth queen who was decked out in black leather pants and a black bell-sleeved shirt. This was what he knew. Thank God, he was home. "What'd you do, Tabitha? Run me over again?"

She duplicated his frown. "When did I run over you the first time?"

Selena slapped at her arm. "I told you, Tab. He's from an alternate place where he knew you."

Nick winced at Selena's disgruntled voice. Dang, it hadn't been a dream, after all. He was really here.

With *them*.

Worse? They'd multiplied. There was now a total of five Devereaux sisters. Tabitha, Amanda, Tiyana, and Selena he knew. The other one he'd seen in a picture pinned by the register in the store.

"I'm Tiyana," the one closest to him said.

He caught himself before he mentioned that they'd already met here in this store. But that had been in a different life, and in a different time. "And you?" he asked the other one, who was leaning against the counter, looking completely bored.

"Karma."

"The woman who works with bulls?"

Karma snorted. "Yeah. And I'm the vengeful, mean one, too. You'd do well to remember that."

"Duly noted." Nick sat up slowly with Selena's help. He felt weak and dizzy. Disoriented.

What had happened to him?

"Now that *is* wicked."

He frowned at Tiyana, who was staring at him like a lab experiment that had just sprouted a new head from its belly button. "What?"

"Your aura. It's . . ." She locked gazes with Selena. "He's not crazy. What he told you is true. He doesn't belong here. We have to get him back to his realm or something terrible will happen there and here."

"I don't know. He's kind of cute. Can't we keep him?"

"He's not a puppy, Tabby."

Tabitha smiled. "Maybe, but he'd look awesome in this spiked dog collar I have at home."

Nick moved over to Amanda, who seemed to be the safest bet in this family of homicidal loons.

Amanda glanced at him over her shoulder. "For the record, if they attack, I'm throwing you at them and running for the door."

"Gee, thanks."

She shrugged. "How you think I've survived so long in *this* family?"

Tabitha cocked her head as she studied him with unsettling scrutiny. "So what are you, exactly?"

"How you mean?" Nick asked.

She approached him slowly until she had him pinned between her and Amanda. "You look human, but . . ." She took a lock of his hair between her fingers and studied it. "I know you're not the undead. You're blond, yet you're not a Daimon. Demon, maybe?"

To his shock, Amanda leaned forward and smelled him.

Stepping away, Nick screwed his face up at her. "Hey! That's gross."

Amanda shook her head. "Can't be demonspawn. He lacks their stench."

"Yeah well, I did have my biweekly bath this morning."

Amanda gave him a dry stare. "You still haven't answered my sister's question. What are you?"

"Mostly confused and, honestly? A lot scared."

Karma laughed. "At least he's not stupid."

Shaking her head, Tiyana snorted. "Karma and Tabby, don't bleed him until we know what we're dealing with. His blood could be potent. 'Cause let's face it. Things are only sent into alternate realities for one of two reasons."

"To hide," Amanda said.

Tabitha folded her arms over her chest as she eyed him with an unsettling intensity. "Or to be killed in a realm where they're weak."

Nick started to deny it. But like it or not, he was probably here to die and they were the closest things to protection he had, and while Tabitha was extreme, she could fight. "It's definitely one of the two. And if I knew how I got here, I'd know which one was right."

Karma pulled out a knife that was similar to Nick's Malachai dagger. "You threaten my family, and I *will* end you."

Tiyana pulled Karma's hand back. "Don't bleed him," she repeated through gritted teeth. "Blood has power and we don't know what blood *he* holds. Until we do, we need to keep him whole."

Karma put her knife away.

Shaken and trying not to show it, Nick turned back toward Tabitha. "Do you stalk vampires and Daimons here, too?"

"Yeah. Your point?"

"The paranormal exists here in your world, like

mine. Maybe we can find some of it to help me get back home."

Tabitha looked past him to Karma. "Sounds like we should take him to your house."

"Worth a try, I guess." Karma turned her head to Tiyana. "Unless Her Supreme Majesty objects."

Tiyana rolled her eyes. "You're such a bitch."

Unaffected by the insult, she smiled. "That's Karma, baby."

With a pain-filled groan, Tiyana headed to the register. "Take Tabby and Mandy with you in case there's trouble. Selena, stay with me and we'll search through our grims and see if we can find something about this."

Nick thought he was safe until Amanda held her hand up and a knife came flying out from the counter to land in her palm. She tucked it into her back pocket.

Gaping, he was stunned.

"Telekinesis," she explained nonchalantly as if that was an everyday thing.

Which, to him, it actually was.

"Yeah, I know. I'm supposed to have it myself. But where I come from *you* don't believe in any of this."

"Who says I believe here?"

He didn't comment on that dichotomy as Amanda led him outside to her white Toyota. He got into the back while the twins took the front seat. Karma eyeballed him with blatant hostility through the window before she went to her red Honda Nighthawk and pulled on her helmet so that she could follow them.

After belting herself in, Tabitha turned around to pin him with an intense stare. "Shouldn't you be in school?"

"I cut class."

Amanda pulled away from the curb. "You shouldn't do that."

"I know, and I don't normally, but extreme circumstances led me to the path of juvenile delinquency this morning. Besides, I didn't even know what my classes were or where they were. I didn't want to look like a complete idiot." He didn't mention the fact that he'd almost passed out at school like he did in their store.

Something was tugging at him and until he knew what, he didn't want to be around innocent victims who wouldn't know how to protect themselves from the paranormal should it appear and pick a fight. For that matter, he wasn't sure if whatever it was was trying to pull him back to his realm or join him in this one.

"So what am I like in your world?"

He smiled at Tabitha's question. "Very similar to here. But your hair is shorter and you wear tighter clothes."

That seemed to please her. "And Mandy?"

"She doesn't have any powers where I come from. At least none that any of you have talked about. She's the normal to your eccentricity."

She playfully hit Amanda on the arm. "I guess some things never change."

Amanda glanced at him in the rearview mirror. "What about you? How do you know for sure that you're not you?"

"For one thing, I'm a lot taller in my world. Have dark hair and my father's dead."

Tabitha gasped. "Triple Threat's dead?"

Nick shook his head. "No. In my world, he's a friend, not my dad. The man who fathered me is the one who died. Not Bubba."

"Interesting."

Nick didn't miss the underlying note in Tabitha's voice. "What is?"

"That he and you would be so different while we're not."

"Yeah, I know, right? I can't figure that out. And people I know for a fact are demons in my world are regular humans here. Why is that?"

Instead of answering, Amanda sucked her breath in sharply. "That's what you really are, aren't you?"

"Yes, he is," Tabitha said before he could even part his lips to speak. "You should have seen the dance his aura just did over that question."

Nick gasped out loud as he was pinned to the seat with an invisible hand. "Hey! I'm not like that."

"How do we know?" they asked simultaneously.

"Do I look evil?"

Tabitha narrowed her gaze on him. "Evil seldom looks it."

"Yeah," Nick choked out as the grip around his neck tightened, "but we all fight with *you*. And I work for a Dark-Hunter."

Tabitha scowled. "What's a Dark-Hunter?"

Of course she wouldn't know that. He'd forgotten

that unlike him, Tabitha wasn't really part of their hidden world. "Immortal warriors who are owned by the goddess Artemis. They spend eternity fighting Daimons and anything that threatens the safety of this world . . . or my world, rather."

"He could still be lying," Amanda said to Tabitha.

She shook her head. "No. His aura says he's not. I believe him. He has this whole innocent puppy look."

Great. That was so the image he was going for. He might as well be dressed as a dork again.

Finally, Amanda released her death grip on him. Nick rubbed his neck, grateful he could breathe finally. Coughing, he straightened his clothes.

"So what's it like to be a demon?" Tabitha asked.

"Like being human, except I have a lot of scary things who want to kill me and suck out my powers. Or worse, stick me in a cage so I can serve them."

Tabitha snorted. "Sounds a lot like my life."

"You think that's why you were sent here?" Amanda asked as she turned a corner. "Something's trying to capture or kill you?"

"No idea. We tried to bind my powers last night.

I'm thinking maybe the spell we used might have backfired."

Tabitha shook her head. "No. It takes something with serious juice to rip someone from their universe and put them in another. Definitely not a misfire or runaway spell. Had to be done intentionally."

That did not make him feel better. Kind of like a nail through his shoe. And if it was done intentionally, where was the responsible party?

Nick looked around nervously.

Amanda pulled into the narrow, tiny driveway of a small white shotgun. They got out as Karma parked her bike on the street in front of the house. After dismounting, she took her helmet off and held it by the strap as she joined them then led the way to her front door.

After she unlocked it, Nick followed them inside. "So why exactly are we here?"

No sooner had he asked the question than a bowl went flying at his head. With reflexes honed by fighting the worst of the paranormal world that liked to ambush him, he ducked.

The bowl shattered against the wall.

Tabby gave him an impressed smile. "Nice reflexes."

"Hey!" Karma shouted out in a hostile bark. "What have I told you about that? Until you learn to pay bills again, lay off my stuff!"

"Who's she talking to?" he whispered to Tabitha.

"Henrietta, I think."

He frowned. "Who?"

"An irritating ghost." Karma set her keys down on the small table in the foyer before she placed her helmet on the coat tree. "She came with the house and we've been at war ever since she told me to get out."

Nick arched a brow at her bravado. Had a ghost told him to hightail it, he'd vapor off so fast, all he'd leave behind was a blur. "Why don't you?"

Karma looked at him as if *he* was the one who was insane for asking a logical question. "My house. I told her when she learns to pay the bills, I'll move out. But I'm not taking a hit on the price just because she's too lazy to pack her things and move on. And let's face it, she has a lot less to pack." Karma tilted her head back to speak to the ceiling. "Start with me, and I'll break out the ghost torment equipment again. See how y'all like that, huh? I'll knock down walls, move furniture, and I'll start playing Bauhaus on all the speakers. I know what a big Peter Murphy fan you're not."

"Okay." Nick took a step closer to the door.

Amanda laughed. "Relax, kid. We're here for Karma to commune with the spirits and see if they know what's after you and why you've been yanked from home. With the exception of the Lalaurie mansion, her house is the most haunted in the city. There have been more murders here than anywhere else in Louisiana."

Nick was aghast at her nonchalant tone over something that traumatized him. No wonder Madaug was always complaining about his older brother and the family Eric wanted to marry into. Madaug was right. All the Devereaux sisters were nuts. "Are you serious?"

Nodding, Tabitha pointed to the living room. "There was still blood on the walls from the last double homicide when she moved in."

His jaw slack, he was completely flabbergasted as he faced Karma. "Why do you live here?"

"Any idea how much a house in the Quarter costs? Especially one *this* size? I got it for a steal."

"Yeah, but aren't you afraid?"

Karma laughed at his concern. "Baby, the scariest thing in this house is me. Unlike others, I know how to protect myself from the evil here and to torture it when it gets cute. Trust me, they have more to fear from me than I have from them. And it seriously pisses them off." She headed up the stairs.

Nick *really* wanted to leave.

And I thought my life was whack. . . .

"C'mon." Tabitha tugged at his arm. "We'll protect you."

Yeah, that was comforting. Never.

Nick glanced up at the large wrought-iron light fixture over their heads and remembered when the one in Kyrian's house had tried to turn him into hamburger. He really didn't want a repeat of that. "Just don't let nothing drop another chandelier on me."

With no real choice, he followed them upstairs to a bedroom that had been turned into a meditation room. Except it had an altar in one corner with a collection of African and Native American prayer fans lining one wall, along with leather bags, and rattles made from different animals. A dozen painted rawhide drums hung on the opposite side. The walls around him were painted a light blue with gold and white stamped over it.

Singing words Nick didn't understand, Karma began burning incense on the altar while Tabitha and Amanda sat on burgundy floor cushions that had been arranged in a circle. Karma sprinkled some kind of herb thing over him before she swept the incense toward him with a large handmade feathered fan.

Nick sank down on the cushion closest to him and looked at Tabitha and Amanda. They joined in with Karma's chant.

Some invisible force pulled Nick's hair.

"Hey!" he snapped, rubbing at his head where it stung.

Karma said something in that language he couldn't decipher.

"I hope you're telling it to leave me alone." No sooner had he spoken than another spirit punched him in the back, knocking him forward. His anger rising, Nick hissed.

The spirit jerked his hair again.

Furious, he rose to his feet to confront his unseen

tormentor. But faster than he could blink, something grabbed him by the throat and launched him into the air before it pinned him to the wall, right in the middle of the prayer fans. Insane laughter rolled through the room like thunder.

Unable to move, Nick struggled to breathe as something that felt like a boa constrictor wrapped hard around his body, squeezing it tight.

Out of nowhere, a deep masculine voice whispered in his ear. "Well, well. What have we here? A tiny little morsel, being offered for my daily snack? Don't worry. The pain won't last long before I kill you."

CHAPTER 5

Nick's ears buzzed while Amanda, Tabitha, and Karma tried to pull him free from the wall where he was pinned. But all their efforts did was cause him more pain. Tighten the hold of whatever had him.

I'm going to die.

He had no powers to break free. No ability to fight. And it was obvious the women were every bit as helpless against whatever was attacking him as he was. He tried everything he could think of, but nothing worked. His sight dimmed.

Closing his eyes and knowing it was useless, he called out for Caleb or Kody to come to him. He didn't know what else to do and it wasn't in him to not at least try to fight. Man, what he wouldn't give for one second of his powers again. Even a misfire would be welcomed right now.

All of a sudden, a battle cry echoed in the room. One minute Nick was blacking out, and in the next, he was free.

He hit the floor and landed on his back. Disoriented and paralyzed, he still couldn't move. His head continued to swim as he saw Kody in her sexy warrior armor, battling a twisted shadow. It spat fire at her. She manifested a red shield that held a black phoenix in the center of it, and drove the shadow back.

Amanda, Tabitha, and Karma acted as if they couldn't see her at all. The three of them surrounded him.

I must be dead. Why else would he see Kody and the shadow when the other three didn't?

Amanda tilted his head back so that she could feel for his pulse.

"Is he dead?" Tabitha asked.

"He's turning blue." Amanda looked up. "Karma, call an ambulance!"

She ran to obey.

Even though he couldn't move, Nick could still see Kody as she fought like a boss. In a matter of seconds, she rammed the creature into the wall.

With one last screech, it vanished.

Kody quickly scanned the room for more threats. When her gaze met his, her face paled.

She ran to him and knelt by his side. "Stay with me, Nick." She leaned down and kissed him.

The moment her tongue touched his, her breath filled his chest and he finally could breathe again as her warmth spread through him. Yeah, he'd take a beating for her kiss any day, and line up twice on Sunday.

I am such a sick masochist. . . .

Amanda and Tabitha shrieked and scurried away from his body. Nick opened his eyes to find Kody still with him. Now dressed in a red sweater and jeans, she pulled back from his lips to smile down at him while the twins grabbed weapons from the wall.

Nick reached up to cup Kody's soft cheek in his hand. No doubt about it, she was the most beautiful girl he'd ever seen. And never had he been more grateful for her presence. "You're really real."

She wrinkled her nose at his odd words. "Are you all right? They hit you really hard, didn't they?"

Ignoring that for once, he glanced around to the other women, who were now gaping at them. "I think I'm okay. But I don't know what happened."

Kody didn't respond to him. Instead, she locked gazes with Karma. "We have to get him out of this house. Fast. The longer he stays here, the worse it's going to get and the more attackers he'll have."

Tabitha glared at her. "Who are you?"

"*What* are you?" Amanda asked.

Kody answered neither twin. "Karma, you know I'm right. There are too many souls and demons that call this place home. We have to get him out. Clear us a path."

Nodding, Karma moved to help Nick stand.

With Kody on one side and Karma on the other, Nick rose to his feet. He still didn't know what was happening or why his body didn't want to listen to his brain, but he'd learned better than to hesitate while being attacked by unknown creatures. Best to get clear and then interrogate later.

"How did you get here?" he asked Kody.

She helped him down the stairs. "I think you drew me to you."

"How? I don't have any powers left."

She shrugged. "I don't know any other explanation. I was on Menyara's porch to ask her where you were and the next thing I knew, I was here with you."

Too grateful to question it, he stumbled on the last step and barely caught himself before he dragged all three of them down.

Leaning him against the wall, Karma left his side to open the front door while the twins pulled up the rear.

"I still want to know what you two are," Tabitha demanded.

"At the moment, unwanted guests." Kody glanced around the house with a stern frown. "What kind of place is this? I've never seen so many ghosts and demons in one location in my life . . . not even a cemetery."

Amanda shrugged. "Karma doesn't like to be alone."

Not wanting to think about that, Nick headed out the door with Kody, but as soon as he was through the threshold, she jerked to a stop and stayed inside.

Her face pale, she tried to walk out and couldn't. She kept hitting an invisible wall.

When Nick started back for her, Karma pulled him to a stop. She leveled a malevolent glare at Kody. "You're a ghost?"

Kody ignored her question as she pounded against an unseen barrier. "What is this?"

Nick rolled his eyes at Karma. "She's not a ghost."

"Yes, she is." Karma gently pushed him toward the stairs. "I have a protection spell that prevents ghosts from leaving the house. It stops them at the door."

Tabitha touched Kody's arm. "She feels solid and warm."

Karma gave her sister an irritated smirk. "Step through and see for yourself."

Tabitha moved through the door without a problem. As did Amanda.

Kody still couldn't leave the house.

With an arrogance that was palpable, Karma folded her arms over her chest. "Like I said, she's a ghost."

Unable to believe it, Nick stared at his girlfriend. It couldn't be true. It wasn't possible. "Kody?"

Tears welled in her green eyes as she splayed her hand against the invisible barrier. "The vision you had of the Malachai killing me in battle wasn't a dream, Nick. We bonded that night while I was trying to ground you, and you shared my memories. I died by your hand. You, as the Malachai, killed me."

His stomach hit the ground as total disbelief consumed him. "I don't understand." His dream had been clouded and strange. He'd been both Kody's protector *and* her killer?

"The man you stabbed in your vision, the one who ran to protect me, wasn't really you, Nick. That was my older brother you slew before you used his sword to kill me."

Horror invaded every part of his being as he saw himself in his demon form again in that battle. Cold. Merciless. Uncaring. He'd felt nothing as he cut through his enemies.

Nothing as he cut down Kody and watched her die at his feet. . . .

Dear God, he'd actually laughed while she bled out. *How could I ever find* that *funny?*

No wonder she wanted to kill him. It all made sense now. Well, some of it did. But he still had a ton of questions for her.

"But I've seen you bleed in my world. You were dying . . . like you were real."

Unshed tears made her eyes glisten. "I have a body, Nick. It's just like yours, but it's a little different. And I can die again. There are many ways beings can perish."

Strangely, that made sense to him. "Why didn't you tell me?"

"Would you have believed me had I walked up to you and said, 'Hi, Nick, I'm a girl you killed? Nice meeting you'?" Kody gave him a trembling smile. "You still don't believe me even now. Not quite, anyway." She looked past him to Karma. "You have to get him away from here. I can feel the powers surging again. Take him to St. Louis Cathedral as fast as you can. It's the only place he's safe." She glanced back at Nick and the look in those green eyes seared him. "Stay on holy ground until I get to you. Understand?"

"Yeah," he breathed.

Karma pulled him back and handed him off to

Tabitha. "You get him to the altar. I'm staying for answers."

Nick started to protest, but one look at Tabitha's expression and he thought better of it. She actually liked to punch things. With *extreme* prejudice. He glanced back to Karma. "Just make sure you share those answers after you get them."

"Don't worry. I'll tell you everything she says."

Nick locked gazes with Kody. She appeared so real and normal. So human.

But she wasn't.

And neither was he.

Dang, in all his wild speculations about who and what she was, *this* had never once entered his mind. Who would have thought?

Kody's a ghost.

Not just any ghost—someone he would kill in the future.

His emotions were so tangled right now that he wasn't sure what he felt. Other than lost. Confused. Yeah, that was definitely the primary feeling.

Kody held her hand up to him. That and the sorrow

and fear in her eyes tightened his chest. He should probably hate her. That was the natural state of a Malachai. It was the emotion that came easiest to his species.

Yet he couldn't. They'd been through too much together. And while he didn't completely trust her, he did love her. In spite of common sense and even self-preservation.

With one last look at her, he got into the car and buckled himself in. "Karma's not going to hurt her, is she?"

Amanda backed out of the driveway while Tabitha stared after her sister and Kody.

Nick's last view was Karma entering the house with a determined stride.

"You want the truth or a lie?" Tabitha asked.

"I always prefer the truth."

"I'm sure she's interrogating the ghost even as we speak."

Nick didn't like the sound of that. "Interrogating how?"

The twins exchanged a look that concerned him even more. There was something they weren't saying.

"What?" Nick asked. "What is she going to do to Kody?"

Tabitha turned around in the seat so that she was no longer facing him. "If Karma doesn't like what she hears, she'll banish her."

"Back to our world?"

"No, Nick. Into oblivion."

CHAPTER 6

Kody stepped back as Karma approached her like a hungry tigress. She wasn't afraid of the woman. Not even a little—she'd grown up with Karma as one of her fiercest protectors. But she understood trying to protect what you loved. There was truly nothing more dangerous than a person guarding their family on their home territory. It was a lesson Karma had taught her well. So she would give Karma space and relieve her fears. Unlike Tabitha, who fought physically, Karma was a spiritual warrior. She would know and understand the world Kody came from better than anyone.

"You don't have to be afraid of me, Karma. I'm not going to hurt you or your sisters." They, too, were her illusion

family. And both Amanda and Tabitha had died fighting beside Kody's mother against the Malachai and his army.

Ever mistrustful of those she didn't know, Karma scoffed as she circled her, sizing her up as if they were about to battle. "How do I know that?"

"Because I'm an Arel."

Only a subtle tensing of Karma's body betrayed her knowledge of Kody's species. Still, the woman wasn't about to give away anything else. "You say that like it's supposed to have meaning to me."

Kody laughed nervously at Karma's continued insistence on this song and dance of ignorance. But she couldn't blame her for being cautious. Karma was someone who had mind-traveled through the many ethers and who routinely talked to creatures like Kody. As well as those who were born of darkness. Those who lied and deceived. Those who would use human naiveté to prey on their victims.

Only a master sorceress with finely honed powers and extensive esoteric knowledge could have created the boundary that shielded this house and kept Kody and the others locked inside it.

"You know what it means, Karma." The Arelim were protectors of the highest order. At one time, they had been nothing more than messengers for the Malachai and Sephirii. Celestial gofers for the ancient gods, and their servants. But after the first war of the gods that had ended both the Malachai and Sephirii bloodlines, the Arelim had risen to be the Guardians of Order and Truth. They were charged with ensuring that the human world didn't end.

That the Malachai remained forever dormant.

Karma shook her head. "You can't be an Arel *and* a ghost. They're born immortal."

"As was I. But even immortals can die under the wrong circumstances. And you're right. I wasn't born an Arel. Because of the blood of my parents, I was chosen to be one. I'm a nekoda, and all of my kind are selected from those who've died."

Finally, the light of recognition that they were on the same team sparked in Karma's eyes. "You're a soldier."

Kody hesitated at the label that didn't quite fit. "More of a guardian. I fight when I have to, but that's not my primary role."

Karma cocked her head as she continued to study Kody and read her aura. "I'm still confused. You said Nick killed you, and yet you're here to protect him? Why?"

That was definitely *the* question. And it was one Kody asked herself constantly. At times, she wasn't sure, either. But whenever she looked into those vibrant blue eyes that showed her Nick's soul, she had clarity.

If only it would last.

Sighing, Kody walked around the small foyer that held traces of Karma's past and showed the very things the sorceress valued most. Her family. The walls were lined with pictures of Karma and her sisters and aunts and mother. Many were with their father, who smiled proudly in the midst of his nine daughters.

Tears choked her as Kody remembered her own father looking at her like that, of him holding on to her, afraid of letting her go and more terrified of keeping her with him because of the things that had been sent to kill them. Like Nick, her father had possessed a kind and, oddly enough given the viciousness of his past, innocent soul. Even in spite of the fact that her father had been one of the fiercest ancient soldiers. A general of legend who had fought back the ancient gods until they'd been forced to resort to trickery to defeat him. Maybe that was why she was so drawn to Nick. He reminded her a lot of her father and brothers. A lot of her uncle. That indefatigable spirit that refused to buckle under any fight or obstacle.

Over, under, around, or through, there's always a way. You don't give up and you never *give in. They can scar your body and take your freedom, but only you can surrender your heart and soul. Nothing is worth compromising yourself for. Stand fast and stand true. Always.* That had been her father's motto that had seen him through centuries of horror, torture, and suffering.

It was the motto Nekoda clung to even in her darkest hours.

She faced Karma. "Life is never simple. It's messy, complicated, and at times debilitating. When I fought Nick as a living demigod, I alone drove him back. I had the Malachai and his army on the run."

"Then how did he kill you?"

"I had been wounded in a previous battle and my

brother refused to let me fight alone. While he was a fierce and skilled warrior in his own right, he didn't have the powers I did. And when he died protecting me, I lost all reason. Even though I knew better, I let my anger grab hold of me and I attacked in a blind rage. The Malachai didn't defeat me so much as I defeated myself."

"Is that why you were chosen to be a nekoda?"

Kody nodded. "I'm the only one left who can defeat a Malachai. The Nasaru—"

"The what?"

"The elite Arelim. They are the ones born to their positions and they're the ones who select the nekodi from the fallen. They knew that I alone possess the powers to take down a Malachai, and so here I am."

That suspicious light returned to Karma's eyes. "I know there's more to this than you're telling me. But I still don't understand why you're helping the boy who killed you."

Kody wrapped her arms around herself as her memories of the Ambrose Malachai surged. Even now, she could see that awful day in her mind when Ari had carried her toward safety. Bodies of their friends, family, and army had lined the battlefield. Blood had run like rainwater under their feet.

She'd done her best to tell her brother that she was fine, in spite of her wounds. To put her down so that they could both return to battle.

In true big-brother fashion, Ari had refused to listen to her. *There is nothing I will not do to protect my family.*

Those words had brought a fury to the Malachai's eyes that seared her to this day. With a hell-born cry, the Malachai had headed straight for them.

She'd tried to warn her brother, but Ari wouldn't let her go. Not until he was sure she was safe. By then, it'd been too late. The Malachai had caught up to them, and before Ari could lift his sword, the Malachai had driven his dagger through her brother's courageous heart.

Because of her.

The guilt of that never left her, not even for a heartbeat. Too many lives had been lost in this fight. She couldn't fail them.

But more than that, she couldn't blindly follow orders, either. While they knew what the Malachai would one day do, they didn't know what would happen once he was gone.

Who or what would replace him.

That was the true nightmare that stayed with her. The one that rode her with spurs and without letup.

Kody locked gazes with Karma. "Because it wasn't Nick who destroyed my family. It's what he will one day become." She gestured toward the door Nick had left through. "That boy possesses one of the purest hearts I've ever encountered. He's not like the other Malachai I've fought."

"You're hoping to save him?"

Kody nodded. "And I'm hoping to save myself."

"From death?"

In part. But there were things far worse than death. She knew that better than anyone. "From becoming a monster."

Karma scowled at her. "I don't understand."

Kody laughed nervously as the true horror of what she faced came home to roost. It wasn't something she liked thinking about. Yet it was more than just a possibility.

It was a probability of the worst sort.

"Whoever kills the Malachai will absorb his powers."

"Ah," Karma said as she finally understood. "You're afraid of becoming one yourself."

Again, Kody nodded. "And with the powers I already hold and knowledge I have . . . No one will be able to stop me. I will tear the entire universe apart. But if I save Nick, if I can keep him grounded and human—"

"You will save everyone, including yourself."

"Exactly." Most of all, she could reset the deaths of her family and not lose them. Not have Ari's and Urian's souls imprisoned by a creature who lived to torment them.

Karma pursed her lips. "I'm still not sure I should believe you."

"You've been lied to before by a demon." One that had almost stolen Karma's soul.

"Yeah. It kind of destroys the whole trust factor."

And that was why Karma kept everything in her home locked down. So that no evil would ever be released into the world again. At least not from something *she* did.

"What can I do to convince you?"

"Show me your real form."

Kody tsked at her. "You know I'm forbidden from doing that."

"You're not in your realm and it's the only way I'll believe you. A demon of any species is incapable of assuming the form of an Arel."

Because they were the essence of good. Only the purest of hearts and most uncorrupted soul could be one. Therefore a demon had no way of duplicating their forms. They couldn't hold it without being burned from the inside out.

If it was anyone else, this would be off the table. But Karma was a human version of the Arelim. What harm could there be in allaying her fears?

Kody inclined her head to Karma before she stepped back and spread her arms wide. White light engulfed her as she unfurled her white, iridescent wings that matched her skin and hair. Snow-white armor covered her entire body.

Gasping, Karma stumbled back, falling against the wall behind her. "Oh my God, it's true!"

Kody leaned her head back and allowed her form to return to that of a high school girl. To the face and body that had been hers before the Malachai had killed her.

When she returned her gaze to Karma, she saw the fear and resolve inside the woman. "Release me from your home. I have to get to Nick and protect him."

"We might have a problem with that."

Kody scowled at the note in Karma's voice. "How so?"

Karma glanced up the staircase. All of a sudden, there was a raw, unmistakable presence of evil in the room. It made the air heavy and tainted it with the sour stench of sulfur.

Dread filling every part of her, Kody turned to see what Karma was looking at.

Kody's jaw went slack as she saw the last thing she wanted to deal with. Tall, blond, and stunning, the demonspawn on the stairs had eyes so green they all but glowed. Even on his best day, he was hard to deal with and viciously unpredictable. Acerbic and sarcastic.

And with every step he took toward her, the air grew heavier.

Deadlier.

"What are *you* doing here?" Kody asked.

He arched a brow at her question as he slowly descended the stairs with an arrogant swagger that harkened back to the days when he'd been an early medieval warlord who had led his army on a voracious killing spree throughout all of Europe. "Do we know each other?"

Kody hesitated as she reminded herself that the people and preternatural beings here most likely wouldn't know her. Aside from the fact that this wasn't her world, this wasn't her time. She wouldn't be born for many more centuries.

And Thorn had no idea that one day he'd be reading her bedtime stories and rocking her to sleep.

That memory was so incongruous with the fierce, powerful demon lord in front of her that she had to bite back a smile. "I might have you mistaken for someone else."

Karma laughed until she met Thorn's gaze. "She's the Malachai's protector."

A slow smile spread across his face. "So this is what he summoned as a protector while he was fighting me? Really? She seemed bigger when she slammed me into the wall."

Karma slid a sideways glance toward Kody. "She's an Arel."

Thorn's eyes turned the color of blood as his fangs descended. There was a cold spark of delight in his green eyes. "An Arel . . . it's been a long time since I fed on one of those."

Fear rose up inside Kody as she realized the horrendous mistake she'd made because of her memories and her past with these people. All of that had happened in a different realm, and none of the people she knew in her past were the same here as they'd been in her world.

Karma and her sisters weren't her allies. And neither was Thorn.

In this realm, they were her enemies.

And Nick was alone and defenseless, in the custody of two people who would now hand him over to the very things her family had died fighting against.

By trying to save Nick, Kody had just unleashed

the Malachai in a world where he would do even more damage.

And into the hands of people who wanted to use him for evil.

CHAPTER 7

Something wasn't right. Even though Nick lacked his powers, he knew it with every molecule of his body. And when the twins stopped at Erzulie's, that feeling multiplied.

Confused, he scratched his head as Amanda turned off the car. "I thought we were going to the cathedral."

Tabitha unbuckled her belt. "Quick pit stop for supplies. You don't want to be defenseless there, do you?"

Honestly? He didn't want to be defenseless anywhere. It was never a good idea, especially when you lived his fun-filled life of epic madness. He couldn't even trust the shadows not to try and end him. Many people were afraid of the dark. Nick had been attacked by the dark, the light, and everything in between.

"Guess not." Still, he hesitated as they got out of the car. There was a sense deep inside his gut that made it tight and apprehensive. What did he feel? What was the universe trying to tell him?

Caleb had warned him to always listen to his instincts, not his human rationale. And Madaug—the son of two neurobiologists—had further elaborated on why. The subconscious mind, whether human or preternatural, took in more stimuli than the brain could process consciously. Unbeknownst to the individual, their brain, like a supercomputer, ran those billions of details from all five senses against its experiences and knowledge base, and then produced the chemicals that made a person cautious or wary, depending on the environment they were in. Those "gut feelings" were actually the brain picking out minute danger signs and trying to warn its host that it was time to run or to fight.

Even when the person saw no logical reason why.

It was all primal instinct. *A dog doesn't know why it barks or growls. It just knows something about its environment isn't right and it reacts.*

Yeah, that was what he felt right now. His gut was barking like a stressed-out terrier sensing a storm before the clouds rolled in. But unfortunately, he wasn't a dog. He didn't want to look like an idiot without good reason.

And still the hair on the back of his neck stood on end.

Wishing he understood it, he rolled out of the backseat while they waited on the curb. As he started to take a step, he remembered something his mom had told him repeatedly when he was a kid. *Beware of anyone, known or unknown, friend or foe, who wants to separate you from the people you're with. Don't ever let them get you off by yourself. No good comes from those who don't want an audience for their behavior.*

Nick had grown up alone on these city streets while his mother was at work. And though she was young, his mom held a lot of wisdom that had never failed to keep him safe.

Why wouldn't the twins have taken him to the cathedral and then come here for weapons *after* he was secured? Given the severity of his attack at Karma's house, and Kody's warning, why would they bring him to where their family was . . . and their personal store? Why endanger what they loved? And given the ferocious attack on him and Kody, they were really calm and collected about it all. Accepting.

Something Tabitha wasn't. Ever. She was hostile and reactive. Volatile, especially whenever something came after her, and never more so than when her family was ambushed. Why wouldn't she be asking more questions about Kody and the attack on him?

That was what his brain had been trying to tell him. They were acting suspiciously, and way out of character for them. And while they were different from the women he knew at home, they weren't *that* different.

Time to act stupid.

Without a word of warning or intent, he turned and ran as fast as he could down St. Ann toward the Square. He shot across the street to where cars were parked on the right side and put them between him and the twins, who were now in fast pursuit.

Dang it! Where were all the tourists? For once, there was little pedestrian traffic on the street he could lose himself in, and Tabitha was quickly closing the distance between them.

Why couldn't she be out of shape in this world? Was it really too much to ask for a Couch Potato Tabitha?

He considered running into the Place d'Armes Hotel, but then reconsidered it. Like Karma's house, it was haunted. And he didn't want them to corner him.

"Stop! Thief!" Tabitha screamed.

Now that was just dirty mean.

Putting his head down low, Nick ran with everything that had made him a prized fullback for his school team. He jumped over four black bags of trash by the corner stop sign and dodged past a do-gooder who tried to block his path. He cut right and shot between the St. Ann light post and the Presbytère entrance.

Unlike the street, the Square was crowded. Tourists scattered out of his way and shouted, but Nick didn't slow down. Not until he ran up the steps and through the open door of the cathedral, into the dark foyer, where several people turned to scowl at him.

He flashed them a grin as relief swept through him that he'd made it without getting caught. "Hallelujah! Felt the Lord calling me to prayer and I couldn't get here fast enough. What can I say, ladies? It's good to be alive."

They rolled their eyes at him and scurried away as if they thought he was on something other than the adrenaline rush from another near-death encounter.

Out of breath and sweating, Nick beelined for the small font of holy water on the left, just outside the interior doors, and crossed himself with it. Only then did he turn around to find the twins outside the threshold of the church. They eyed him with malice, but for whatever reason, didn't step one foot onto holy ground.

Thank you, God, I'm safe.

Take that evil and choke on it . . . in your fugly face!

Overconfident and euphoric, Nick strutted back and forth, taunting the twins, who couldn't reach him. "That's right, bitches! I made it. Hah!" He cringed as he realized what had just come out of his mouth.

In church.

Horrified, he glanced over to the gaping volunteer

who was running the gift store cash register. "Sorry, ma'am. The devil's an evil beast. It's why I came to pray."

Stiffening her posture, she narrowed her eyes with disdain. "Make sure you add your shameful language to your confession on Saturday, Mr. Burdette."

"Yes, ma'am."

Tabitha threw her hands out as if she was cursing him. Nick started to return that with a gesture of his own, but he'd already shamed his upbringing. He wasn't about to add more to it.

Grateful he was safe, he went into the tiny gift shop and bought candles. No one would mess with him so long as he was praying.

The clerk glared at him the whole time. Like she'd never screwed up in her life. Umm-hmmm . . .

"Judge not lest ye be judged," he said with a smile as he handed over the money then took his candles to the prie-dieux so that he could light them and pray while he waited for Kody.

Please get here soon. He had no idea what he'd do if she failed to show.

Nick had barely begun the third round of prayers before a shadow fell over him. Looking up, he saw a cop.

"I need you to come with me. Now."

Nick gestured to his candles. "Dude, I'm in the middle of prayer here."

"And I have two women who claim you shoplifted from their store."

Anger over the fact that the twins would accuse him of something so foul widened his eyes and made his jaw tic. "Yeah, right." Nick stood up and pulled his pockets out for the officer to see what he had in his possession. "I don't have nothing but my wallet and the two candles I paid for."

"Well, that's not the story they're telling."

"Then they're lying."

"Why don't you come with me and we can straighten this out at the station."

Nick shook his head. "I didn't do anything and I'm not going anywhere."

"Is there a problem, officer?"

Nick looked past the cop to see the rector, who

thankfully was the same one who presided over the church in his realm, too.

The cop bristled. "This doesn't concern you."

Father Jeffrey smiled patiently. "You're in my church, officer, disturbing the faithful who are here to pray, so it would seem that it does."

Nick stepped toward the priest. "I didn't do anything, Father Jeffrey."

The priest patted him on the arm while he continued to speak to the cop. "Do you have any probable cause?"

"Two witnesses claim they saw him steal merchandise from their store."

"And what store is this?"

"Erzulie's."

Father Jeffrey gaped. "The Voodoo store on the corner?"

"Yes, sir. He ran in here after they caught him and told him they were calling the police."

The priest turned to Nick with an arched brow. "Nicholas?"

He met the priest's gaze dead on, without flinching or faltering. "They're lying. Father, you know me. I'm not perfect, but there's nothing in this world I want bad enough that I'd make myself out a thief to have it. And if I ever did, you'd be the first one I'd tell about it on Saturday."

Father Jeffrey smiled. "And your mother would be beating you every step of the way to the confessional." He returned his gaze to the police officer. "He's right. I've never known this boy to take anything from anyone."

In more ways than one.

"Well, I have a complaint."

"And I have a phone. What say we call Nicholas's parents and have them escort him to the station for you?"

The cop bristled. "I don't have all day."

"It won't take all day, officer. They both work here in the Quarter. For that matter, his mother's office is just around the corner and his father's is less than two miles away. It'll save you paperwork later." Father Jeffrey pulled out his cell phone and handed it to Nick. "Call your parents, son."

Nick reached for it before he remembered that he had no idea what the numbers were. For that matter, he didn't know where his "parents" worked.

The cop eyed him coldly. "Is there a problem?"

"I don't have their work numbers memorized. They're on my speed dial and I don't have my phone on me." It was in the backpack he'd thrown into Caleb's arms before he left school.

Father Jeffrey stepped between Nick and the cop, who was quickly losing patience with them. "Then I can look it up. It won't take but a moment. Both of his parents are frequent volunteers here and their numbers are on my desk."

It was obvious the officer didn't want to wait, but he didn't say anything more.

Nick followed Father Jeffrey to his office, but with every step he took, he couldn't help wondering what was happening with Kody. What was taking her so long to get here?

And what would happen to him once the cop got his way and hauled him out of the building?

This was the first time in Nick's entire life that he'd ever felt truly defenseless. Even when Alan and crew had held him on the ground and shot him, he'd felt more in control of himself and his fate.

But this . . .

How do I fight against evil when I have no powers?

For all intents and purposes, Amanda and Tabitha were human and female. He couldn't even hit them to protect himself. There was nothing he could do. The moment he left here, they would be on him like spice on sausage. And there was no telling what they planned to do with him once they had him alone again.

Why did I tell them I was the Malachai?

Because they were supposed to be your allies.

Yeah, in a different time and place. Now he'd trapped Kody *and* himself.

What would Acheron do?

Stupid question. Ash could teleport. He'd never be in this position. He'd simply wave his hand over the women or the cop and they'd forget that they'd ever seen him. *These are not the droids you're looking for.* Ash made those powers seem so easy to command and yet Nick screwed them up every time he tried.

I'm so not Ash.

Nor was he Kyrian, who could fight or talk his way out of the worst event.

His stomach tightened to a painful knot while the priest called and Nick sat in a chair, waiting for the rest of the preternatural world to come get him.

C'mon, Nick. Think. . . .

There had to be some way out of this.

Father Jeffrey hung up the phone. "His mother is showing a house in the Garden District and his father's in a meeting."

"Then they can pick him up at the station." The officer pulled out his handcuffs.

Nick bolted to his feet. He started to protest, but was distracted by the door behind the cop that opened to show what had to be the baddest of bad. Standing a good six-eight, this newcomer oozed the kind of feral power that Acheron held. Massive. Terrifying.

Lethal.

That don't-cut-your-eyes-at-me-if-you-want-to-keep-breathing-human stance.

With short dark hair and a goatee, the man had eyes so dark a blue they appeared purple in color. He was dressed black on black and held himself like a predator. Head low, eyes alert to every single thing.

When that deadly gaze locked on him, Nick felt like he'd just been targeted by a nuclear device of some kind. One that would take no mercy on him.

"Come with me, kid."

It was only then that Nick realized both the priest and the cop were frozen.

Ah man, this can't be good.

What now?

"Who are you?" *What* was he?

A slow, arrogant smile curved his lips. One that said he enjoyed Nick's fear a little too much. "Your only hope."

Last time he heard something like that was in *The Terminator* movie.

Not a good analogy.

Nick stepped back at the same time another person joined them in the room. One who lacked Nick's self-preservation as she playfully slapped the supernatural being on his arm. It was tantamount to popping a rabid lion on the nose with a newspaper and telling it to shush. "Savitar, stop. He's traumatized enough."

Nick let out a relieved breath at the sweet, soft tone that meant everything to him. He was so glad to see her that it left him weak in his knees. "Kody, thank God you're all right."

It wasn't until she stood in front of him that he saw the bruises on her face where someone had hit her. Hard.

His vision darkened as he gently touched her cheek. "Who did this to you?"

She covered his hand with hers and offered him that tender smile that always made it hard for him to breathe. "Long story, and we don't have time for that now. We have to get you out of here before Tabitha and Amanda tell everyone where you are. Right now, they think you're about to be led out to them."

In spite of the danger, he had to hug her, just to make sure she was really all right and here. The sweet scent of her hair went a long way in soothing his ravaged nerves.

"Break it up before I throw water on you two to separate you."

Laughing, Kody pulled back and ruffled Nick's hair. "How did you get away from them?"

"Ran screaming like a cheerleader in a horror film. You?"

"Fought like a demon."

Nick laughed at her joke. "Are you really a ghost?"

"We'll talk about it later, okay?"

Nodding, he took her hand and allowed her to pull him toward the back of the church where a side door let them out onto Pirate's Alley. Savitar pulled up the rear and herded them down the Cabildo Alley to St. Peter.

As soon as they reached the curb, Nick slowed to a stop. Bubba was waiting for them in his large black SUV.

Without warning, Savitar literally picked Nick up and threw him into the backseat. Kody climbed into the back with him while Savitar took shotgun.

"Buckle up, Nick, or Mom will kill me." Bubba didn't wait as he pulled away from the curb. "Did you have any trouble?" he asked Savitar.

"No. They had no idea we were there."

"Good."

Completely baffled, Nick rubbed his head as he struggled to catch up to this newest and most bizarre turn of events. "Pardon, but I think I left my sanity in church. We might need to go back and get it."

Bubba laughed. "He looks and sounds just like my boy. Are you two absolutely sure you're right about him?"

"I'm positive." Kody took Nick's hand and squeezed it. "And we stupidly informed the Malachai's šakkan in this realm what Nick really is."

Now there was a term Nick had never heard before. "My what?"

"Šakkan," she repeated. "He's the head general who leads your strongest forces in battle. And he's going to come for you, full force, so that he can take your powers and use them as his own."

Bubba cursed. "Like we needed anything else to fight."

Kody expelled a heavy sigh. "I know. Sorry."

"So who is this šakkan?" Nick asked, wanting to make sure he cut the beast a wide berth.

"In our world, he's someone you haven't met yet. He was imprisoned until your father died. Here in this realm, the šakkan who leads their dark forces is Thorn."

Nick frowned at the name of someone he thought was friendly . . . *ish*. "The scary dude who helped me out when I was imprisoned in the Nether Realm?"

She nodded.

"Dang, I really liked him, too." He shook his head. "I don't understand why he'd be our ally at home and against us here."

"Free will."

Nick cocked his head at Savitar's words. "Say what?"

Savitar ran his hand over a vicious scar on his forearm. "For better or worse, every decision we make, good or bad, small and large, puts us on a course to nightmares we don't see coming until they're in our face." Savitar turned his gaze to the road. "In every universe, we play out different decisions we've made for whatever reason. What breaks one person at one time can make them strong at another. And one small variable can have devastating consequences. Timing is everything, kid."

Kody nodded. "In our world, your mother was attacked by the Malachai and you were born. In this one, there is no Malachai so she was able to live out her life under more normal circumstances."

"But she still had me."

"And Bubba's still your father."

Nick fell silent as he considered that. In many ways, Kody was right. Bubba was the closest thing to a dad Nick had ever known. And though they weren't blood related in his world, they were still family. "But what about Kyrian?" He was as much of a mentor and father for Nick as Bubba. "I found out this morning that he's dead in this world."

"Nick Burdette didn't need to meet a Dark-Hunter to put him on the right path, away from the darkness that was trying to claim him. He has Bubba here to keep him straight. He doesn't need Acheron to watch over him. Or Caleb to guard him from forces he's not strong enough to fight yet."

He was struggling to make sense of it all. Everything she said was valid, but . . . "What about Amanda and Tabitha and Karma? Why are they good in our world and not in this one?"

Kody sighed. "In both worlds, they, like you, were born to walk the line of shadows. One foot in the light and one in the dark. A few are scared enough of both that they stay in the middle and never pick a side. Others are strong enough to choose the light and stay firmly planted there, even while the darkness tries to claim them. And others are too weak or blind to fight the lure of darkness. It overwhelms them with false promises and before they know what's happened, it owns them. Sometimes, like the Thorn you know in our world, they can battle their way back to the light and put the darkness behind them even though it continues to try and reclaim them. But those people are very rare. I don't know what kept our Tabby and Amanda on the right side in our world nor do I know what corrupted them here. As Savitar said, it's a matter of free will. Decisions made at the wrong or right time, for the wrong or right reasons."

Nick picked her hand up from the seat and studied the scars on her knuckles. Even though she was a veteran warrior, her hands were soft and tiny. Delicate. And yet they held a strength that was unfathomable to him. "How old are you, Kody? Really?"

"I had just turned nineteen when you killed me."

He sucked his breath in sharply as her words slapped him hard. He wasn't that far away from turning nineteen himself. Just a little over two years. "And you were fighting the Malachai at that age? Why?"

She snorted. "By the time my father was nineteen, he was an experienced war veteran and a feared general."

"And he was okay with you following in his footsteps at that age?"

"Not really, but he had no say in it. I became a soldier after you killed him."

He winced and wondered how she could stand to be in the same car with him right now. Why she didn't try to claw his eyes out every time she looked at him.

Kody squeezed his fingers as if she knew what he was thinking. "As an infant, my oldest brother was taken from my parents and they weren't allowed to raise him. For centuries, my father thought him dead while my mother . . . well, both of them really, were imprisoned by different gods. When they were finally reunited, long after my oldest brother was grown, they had my brother Ari right away." A bittersweet smile curled her lips. "They were so overprotective of him that I'm told it scarred him for life. And for the longest time, they were afraid to have another child. They just wanted to protect the two they had and make sure nothing bad happened to them."

"Were you an uh-oh baby?" Nick teased, trying to ease the grief in her eyes.

She wrinkled her nose at him. "No. I wasn't an uh-oh." There was a hint of laughter in her voice. "Many centuries later, after Ari was grown and married, my parents decided that they were finally ready to have another baby to viciously overprotect."

The light faded as sadness darkened her eyes again. "I was only two when something happened to you. I don't know what. But it unleashed the Malachai and you went crazy on the world. I was sent into hiding and trained to battle your forces while my family rallied their allies and did what they could to keep your army at bay and protect the world."

Nick ground his teeth at the horrors of her life. Horrors *he'd* caused for her and all the people they loved. He'd never hated himself more than he did right now. "I'm so sorry I hurt you."

"*You* didn't."

That wasn't true, but he appreciated her saying it. At the end of the day, he was the Malachai. Whatever his future self did, it was him, too.

Now he understood why Ambrose was so desperate to change the past. His future self had told him that he could feel the last of the goodness inside him dying. That any day, he expected the Malachai to devour his conscience and render him a merciless monster. Because of it, Ambrose was barely sane at times as he tried to keep Nick from making the same mistakes he'd made at Nick's age. To steer Nick onto another path that kept him firmly planted in the light.

And once that decency was gone, the Malachai would take over and kill everything and everyone. That was what his species had been born to do.

Man, it sucked.

"You should have told me the truth before now, Kody."

"You weren't ready to hear it, and you definitely weren't ready to accept the reality of what you're headed toward."

Who would be? No one in their right mind wanted

to be told that they would one day destroy the entire world and everyone who lived in it. That they would kill or cause the death of every being who mattered to them.

And so what if she was right? It still stung that she'd lied to him and kept such a huge secret. "Is that why you came to see me in the hospital after I'd been shot? Were you planning to kill me?"

She looked away. "I was supposed to kill you that first day we met at St. Richard's."

That news floored him and flooded him with memories. Even now, he could visualize her clearly that day in his mind when he'd first seen her standing in the office—it seemed like a lifetime ago. She'd looked like a vision. So sweet and innocent. Confused by her new school, or so he'd thought. Meanwhile, there she'd been with the intent of ending his life. "Why didn't you?"

She laughed bitterly before she met his gaze. "You were so not what I thought you'd be. I went there expecting a cruel Malachai to battle to the death. Someone like Stone." The bully who'd caused him to be sent to the office. "And instead I found a sweet, bashful, respectful boy who wore the tackiest shirt imaginable just to make his mother happy and not hurt her feelings, even though everyone else mocked him for it. One who gladly took a beating to protect his saintly mother's reputation. An innocent soul who found humor at the worst of times and who held himself up with hard-won pride even when everyone else was relentlessly trying to knock you down. You have inside you a purity that is so rare. The capacity to love unconditionally and completely. In spite of what you are, and as unbelievable as it is, you are truly decent."

Swallowing hard, she wiped at her eyes. "Gah, it gets so confusing for me. I just can't reconcile the creature I know you will become—the heartless beast I have battled—with the man you are, here and now."

Savitar handed her a tissue. "Life hammers us all. Too many times we become things we never thought we'd be. For many reasons."

Kody drew a ragged breath as Nick pulled her against him and held her.

He buried his face in her hair and inhaled the sweet, precious scent. "But now that I know, Kody, I won't hurt you. How could I?"

She shook her head. "You don't understand, Nick. When your blood takes over you, you won't be able to stop. The Malachai will control you, not the other way around. If you could stop it, I wouldn't be here. I'd be snatched back to my time to live out the life I should have had. But the mere fact that I continue to exist as a ghost says that you will ultimately kill me."

"I refuse to accept that."

She patted his chest. "You are ever a stubborn Cajun."

"Dat right, *cher*. Born on da bayou, with boudin in one hand and gumbo in the other, and riding a gator."

That succeeded in getting her to laugh. "You were born on Menyara's couch and you hate those stereotypes."

"Yeah, but I am proud to be Cajun and I happily embrace my stereotype . . . sometimes."

Bubba shook his head. "It is so disconcerting to hear a stranger speaking out of my son's body. Talking about things I know my boy has never seen or done. How are *you* coping with this?" he asked Kody.

She straightened up in the seat. "I don't see your son when I look at him, Michael. I see the lunatic I'm in love with. Blue eyes, dark hair, big ears, and a goofy grin ringed by dimples."

Nick gasped in indignation. "I don't have big ears."

"Yeah, you do." She reached up to touch one. "Not in this body, but the one at home . . . total Dumbo. You really don't need your wings to fly. You could just wiggle the ears and catch a breeze."

He pretended to be wounded by her teasing. "Now that's just cruel, woman."

With an innocent expression, she held her hands up to her ears and waved her fingers like wings.

Savitar rolled his eyes. "You know what truly terrifies me, Michael?"

"Very little?"

"Well, yeah . . . that's true. But for the moment, it's the fact that the fate of the entire universe rests in *their* hands." He shifted his gaze to Kody. "You really should do us all a favor and end him while you can."

She scoffed at words that seriously offended Nick. "Don't take it to heart, hon. Savitar had a chance to kill you himself and instead, he taught you how to surf."

Savitar screwed his face up as if surfing was the most repugnant thing he could imagine. "Surf?"

She nodded. "I asked you once why you didn't kill Nick during the two years he spent with you on your island, and you know what you said?"

"I'm an idiot?"

"No," she said with a laugh. "You told me it wasn't your place or his time. That he still had good he needed to do and that if you'd killed him then, people you love would have suffered because Nick wouldn't have been there to help them when they needed it. But what you didn't say was what my father told me later. That in spite of all your denials and gruffness, you, like my father, carry hope. You curse it, but for whatever reason, no matter what the world does to you, you can't let it go."

Savitar made a sound of ultimate disgust. "I take back what I said. Your father's the idiot."

"No, he wasn't. He was the most intelligent man I've ever known. Even *you* respected him, Mr. Hostile."

"And I find that impossible to believe."

Nick took a moment to study Savitar. He knew from his future self that Savitar would be important to him one day. But he didn't know when or why. Only that this was an extremely powerful being.

A shiver went over him as he leaned to whisper in Kody's ear. "Are you sure Savitar is on our side?"

"I can hear you, kid," Savitar growled. "And yeah. I'm on your side."

"Just checking. My other former allies turned out to be myths. And you," Nick said to Bubba, "are supposed to be in a meeting right now."

"I *was* in a meeting when the priest called. With Savitar, who was explaining you and Kody to me."

Nick scowled. "You already knew Savitar?"

The men exchanged an amused look.

"Yeah," Bubba said. "For a long time now. We've headed off many a Daimon invasion."

That was an interesting turn Nick hadn't expected. "So you're as crazy here as you are in my world?"

Kody laughed. "No. Michael's much more sane here, but he does stalk the night, protecting what he loves . . . with Mark."

"What about Mom? Does she know any of this?"

Bubba shook his head. "I've kept all my nocturnal activities away from you and your mom. After the way she reacted when we were attacked years ago, I knew better than to let her in on anything me and Mark do. Not to mention, I didn't want to endanger either of you."

"What attack?" Nick asked.

"When you . . . or rather my son, was a baby, y'all were at home alone. I came in just as the Daimon grabbed your mother. I fought him off, but she had a hard time coping with what had happened. With the fact that her attacker wasn't human. But after that, I knew I couldn't just stand by and do nothing while those creatures ran loose on innocent people. Sometimes, you've just got to take a stand. For yourself and for others."

Nick smiled. "You've said that last bit to me a lot over the years . . . that and don't double tap when you can pull a triple."

"And that you'd rather be judged by twelve than carried by six," Kody chimed in.

Savitar snorted. "Sounds like you're basically the same in both worlds."

"I guess so," Bubba drawled. "Dang, and here I always thought I was original. One of a kind."

While they drove through the city, Nick wondered if that event Bubba had described was what had killed Bubba's family in his world. When Kody had told him Bubba's wife and son had been murdered, he'd assumed the assailant had been human. But if it'd been something supernatural . . .

It would definitely explain a lot about Nick's favorite lunatic.

As they turned onto Ursulines, the sky above them darkened with clouds. And it came on fast.

They collectively sucked in their breaths.

"That's bad, isn't it?" Nick asked.

Kody nodded an instant before lightning struck their SUV and sent it careening. To Bubba's credit, he kept it upright, but it was toast as they came to a harsh stop, and barely missed hitting a parked car by the breadth of a hand. Bubba tried to start the engine.

It wouldn't even turn over.

Nick ground his teeth as he heard an all-too-familiar sound from far away. One that was drawing nearer. "Please, someone, tell me those aren't wings."

"We can say that, but we'd be lying." Savitar opened the door and sent a blast of fire into the air.

Nick unbuckled his belt and opened his door. "Can we make it to Sanctuary?"

Kody shook her head. "There's no Sanctuary here, Nick."

His jaw went slack with her news. No. It wasn't possible. How could there not be a Sanctuary in New Orleans? "What?"

"They don't have Were-Hunters in this realm."

He was even more aghast. "None? Seriously?"

"None," Savitar repeated as he grabbed Nick from the SUV and shoved him toward the curb. "Michael, get the kids to the convent. I'll cover you."

Bubba pulled out a gun the likes of which Nick had never seen before as they ran down the street. Nick looked up at the dark sky and gaped at the sight of a thousand winged demons that were headed straight at them.

"Run!" Savitar barked as he sent more fire blasts at the demons.

Nick didn't hesitate.

As soon as Nick reached the convent wall, he heard

shots. He started to look back, but he knew better. That fool always got eaten in movies. And Nick didn't want to be on anyone's menu.

Except maybe Kody's, but not when they were on a death run from things out to kill them.

He dashed to the gate, and tried to open it. It was locked tight. And the demons were landing on the street in front of the church entrance.

Shooting her own fire blasts at them, Kody met his fearful stare.

Without thinking, he grabbed her and threw her up on the wall as high as he could.

She scrambled over the top then leaned back and held her hand out to him. "Come on, Nick."

He took a running start and leaped for it. His hand touched hers an instant before he was thrown to the ground, on the wrong side of the fence.

"Nick!"

Dazed from the impact, Nick kicked the demon off him. But as he tried to rise, three more landed on his back and drove him to the ground again. His ears rang with the sound of their hisses and flapping wings.

Something warm and wet covered his face.

Blood. *His* blood.

He grimaced as pain consumed him. So this was how his life ended. Not with some great battle against horrible odds, or from some noble sacrifice for the ones he loved.

It ended with hell-monkeys slobbering all over him.

CHAPTER 8

Nick was still trying to get free when all of a sudden something knocked the demons off his back and sent them flying. And not with their wings.

"Get your filthy paws off my son, *feet pue tan!*"

Nick's eyes widened at the Cajun insult his mother hurled at the demons as she literally batted them away from him. Where had she learned *that*? He hadn't even known she'd ever heard such. For that matter, she once washed his mouth out because he called someone an idiot.

Impressed, and terrified of her, Nick held his hands up to shield his face as she came a little too close with her frenetic swings. "Ma! I'm under here. Don't kill me!"

She jerked him up from the street by his arm and shoved him toward the convent, where Kody had opened the small pedestrian gate. "Get inside, Boo."

He swung his mother up to carry her to safety as he ran inside. Once Kody closed the gate behind them, he set his mom on her feet. But he was far from safe. As soon as his mother was assured the demons couldn't follow them in, she turned on Nick with the wrath of the Furies.

"What do you think you're doing?" She poked her tiny finger into the center of his chest hard enough to hurt. "You're supposed to be at school, boy. Instead, I get a call saying you're about to be arrested and then I find you covered in demons. What is wrong with you? What were you thinking doing something so reckless?"

Now there was the angry Chihuahua he was used to facing, but it'd been awhile since he stood eye-to-eye with her. He'd forgotten how scary it was to be within her actual striking range.

His mother growled at him. "What have you to say for yourself, boy?"

"Sorry, Ma, I'm a sexy demon magnet?"

She actually pulled the bat back like she was planning to hit him with it.

"Cherise!"

She swung around, ready to battle until she saw the massive, muscled Bubba nearing them with the same fear in his eyes Nick was sure he had. "Don't you even take that tone with me, Mr. Triple-Threat-I-don't-have-to-listen-to-anyone-because-I'm-the-size-of-a-tank. You're in the doghouse, buster. You might as well pack a bag 'cause you're going to be in there so long your name's going to be engraved on the mailbox."

Bubba placed his hand over his heart as if her words wounded him. "Ah, what'd I do, *cher*?"

"You dragged my baby into danger, and *you*—" She turned on Savitar then. "Are you one of them?"

Savitar actually took a step back from her. "I'm going with whatever answer doesn't get me swatted with that bat."

Bubba disarmed her. "Cherise, calm down. What are you doing here?"

"What do you think? I'm protecting my boys. Both of you . . . Because Mark values his own life and in particular his male body parts, he called me after he got off the phone with you to tell me what the two of you were doing." She raked Bubba with an angry glare that made Nick take a step closer to Kody for protection. "You didn't honestly believe that I've been ignorant of what you and Mark do at night all these years? Did you?"

Bubba shifted nervously. "Um, yeah."

"Well then you're a fool, Michael Burdette. And I'm not." With a disgusted sigh, she gestured up at the sky where the demons circled like vultures. "And how do we get rid of *those*?"

"Not easily, and we need to get into the building before they start throwing—" Savitar's voice broke off as a car came hurtling over the wall at them. Barely missing them, it rolled across the manicured shrubs and slammed against the wall on Nick's left. "–things at us."

With Savitar leading the way, they ran for the old convent. Savitar used his powers to unlock the door. Nick stood back to allow Kody and his mother to enter, but then Savitar shoved him in headfirst.

"Hey!"

Savitar curled his lip. "Don't hey me, kid. Not after the hour I've had because of you."

Bubba locked the door behind them. "That'll keep the demons out, but the humans are another story. Holy ground won't stop them from coming in after us."

"I don't know . . . it stopped Tabby and Amanda earlier at St. Louis."

Bubba gave him a droll stare. "What say we don't bet our lives on whether or not humans can get in? We'll just hedge our bets and assume they can. That okay, punkin?"

Nick snorted. "Yeah, sure."

Kody agreed with Bubba. "And let's also assume they'll head straight here as soon as the demons tell Thorn where we are." She let out a half-hysterical laugh. "Or they could just follow the circling demonic cloud over our heads. Surely they have to know *that's* not normal. Even for New Orleans."

Savitar sighed. "Too bad they know you're a ghost. We could have used that advantage. Now it's just a liability."

"Yeah." She glanced at Nick. "It wasn't information I'd ever planned on being free with. Extenuating circumstances and all that." She ground her teeth in anger. "I knew better than to let my guard down. I can't believe I was so stupid!"

Cherise patted her on the back. "Don't be too hard on yourself, Boo. We all have moments of stupid."

"Yeah," Bubba agreed. "How you think Cherise ended up with me for a husband? I swear, that woman needs better lawyers. A really good one could have had her off for good behavior by now."

Cherise walked into his arms and hugged him. "That wasn't stupid, Michael. A bit masochistic, no doubt, but definitely not stupid."

Ignoring them, Savitar grabbed Nick's chin and held him by his side.

Her eyes flaring with anger, Cherise started for them, but Bubba caught her. "Don't, baby. While that's our son's body, that ain't our boy."

"What?"

Bubba nodded. "Our Nick was switched out with another soul."

Dumbfounded, Cherise couldn't speak as she sputtered.

Savitar narrowed his gaze on Nick while he turned Nick's head from side to side to study him. "And whoever did this to you, boy, knew exactly what they were doing. There's no sign of your bloodline. I didn't even know it was possible to hide a Malachai so completely."

Kody folded her arms over her chest. "You should be with him in our world. He has stood next to Acheron Parthenopaeus many times, and not even Ash can tell."

Savitar finally released him and stepped back. "You're sure he's a Malachai?"

Kody lowered the neck of her sweater to show a vicious scar over her heart. "I was looking him in the eyes when he killed me. It's him." She paused before she continued. "Well, not *him*, but it will be one day." Biting her lip, she faced Cherise, who was still struggling with the unbelievable reality. "Have no fear for your Nick, Mrs. Burdette. Your son is safe in my world. He couldn't be more protected. I promise you I left him with two powerful men who would die before they allow him to be harmed."

Finally, Cherise found her voice again. "How do we swap them back?"

Kody sighed. "I wish I knew."

Savitar moved to a window to check on the location and activities of their demons. "We have to find the one responsible. It's our only hope to undo this and get him back to your world before it's too late."

"Well, I can tell you it's not Thorn. He had no idea the Malachai was here until I accidentally told him."

Too grateful that she'd survived the attack to mind her slip to their enemies, Nick took Kody's hand. "How did you escape Karma?"

Savitar glanced back at them. "She summoned me."

That surprised him. Especially given the trap they'd both walked into with the Devereaux sisters. "How did you know to call for Savitar?"

"I took a wild guess and bet our lives on it. I was hoping he'd be strong enough to be on our side, even in this world. So glad I wasn't wrong."

Nick, too. Still, it didn't answer what he was really asking. "But how do you *know* him?"

She hesitated like she normally did whenever he asked her a point-blank question. Instead of her usual hedge, for once she answered it. "He's my godfather."

Savitar held his hands up as if those words offended him. "Yeah, I had a hard time with that one myself. I'm not exactly a people person and I have never met her before, but she told me things no one else could possibly know. Things my own family doesn't know about me . . . yet. I apparently get a looser tongue in the future. Like you becoming the Malachai, I can't imagine what damage I'll live through that would allow that to happen. Guess we're all future fools for something."

Kody swung Nick's hand between their bodies. "I'm just glad those events happened in both worlds. Otherwise, he'd have left me to die under torture."

"Savitar!" Nick reprimanded.

"Don't take that tone to me, kid. I'm not that fond of you. As for your girlfriend . . . I learned the hard way not to put my butt in a sling for anyone. It's a debt they seldom repay."

Something began striking the walls around them.

Nick growled in frustration that he couldn't have a minute's peace. "Can't you teleport us somewhere?" he asked Savitar.

His eyes burning with regret, he shook his head. "I'm not the Chthonian I used to be."

"Meaning what?"

Kody answered Nick's question. "With every god a Chthonian kills, it weakens them. . . ."

Savitar nodded. "A few centuries ago, I had a really bad day."

When he didn't elaborate, Nick prompted him. "And what did you do?"

"I. Had. A. Bad. Day." He enunciated each word slowly and with great irritation. After a second, he calmed. "Let's just say I did some things I seriously regret. The biggest of which being the powers I lost as a result of my tantrum. Some of them definitely weren't worth it."

Nick hated hearing that. For many reasons. "Are there any other Chthonians left?"

"Just Zebulon, and he's even weaker than I am."

Great. Raking his hand through his hair, Nick took a mental inventory of possible allies.

"What about the Charonte?" Kody asked Savitar.

"All enslaved."

"Even Simi?"

Savitar winced as if that question sucker-punched him. "Simi died a long time ago."

"Nuh-uh," Nick said, denying it immediately. "She was at school with me. I saw her."

Savitar shook his head. "I know Simi and I was there when she was killed. I burned her remains myself. She's gone, kid. Long gone."

Then who'd been in his school with him? She'd even answered to Simi's name. That was just weird.

"What about Menyara?" Kody asked.

"Imprisoned."

Scowling, Kody let go of Nick's hand. "Wait . . . what month and year is this?"

His mom was the one who answered her. "April 2002, why?"

Kody let out her own sound of gross frustration as she started pacing. "I was hoping we could get to my father, but he would still be imprisoned in the Greek Underworld."

"*If* he's alive here," Nick reminded her.

She disregarded his warning. "If the Harbinger lives, he lives."

Savitar snorted. "And the Harbinger is definitely alive, but mentally unwell."

Neither knowing nor caring who this Harbinger was, Nick sighed as he continued to think through an escape route. "What about your mother?" he asked Kody.

"Imprisoned, too. Only my oldest brother would be free and grown right now, and trust me, he won't help us. He's knee-deep in Daimon drama."

That was a serious and most unexpected kick in his stones. "Excuse me? Your brother is with Daimons even in our world? Who are your parents?"

"Long story, Nick."

Okay, he put that in the to-be-pursued-later bank. "But maybe he's not evil. I mean, Tabitha and Thorn switched sides. It's possible your brother did, too. Right?"

Savitar rubbed his hand down the line of his jaw. "Who's your brother?"

"Urian."

Savitar choked on the name. "The head general of the Spathi Daimons?"

She nodded.

"Yeah, that's a lost cause. He's evil to the core of his rotten heart. I don't care if you are his sister, he'd still rip your head off and use it for a basketball."

Kody bit her lip. "Unless . . ."

"What?" Nick asked her hopefully.

Shaking her head, she paused in her pacing. "Phoebe. He should be married to her."

"And that helps us, how?"

Raking her hand through her hair, Kody groaned in frustration. "You're right. It doesn't. I keep thinking everyone is the same here as they are in our world. For all I know, Phoebe's gone Daimon, too, and is helping him."

"Or she's dead," Savitar mumbled.

And still the something pounded on the building for entry.

Bubba's cell phone rang. He pulled it out of his pocket and moved away from them to answer it while they continued to futilely explore the path of lost causes.

Kody paused again as she faced Savitar. "If Nick brought me over, do you think we could do that to someone else?"

"What are you thinking?"

"Maybe I could summon a Charonte. Do you think I'd be able to bring *our* Simi here?"

Savitar shrugged. "You can always try."

Closing her eyes, she leaned her head back with the most peaceful of expressions on her beautiful face. The storm outside picked up fervor while they waited.

Nick held his breath, praying this worked. They needed backup in the worst way imaginable. But more than that, he'd sell his soul for just a tiny bit of his powers to work.

If I ever get them back, I will never complain about them again. Even if they turn Madaug into another goat. Heck, at this point, he'd even kiss the surly spirit that inhabited his Malachai grimoire.

"Mark's just down the street, but he can't make it through the demons to reach us." Bubba returned to frown at Kody. "What's she doing?"

"Unfortunately, nothing," she said with a sigh. "It's

not working. I can't reach anything on our side. I'm completely blocked, which should be an impossibility."

Closing the distance between them, Nick ran his thumb down her jaw. "*Ca c'est bon, cher t'bebe*. We have *you*."

Kody scoffed at his blind optimism, even though that was one of the things she loved most about him. "What can I do? I'm only one person."

Nick tsked at her in true Cajun fashion. And when he spoke, his accent was thicker than frozen roux. "Now who's making excuses, eh?"

She wanted desperately to be irritated at him, but he made it impossible. The boy was way too charismatic for his own good. And unfortunately, it wasn't just his demon's glamor that made him so irresistible. "Don't make me take your mother's bat to you, boy."

He gave her that charming grin that never failed to set her heart pounding. Even in this incarnation when he lacked the incredible good looks she was used to. There was just something about him that was absolutely compelling. "Come now, *cher*. No fret on that face *de jolie*. You done stood toe-to-toe with the

Malachai. What's a few thousand generic demons compared to that?"

"A slaughter."

His grin widened. "That's the spirit."

"No, Nick. Slaughter for *us*. Feast for them."

And still that grin warmed her as he took the bat from his mother and hoisted it over his shoulder. "Ah now, *cher*, I plan to pass a good time. Besides, you know the old saying. When the going gets tough, the tough get napalm."

Heck of a time for him to lose his mind. Couldn't he have waited a little longer before he totally gave in to insanity? "What are you talking about?"

Nick examined the end of the Louisville Slugger. "Contrary to what you and Caleb and Madaug think, I am actually literate. And between the marathon runs of Let's-Kill-Nick, I've been studying my grimoire and taking notes. We're currently on holy ground with Malachai blood. What say we practice a little chemistry?"

She wasn't quite following his lead. "How do you mean?"

"What do you get when you mix my blood with holy water?"

She sucked her breath in sharply at the mental image that evoked. "Demon napalm."

Nick winked at her as he walked backward through the hallway toward the church that was attached to the convent. "That's right, *cher*. I was an altar boy for three years here and at St. Louis . . . I know where all the good stuff is kept."

He opened the doors with a grandiose flair. "We can mix it together and use a thurible and aspergillum to sling it at them." Then he bit his lip as if the mere thought of it caused him pain. "Man, I'm going to give the monseigneur a stroke this coming Saturday when I lay this confession on him. I'll be saying my Acts of Contrition and Hail Marys from now until I'm too feeble to kneel."

His mother sighed wearily as she took the bat back from him. "Or get us excommunicated."

Nick nodded glumly. "Bubba—"

Bubba growled, cutting him off. "Why do you keep calling me that? I detest that nickname."

"Sorry," Nick said sheepishly. "In our world, it's

the name Michael you detest, and I can't really call you Dad 'cause that's just creepy and weird . . . anyway, can you sit tight on my mom while we do this?"

Cherise took a step toward him. "Nick—"

"It's all right, Ma. This is not the most dangerous thing I've done . . . even today."

"Is that supposed to be comforting?"

"Yeah, it sounded better in my head than coming out of my mouth." Nick moved forward to hug Cherise and kiss her cheek. "Don't worry, I'm not going to die until I return your Nick to you and I get back home to my mother who needs me. Poor thing, I'm all she's got."

Cherise cupped his face in her hands. "For the record, I'm proud of both my Nicks."

"Thanks." He took her hand and placed it in Bubba's before he turned around and vanished into the hallway that connected the convent to the church.

Unsure of what was happening, Kody followed after him. Something about Nick was suddenly very different. He held a new confidence in himself that hadn't been there before. It was as if he no longer felt guilty for ruining his mother's life. As if he realized that he had real value to the world and wasn't the loser other people had called him all his life.

Strange that he would find it now when he had no powers to draw on. No real protectors to keep him safe from harm.

And yet it was there. And it was undeniable. Inside, he wasn't the same Nick he'd been when all this started.

Bemused, she watched as he gracefully genuflected and crossed himself in front of the nave before he went to where the keys were kept.

Savitar came up behind her and leaned down to whisper in her ear. "Are you absolutely sure he's the Malachai?"

"I am."

"Then you were right. He's not like any that has come before him."

"No, he's not. And I can't even begin to fathom how this boy becomes the beast that killed me. He's so . . ."

"Human."

She nodded.

"People change."

Kody bit back a smile at the irony of that coming out of the mouth of someone who was so very different himself. This Savitar wasn't anything like the acerbic Chthonian who'd taught her to surf before she was out of diapers. The Chthonian who'd trained her on how to call and command Charonte. Deep inside, she ached for those long-lost days of innocence.

Even though they weren't related by blood, Savitar had been like a grandfather to her.

"Would you mind if I hugged you?"

Savitar quirked a brow at her sudden request. "Why?"

"Because I've missed you. A lot, and I haven't seen you in centuries."

"But I'm not the same as the man you knew."

"You're more alike than you think, and right now, I could really use it."

Nick paused as he saw Kody with Savitar. She threw herself against him like a small child with a parent they hadn't seen in a long while. And it was obvious from Savitar's awkwardness that he wasn't used to being embraced by anyone. It made Nick wonder if the Savitar in his world was the same.

And he still had so many questions for Kody that he needed answered. What was Savitar to her? Really? Because what he saw right now said that she loved and adored the man. All the time he'd known her, she'd never trusted anyone. Not really.

Yet she'd trusted Savitar, even in this realm.

Trying not to think about it or be jealous, Nick ran holy water into the large plastic bin the volunteers used for storing cleaners. And even that made him feel guilty.

It'd been drilled into him from birth that holy water was sacred. They even had a special, separate drain they poured the excess down so as to keep it away from regular water.

No matter how much it meant for their survival, Nick couldn't bring himself to desecrate anything holy. His conscience was already flogging him over what he was doing. But he'd left money in the cupboard to pay for the blessed salt and the thurible and aspergillum he'd taken. It was for the survival of the world, after all. Surely he'd be forgiven for this little bit of unsanctioned use.

Nick carried the bin to the back pew where Savitar

and Kody were huddled in the shadows. "Kody? Do you have a knife on you?"

She pulled one out of her pocket and handed it to him.

Without comment, Nick rolled his sleeve back and cut his forearm.

Screwing his face up, Savitar hissed as Nick allowed his blood to drip into the bin. "You act like you've done this before."

"Not quite, but I did assist an exorcist once. We took blood from my hand for that and it made it hard to grip or make a fist. I'd rather my arm throb than my hand be rendered useless for the fighting I'm sure we're going to have to do to get out of this."

As soon as Nick was finished, Kody wrapped a cotton towel around his cut and used her powers to stop it from bleeding.

With his hand, Nick mixed the water and blood then poured it into the thurible and aspergillum. As soon as the mixture touched the holy objects, there was a subtle hissing.

Snorting, Nick looked at them. "Should I be offended at the sound it's making?"

Savitar shrugged. "Well, you were born of the darkest powers."

"But he's also born of innocence and good."

Nick smiled at Kody's rapid defense of him. She never allowed anyone to insult him or put him down in any way.

Not even himself.

Still, he hated how he'd been conceived. The misery he'd caused his real mother because she dared to keep him when any sane woman would have given him up for adoption and walked away without ever looking back. She deserved to be like the Cherise in this world. Treasured and loved.

Rich and affluent.

Instead, she'd been saddled with him, and to her credit, she'd never once made him feel like the worthless burden he was.

I love you, Mom.

Nick glanced to Kody. "My mother's heart and my father's curse. . . . God forgive me," he whispered before he handed Kody the aspergillum and headed for the doors to the outside.

Worried about Nick, Kody picked up the bin and

carried it after him while Savitar followed her. She held her breath, hoping this actually worked.

As soon as Nick was on the curb that was off holy ground, the demons came for him. Like a fearless gladiator, he waited until they were closer before he slung the thurible up and bathed them with the mixed water.

Kody bit her lip, waiting for them to explode.

They didn't. In fact, it had no effect on them at all.

Her stomach shrank painfully as she realized why. "Nick! Your blood isn't the Malachai's. It's the other Nick's blood. You're human here."

"Then why did it hiss?" He looked up at the demons and had the same "oh crap" expression she was sure was on her face. "Ever have that feeling that you're a complete and utter nimrod? Yeah, I'm there right now. . . . It was a good idea. Just a real bad execution."

"Nick!" she screamed as the demons dive-bombed him. He ran toward her as fast as he could. She opened fire on the demons with every fire blast she could manage.

Savitar joined her, but the demons were all over Nick, dragging him away from them.

"Get Kody to safety!" Nick shouted as he punched and fought against the winged demons.

They both ignored him and rushed forward.

It was too late. Before they could take more than a handful of steps, demons picked him up and carried him off.

Disbelief speared her as the demons vanished with Nick and the sky above cleared up. The sun returned to shining as if the worst thing imaginable hadn't just happened.

The Malachai's soul was in the hands of his enemies and he was powerless against them.

CHAPTER 9

"Kody!"

Dazed, she heard Savitar's fierce shout, but all she could do was blink as memories ripped through her and shredded every last piece of her sanity. Over and over, she saw her family die. Felt the stabbing agony of losing what she loved most.

Of watching her world torn apart while she was powerless to stop it.

No longer in New Orleans, she saw herself standing in front of Sraosha, Suriyel, and Adidiron after she'd died. Their spartan office had been bright and austere. Clinical.

As were they.

Like his brethren, Adidiron was dressed in his ancient bronze armor. Golden fair, he'd been so beautiful that it was hard to look upon him at all. "Will you serve us?" he'd asked her.

Their request to join their league and fight against the Malachai had floored her. "Why would you want me? I failed."

His hands folded in front of him while his wings were spanned out, Suriyel had stepped forward. Unlike Sraosha and Adidiron, he had short dark hair and vibrant gold eyes. His skin was a deep caramel that was almost the same color as her mother's. "You are the only one who has ever forced him into retreat. For three years, you managed to hold him back. And you're just a child. In all these centuries, with all the Malachai, no other general ever managed that."

"But I failed," she repeated.

"No," Sraosha contradicted. "Your anger betrayed you. Had it stayed in check, you would have succeeded."

Maybe. She wasn't as sure about that as they were. All she remembered was the hatred blazing in bloodred eyes as the Malachai delivered blow after blow to her.

He'd been relentless and huge. Nothing had daunted him. It was as if the rage inside him was so great that nothing could quell or lessen it.

Honestly, she didn't know if she was up to a rematch with that monster.

Suriyel placed a kind hand on her shoulder. "You're the only hope we have. We can send you back to the first Malachai. Kill him and reset the time sequence. Let the world know what it's like to exist without such evil in it."

She'd frowned at his request. "What about the balance?"

With a heavy sigh, Sraosha had folded his arms over his chest. "Another will rise, but whoever it is, they won't be as powerful an enemy. We will be able to keep them in check."

Still, she didn't want to go back. Even though she'd barely lived nineteen years, she felt ancient. She was so tired of fighting. Tired of watching people around her die and not being able to save them. "I don't know. . . ."

Adidiron had spread his hand toward the windows that looked out onto a clear sky. They darkened to show her the world she'd just left. Human survivors screamed out for help and death as the Malachai's army dragged them into chains to serve them.

But the worst was her aunt Artemis—the Greek goddess of the hunt who had once ridden Kody through the skies in her golden chariot. For centuries, Artemis had been Nick's sanctuary. Had sheltered and protected him.

Now, he kept her caged like an animal. Bruises and bleeding welts marred her beautiful features as she wept in hopeless despair. Just as he'd done with her uncle and father, the Malachai had stripped all of Artemis's powers and left her to suffer at the hands of his army.

That was harsh, but harsher still was the fate of Kody's cousins and the once proud goddess Apollymi. Their cries for death shredded her, heart and soul.

"Stop!" she'd screamed as she turned away from the horrors she couldn't stand to see.

But Suriyel had refused to take mercy on her. "They are immortal. The Malachai intends to keep them like that. Forever. Is that what you want?"

No. What she wanted was to go back before all

this started and have her family alive and safe. To see Urian and Ari teasing her while she played with their children. To feel her father's arms wrapped around her while her mother sang to them. To eat barbecue-drenched ice cream with Simi. . . .

Sraosha narrowed those eerie green eyes on her. "The balance hasn't been broken. It's been shattered. Think you that animal cares that he has destroyed everything good in this world? That he has left us with nothing? Left you with no one?"

Adidiron had lifted her chin until she met his gaze. "If the balance is to be tipped, is it not better for good to reign than the Malachai?"

He was right and she knew it.

Tears had flowed down her cheeks. "Send me back and I will end this. Whatever it takes!"

"Kody!"

Blinking, she left her past and found herself back in New Orleans with Savitar shaking her. She shrugged off his hold and stepped away from him so that she could think.

"Are you back?"

She nodded. "Sorry. I'm just a little overwhelmed."

"Understandable. It's not every day you get to watch a herd of demons drag off your boyfriend."

Her sanity snapping in half, she started laughing hysterically.

Savitar took a big step back. "Do I need to get you a doctor? Ambulance . . . straightjacket?"

Covering her face with her hands, she brought herself under control. "No. It's just . . . not the first time I've watched demons drag off my boyfriend . . . or my family." She closed her eyes and tried to get a handle on the situation and her slipping sanity. "And the saddest thing is I don't know what scares me most. The fact that they will most likely kill him and end the world before we can find him, or the fact that we have to walk back into that building and tell Cherise we let demons take her baby."

"Yeah. I'm going to leave that to you. I've already been on the losing end of a mother's anger. Not real anxious to repeat the experience."

Her stomach in knots from terror, Kody headed up the walkway to face Cherise. But that wasn't really her fear. Her nightmare was that she'd fail again. Fail the world, her family . . .

And the man she'd been instructed to kill who owned her heart.

CHAPTER 10

Nick came awake to a pounding ache in his head. Every inch of his body throbbed as he recalled being captured by the demons and dumped in a cage.

I'm really getting tired of this crap. It seemed like every other day, he was being taken by something and locked up someplace weird. If it didn't hurt so much, he'd laugh at just how routine crazy had become in his daily life.

Slowly, he cracked open his eyes and did his best not to show any sign of alertness until he knew where he was, and who or what was around him.

"You might as well sit up. He knew you were awake before you did."

Nick frowned at the familiar voice. Bracing himself for the pain, he rolled over on the small bed to find the Ash from his school sitting on a chair in the corner. He ground his teeth to stave off the pain and pressed his thumb to his temple. "What are you doing here? You a prisoner, too?"

"Depends on the definition, I guess."

Rubbing his head, Nick was having a hard time focusing either his sight or his thoughts. "Where am I?"

"It's called the guest room, but no one ever wants to stay here."

Yeah, it was a little cold and creepy. Four gray stone walls, no door or window. Just a bed and a chair. While there were probably some people this might appeal to, Nick was definitely not one of them.

He tried to stare at Ash, but he could barely keep his eyes open from the pain that cleaved his skull. "If you're just going to evade my questions, why are you here?"

"In case you were injured, I didn't want you to wake up alone. I know from experience that they can be really rough when they bring you in."

"The slobbering hell-monkeys?"

Ash let out a nervous laugh. "Yeah. Good term for them."

Nick leaned back against the headboard as a wave of nausea consumed him. "Do you live here?"

"Unfortunately." Panicked and nervous, Ash stood up fast. The moment he did, the chair he was in melted into the wall. "He's coming."

"Who?"

Ash didn't answer. Instead, he vanished at the same time a door appeared in the wall to Nick's left. A tall, dark shadow entered. At first, Nick thought he was hallucinating.

But no, it was real.

Throwing his head back, Nick cackled with laughter at the last thing he'd ever expected to walk into this room. Now this . . . this he had not seen coming.

The ancient Atlantean he knew so well paused at the foot of his bed with an arched brow. Standing at the almost seven feet in the height Nick was used to, Acheron was back to his in-your-face bad on bad. The only thing different was his long blond hair. But the swirling, inhuman silver eyes were there, along with the black Goth clothing.

The "real" Acheron Parthenopaeus narrowed those swirling silver eyes on Nick. "That's not the reception I'm used to receiving."

And still Nick laughed. "Yeah, well, I'm an idiot."

"Apparently." Acheron waited several more minutes while Nick continued to laugh. "Are you planning to stop that anytime soon?"

Nick held his hands up as he struggled to control himself. But every time he looked at Ash, he lost it again. He just couldn't stop laughing.

Until something grabbed him by the throat and lifted him from the bed to pin him to the wall. Yeah, that sucked the humor right out of him.

"Better." Acheron folded his arms over his chest. "Now that I have your full attention, tell me why Thorn is so eager to lay hands to you."

"I'm irresistibly cute."

"And you're about to be a stain on my wall."

"Sure you want to do that? Blood's so dang hard to paint over. Makes reselling a bitch."

Acheron scowled at him. "How is it you're human and not afraid of me?"

"Told you, I'm an idiot. Cute one. But idiot nonetheless . . . Just ask my girlfriend. She will gleefully corroborate my rampant stupidity and probably add many more examples of it."

The invisible grip brought Nick forward until he was hanging in front of Acheron, who eyed him pointedly. "You don't want to play with me, kid. I've been known to tear the limbs off things that annoy me."

"And I've been known to send grown adults into therapy, especially anger management."

The expression of irritated disbelief on Acheron's face was almost enough to make Nick laugh again, but self-preservation kept him from doing anything more than staring at the ancient being. "What gives you your strength?"

"If I said Wheaties, would you let me go?"

The grip loosened and dropped Nick straight to the floor. "I should hand you over to Thorn and let him dissect you."

"That would probably make him happy . . . me, not so much."

"And again, I ask you why."

Obviously, this Acheron wasn't as clairvoyant as the one Nick knew at home.

Time to do what I do best. Play stupid and see what Ash knows about all this.

"He thinks I'm the Malachai."

It was Acheron's turn to burst out laughing. "You?" Could he have put any more disdain into that single word?

But Nick wasn't offended. He found it rather amusing himself . . . at times. "I know, right? I think Thorn was sniffing fumes or something. Inhalants rot the brain and shrink the important equipment. Make you delusional and cause you to drool."

Acheron ignored his segue. "Why would he think that?"

Nick shrugged with a nonchalance he definitely didn't feel. "I told you. Inhalants. Bad bad stuff, that."

Indecision was plain in those eerie swirling eyes. It was obvious Acheron was trying to discern the truth. "I know you're lying to me about something. I just can't tell what." His eyes flared red. "Tell me what frightens you."

Nick felt his head starting to swim. Ash was in there, picking around his thoughts.

Let's hear it for us stubborn Cajuns. Malachai powers or not, Nick was the most obstinate and steel-willed creature ever born. No one picked his brain without his consent. Not even the great and mighty Acheron. "My worst fear? Being like everyone else. So I usually battle it with my extraordinary powers of awesomeness."

Ash curled his lip. "You think you're amusing. . . . Tell you what, let's see just how long you can keep this up in the cage."

Nick mentally winced. *Ah man, this can't be good. I should have kept my stupid mouth shut.*

One instant Nick was in the "guest room," and in the next he was dropped into the center of a fighting ring that was enclosed with steel bars. *Welcome to the Thunder Dome . . .* Rising to his feet, Nick bit back a smile. "What? You're going to cockfight me?"

Acheron walked around the outside of the cage. "Not me. I don't want to get blood on my clothes. I think I'll let my pets have a go at you first."

Nick cracked his knuckles. "Fine. Send in the hell-monkeys. I've got a score to settle with a couple of them, anyway."

"Since you're so eager to get started . . ."

A bright flash blinded Nick an instant before smoke filled the area in front of him. His jaw dropped as it cleared to reveal a huge Aamon demon—the same kind of beast as Zavid. And as with Zavid, this one was dark-haired and seriously pissed off.

Bracing himself, Nick stood steady. He refused to show fear to any creature. It just wasn't in him. "C'mon, Lassie. Let's go check out the well."

G randpa! Please, stop. You'll kill him!"
Holding back the demon that was trying to bite him, Nick turned his attention toward Acheron and the girl who held on to his arm. It took him a second to recognize the Simi from his school.

Acheron glared at him for a long minute. Then he glanced down to the angelic face of his granddaughter and snapped his fingers.

The demon on top of Nick vanished instantly.

Man, wish you'd done that an hour ago. His breathing ragged, Nick tried to push himself up, but his body was finished. It wouldn't do anything more than throb from the strain of holding the wolf away from his neck. He had a few bites on his arms and shoulder and a busted lip, yet all in all, it could have been a whole lot worse.

Acheron walked over to him. He reached through the bars to touch the blood on Nick's face. His gaze never wavering, he pulled his hand back so that he could taste Nick's blood.

Nick grimaced in distaste. "Dude, that's so nasty. You could get like hepatitis or parvo or something. Rabies even. Has your dog been vaccinated recently? I would also suggest some neutering and doggie breath mints."

His gaze darkening while he ignored the question, Acheron rolled the blood around his tongue. "You're absolutely human . . . something about this is very wrong." Without another word, he walked toward the door.

Biting her lip apprehensively, Simi approached Nick. "I'm so sorry. He's really not as bad as you think." She reached out to touch his hand. "He's just—"

"Simi!" Acheron barked.

She jumped away. "Coming." Without a backward glance, she ran after Acheron.

Sighing, Nick thought they'd forgotten him completely until he was flashed from the cage back to the doorless guest room. Well, at least Acheron put him on the bed. He'd take that for now.

Bewildered and tired, Nick stared up at the ceiling and tried to make sense of everything. So the short Ash and Simi were Acheron's grandkids in this world. But it begged the question, who were their parents?

As if on cue, the Ash from school flashed into the room. He visibly winced at the sight of Nick's torn clothes and the blood that stained them. "I'm sorry."

"That's what your sister said."

Kid Ash moved to stand next to the bed. He waved his hand over Nick and the pain went away instantly. Too bad the injuries didn't go with it. But hey, he'd take it. "Why didn't you just tell my granddad what he wanted to know?"

"Because I don't know the answer." It was mostly true.

"Then I'm doubly sorry."

Nick swung his legs over the edge of the bed to sit up. "Why do you live here with him? Where are your parents?"

Sadness darkened Ash's eyes as he moved away from the bed. "They died a long time ago. It's why my grandfather is the way he is. After my parents were killed, he turned on everyone, especially anyone who was human."

"Why? What happened?"

The wall shimmered before the chair formed out of it. It walked forward, into the room, and stopped beside Kid Ash. As if that was a normal occurrence and not totally whacked out, he sat down on it and sighed. "I guess you've figured out we're not entirely human, right?"

Nick glanced at the chair. "Um . . . yeah. Not like it's hidden here, and the hell-monkeys pretty much blew the lid off it in public."

He nodded. "My father was human. My mother a . . . I know you'll laugh, but she was a goddess." He paused to study Nick's non-reaction. "You believe me?"

Nick let out a bitter laugh. "After everything I've seen today, I'm willing to expand my definition of believable."

Ash glanced away from him. "Yeah, I guess you are. Anyway, she gave up her powers to live in the mortal world with my dad. One weekend when me and Simi were with my grandfather, some men broke into our house and killed my parents. After that, my granddad went crazy and kind of declared war on the entire world."

"I'm sorry."

"Thanks. I'm sorry you got caught up in my grandfather's lunacy. But when he heard that Thorn was looking for you and that you went to our school, he was paranoid you might pose a threat to us. Me and Sim have been on lockdown ever since and we'll remain here until he decides you're not a threat to us or he kills you. He's terribly overprotective that way."

Nick could have respected that, had he not spent

the last hour trying to keep a demon from tearing out his throat. "So what's he going to do with me?"

Leaning forward, Ash appeared to be holding something back. "I don't know. I hope he lets you go."

Nick arched a brow. "You say that like he ate the last person he trapped here."

Oh yeah, that was not a look a guy wanted to see on someone else's face when his life hung in the balance. "I should be going."

"Ash?"

He paused to glance at Nick.

"The Thorn I met earlier is a psycho, but I promise that I would never hurt you or Simi. I don't turn on my friends and I don't cause them harm. My mama raised me better."

"I know. I just hope we can convince my grandfather of that. He's not used to honorable people. Only those who are out to do as much damage as possible . . . and usually to the most innocent." And with that, Ash vanished and left him alone. The chair backed itself into the wall again and melted.

Baffled, tired, and defeated, Nick stared up at the ceiling and tried to remember what life had been like before all the insanity had started. In some ways, he missed the naive assumption that the world was only inhabited by humans. But honestly, it'd been no less evil. Not really. The enemy had only taken other forms in those days. One good thing about demons, they didn't pretend to be your friend. They declared their enmity and attacked accordingly. Full frontal assault.

Humans, alone, pretended to be your friend while plotting ways to stab you in the back and cut your throat. Many times for nothing more than their own petty amusement.

That, he definitely didn't miss.

Closing his eyes, Nick allowed his thoughts to drift back to the world he knew. The friends he could count on. While his life was hard—sometimes impossible—aggravating, and grueling, it was his.

And he missed it. More than he would have ever thought possible.

Nick released a long, pent-up breath and relaxed in spite of the stress of being here. His ears rang as he drifted to sleep.

But no sooner did he feel his body go limp than he heard Caleb's angry curses. Following the sound, Nick suddenly found himself in Caleb's elaborate mansion, which appeared to be under siege.

At first, he thought he was dreaming.

Until he saw the other Nick, cringing on the stairs with his hands over his ears as he cowered. It was the strangest sensation to see himself doing something so out of character.

Zavid was covered with bruises and bleeding cuts as he stepped over the body of three twisted demons that lay in the center of the marble foyer. His breathing labored from the fight, he glared at Caleb. "You and I need to discuss the definition of *protected*, Malphas, because mine is apparently radically different from yours."

"What is *that*?" "Nick" screamed in a tone that could double as a sonic weapon while he pointed to the demon carcasses.

Holding one hand up to his ear, Caleb visibly cringed. "I really miss Gautier. While he might be a major pain most of the time, at least the kid can hold his own in a fight . . . and he doesn't scream like a prepubescent girl who just had a spider run up her arm."

Zavid started to blast the other Nick.

Caleb grabbed his arm to stop it. "Unless you want to carry him in the fight, don't."

Zavid bared his fangs at Caleb. "I think we should hand him over and let them have his worthless hide."

"Don't tempt me. But until we find out what's going on and where Kody went, we need to keep protecting him."

"Why?"

Caleb gave Zavid a droll stare. "Nick's my friend and I don't have many of those. No offense, I don't want to lose him. And I definitely don't want to tell his mom we let him get lost."

Those words stunned the real Nick as he watched them. It wasn't like Caleb to admit that to anyone. And it touched him deeply. Honestly, he'd thought all this time that Caleb would rather cut his head off and use it for a bowling ball than put up with him. At least that's what Caleb had always told him.

The Hel Hound held his hands up in surrender. "Never have understood the mind of a daeve and you're not making this any easier."

Caleb began chanting, strengthening the spell that was supposed to protect his house from preternatural interlopers.

Zavid growled as something hit the window closest to him. "You should have never bound Gautier's powers. If he had them, he could just sneeze the vermin back into their hole."

"It's not that simple."

Zavid scoffed. "How is it not?"

Caleb started toward the other Nick then paused to look back at Zavid. "Do you know how a Malachai evolves?"

"Yeah, they're spawned by mothers who hate them with every breath they take, and are beaten into beasts."

Caleb nodded. "Nick has been shielded from that kind of hatred his whole life. While he's had a few people who despise him, he's had many more love him. The moment any hatred rises around him, his mother negates it. She calms and cares for him. Loves him. It's why Cherise is so important to all of us. She is his anchor. For Nick to be blasted with the full weight of his bloodline . . . we don't know what it'll do to him.

Every time those powers have taken hold inside him, he's blacked out mentally while destroying everything that's in his vicinity. He's not in control. And an out-of-control Malachai is the last thing any of us need. Especially when that Malachai has not only his own powers, but those of his extremely powerful father."

"Highly valid points." Zavid rubbed his hand over his brow. "And you're right. I barely got a taste of Adarian Malachai and that was with him severely weakened. I can only imagine how deadly he was at full strength."

"Don't have to imagine. Was there, and had my butt handed to me after Adarian put it in a sling."

Suddenly, the window behind Zavid shattered. A blast of fire came through it, setting Caleb's curtains ablaze.

Without thinking, Nick started toward it to help put it out. He'd only taken a step before something pulled him back. He reached out with his arms.

It did no good.

Aggravated, he spun away from the sight of them

stamping out flames until he was alone in utter darkness. Even so, he felt a subtle stirring in the air by his side.

"Will you help my brother?"

He turned to find a woman there who bore an uncanny resemblance to Zavid. "Can you see me?"

She nodded. "I'm a ghost, too."

"I'm not a ghost." At least he didn't think he'd died while sleeping.

Scowling, she looked at the fake Nick then back at him. "Are you the real Malachai?"

"I guess I am."

Anger darkened her eyes. "You guess?"

"Yes," he said more forcefully. "I'm the Malachai."

That seemed to appease her. "How did you get separated from your body without being a ghost?"

How he wished he had an answer. "I'm open to any suggestion you might have about that. Ticked off the wrong body-changing god?"

She paused to consider his words. "They must be trying to kill you."

"Most things are, but who are *you* referring to?"

"Your generals." She stepped back. "Something

must have changed. They wanted you to claim and develop your powers from your father so that they could use and control you. But to separate your soul from your body . . . death is the only reason for that."

Nick scowled at her. She had a lot of pertinent information that was missing from his knowledge bank. "Who are you?"

"I'm Zarelda."

That name meant nothing to him, but if she was related to Zavid, that would make her a demon, too. "You're an Aamon?"

She winced at his question. "I was. Then I was betrayed and left to die alone." A tear slid down her cheek. "I just wanted to be loved by someone. Just once in my life. But perhaps you and I are alike in that no one can love our species. We don't deserve it. We are both born to suffer endlessly."

Nick shook his head. She was wrong. She had to be. "I don't believe that. Everyone deserves love."

Denial burned bright in her eyes. "The only one who ever loved me was Zavid. He gave up everything, including the one person he loved above all, to save me. And I ruined him." A tear slid down her cheek.

"His heart is so pure and true. Please. You must help my brother."

"Help him how?"

"Keep him safe from Hel. I should never have allowed him to take my place. It was selfish and wrong. I was scared and stupid. No excuse, I know, and yet I didn't stop him when I should have. But you will help him, yes?"

She was caught on that loop. Not that he blamed her. He'd be the same way if he'd hurt someone he loved.

"Yeah. I'll do my best . . . If I can ever get back to my body."

"You must get your powers back."

She said that as if it were easy and under his control. "If I knew how to do that, I'd have done it already."

Zarelda's gaze burned into him. "You are the Malachai. The most powerful of all demonkyn. Your powers are always with you. They are a part of your very soul . . . not your body. No one, except your son, can ever take them from you. You just have to believe in them and in yourself." She began fading.

"Wait!"

"Save my brother." The words whispered and echoed around him as she vanished.

Nick cursed at the darkness that was now so thick it pressed in on him. Made it hard to breathe.

"You know," he shouted, "if it was that simple, I'd have done it already!" He knew she couldn't hear him, but he felt the need to state that out loud.

Believe in myself and my powers . . .

Sure. Why not?

Sighing, he clenched his fists and in the most enthusiastic voice he could muster he called out, "I believe!"

Of course, nothing happened. Other than he sounded like an Oz munchkin on a helium high . . .

Just follow the yellow brick road. Follow the yellow brick road.

"Gah, I am losing it." Why not? Both places had slobbering hell-monkeys. "Just don't put me in a pair of red ruby high heels." Or drop a house on him. That was all his screwed-up life needed.

But as he drifted through the darkness, one thing crystalized for him. He had to become whole again even if it meant embracing the part of himself he not only hated most, but the part of him that terrified every cell in his body.

And if he had to sell his soul to keep his loved ones safe, he'd draft the contract himself and nail it to the devil's forehead.

CHAPTER 11

Nick jerked awake as the air around him shifted. Ready to battle, he opened his eyes to find the scary Acheron standing by his bed. Yawning, he rubbed at his eyes. "Oh look, it's Mr. Happy-Creepy come to feed me to more of his pets."

"How can you not be afraid of me?"

Nick shrugged. "Guess I knew you in a former life."

Acheron narrowed his spooky gaze on him. He cocked his head as if he was listening to the ether for clues or information. That was yet another unreliable power Nick missed having. "Thorn has offered me quite a bargain to hand you over to him."

"Should I pack my things?" Nick looked down at

himself. "Oh wait, I forgot. Don't have anything to pack." He sighed wearily. "Not even a toothbrush. My dentist would be so disappointed in me."

Ash let out a sound of supreme irritation. Not like that was a first for the two of them. "How can you have no fear whatsoever?"

"The only thing we have to fear is fear itself," Nick said in his best FDR accent, then he shrugged nonchalantly. "Worst you can do is kill me."

Acheron gave him a gimlet stare. "Worst we could do is torture you."

Nick grinned at his threat. "Pain I can take. Really. Doesn't scare me, either."

Acheron rolled his eyes before he pulled something out from under his coat and slung it at Nick. Some kind of wet spider-webby something covered him.

Hissing, Nick wiped the clear, stringy goo off his face. "Ew! What *is* that?" It smelled like Stone's week-old gym socks.

Incredulous, Acheron tucked his vial into his pocket. "Proof you're not the Malachai. That would have seared your demon's flesh . . . which still makes me curious as to why Thorn wants you so badly if you're human."

Nick continued to wipe it away. "Told you. I'm irresistibly cute."

"I should probably kill you, just to be safe."

Pausing, Nick wiped his hand against his jeans. "I'd really rather you not."

"Thought death didn't scare you."

"Roaches don't either, but I don't want to be covered in them. Know what I mean?"

An amused glint lit those weird eyes. "Strangely, I do, kid."

"Grandpa?"

Acheron froze at the sound of Simi's hesitant voice. Before he could move, she appeared in the room with them. Her face pale, she was trembling.

"Simkey?" Acheron breathed, pulling her against him. It was only then that Nick saw the blood on her. Something had cut her in the stomach.

She showed Acheron her blood-covered hands that shook with the weight of her pain. "T-t-they said I was evil. That I-I needed to die."

Tears filled Acheron's eyes. "Who did this?"

Her breathing labored, she couldn't respond as she collapsed. Acheron laid her down on the floor. Now his hands trembled even more than hers did while tears streaked down his face.

"Don't leave me, Simkey," Acheron breathed, taking her hand into his.

Nick was stunned by Ash's actions. Why wasn't he helping her? Where were the glowing hands and . . . stuff that Acheron normally did whenever someone was injured? "Heal her!" he snarled.

Growling, he glared at Nick. "I can't!"

Huh? Nick scoffed at him. "You have the power. I've seen it."

Acheron shook his head. "I've never had the power to heal. Not since I crossed over and became the Harbinger. I lost those powers."

Anger welled up inside Nick as he watched her breathing grow shallower. Her features paled. She wouldn't last much longer. And as the hopeless fury built inside him, his hands heated up to a volcanic level. His heart raced.

She didn't deserve to die. Not like this and definitely not because of him.

In that moment, Nick remembered the words Menyara would use whenever he was sick as a boy—which was a lot, since his human body had been at war with its demonic blood. Time and again, doctors had told his mother that it would be a miracle if he lived until morning.

In true Cajun fashion, Nick had defied them all, and he now refused to let Simi die like this. Without hesitation, he closed the distance between them, knelt on the floor by her side, and placed his hands over her wound.

Letting out an elongated breath, he whispered the words that his godmother had impressed into his memory:

Hear me Isis as I pray.
See her pain and take it all away.
Let the heaven's light shine bright from above.
And wrap her in your most benevolent love.
Let no evil touch this child.

Protect and hold her all the while.
Save her from the darkness, ills and fevers of all kind.
Heal her wounds by your most sacred design.
There is nothing more earnest I can say.
Except please accept my humble heart as I pray.

He'd barely finished whispering those words before his hands heated up even more, to an unbearable level. An orange glow radiated from his hands to her stomach, similar to the one that usually shot out of Acheron.

Simi shrieked. Acheron threw Nick against the wall and gathered her in his arms. He let out an anguished cry of pain that came from the darkest part of his soul while he rocked her.

Rattled and dazed, Nick shook his head as he tried to focus and push himself up from the floor where he'd landed.

"Grandpa, please . . . you're squeezing me too tight. I can't breathe."

Nick wasn't sure who was more stunned. Him or Acheron.

The ancient Atlantean pulled back to look down at

the girl he held. He brushed the hair back from her face. "Simi?"

She made an irritated face at him. "You're still crushing me."

Instead of releasing her, Acheron pulled her against his chest and held her like an infant. Over Simi's shoulder, Acheron met Nick's gaze. "How did you do this?"

Nick shrugged. "Danged if I know. It was just something my aunt used to say over me whenever I was sick or hurt."

Simi tugged at Acheron's sleeve to get his attention. "Grandpa, someone broke in and they attacked me. We have to find Ash and make sure he's all right."

His eyes flared red before he released her. "You stay here with him. I'll be right back." He narrowed his gaze on Nick. "Do not let her be harmed or I will show you unimaginable pain." He vanished.

Simi ran her hand over the tear in her shirt that was soaked with blood. Then, she looked up at Nick. "What are you?"

"Honestly? I don't know. I've never been able to

heal anything and was told I couldn't. No idea what just happened or why. Really. But I'm glad it worked."

"Thank you for saving me." She pulled him into her arms and hugged him. Before she let go, she placed a quick kiss to his cheek.

An instant later, her eyes widened as they both heard the sound of brutal fighting from outside their room. It sounded like two medieval armies going at each other with everything they had. Shouts rang out along with blasts and hissing.

Nick put himself between her and the noise. "Don't worry. I won't let them hurt you again."

Simi placed a hand on his shoulder. "Are you always this gallant?"

"For a lady, absolutely." Nick flashed a grin at her. "Dudes, on the other hand, can slug it out for themselves." He braced himself to fight as a bright light flashed in front of them.

Younger Ash appeared in the room. The panic left his eyes as soon as he saw his sister. He rushed forward to hug her like Acheron had done when he realized she'd been wounded. "Are you all right?"

She nodded. "You?"

"Yeah. I was keeping to the shadows, trying to find you, until Grandpa saw me and sent me in here. What are those things that broke in?"

"I don't know. I've never seen anything like them before."

They both looked expectantly at Nick, who took a step back in apprehension. "What? I have no idea what's making that sound. Unlike you two, I haven't seen them at all."

The entire room shook so hard, it knocked them off their feet. Nick caught himself against the bed. One second they were in the room, the next, they were inside a large, doorless study with Big Scary Ash. His expression said this was not a good time to ask to borrow his car keys or spare your life.

He gathered his grandkids to him and held them against his side while he narrowed his gaze on Nick. The anger inside it was searing. "Do you know how rare Arelim are?"

Nick shifted nervously. "Since I've never heard the term before, I'll go with very. Why?"

"Why is my question for you. Why would they be after a mere human boy?"

Nick shrugged. "My sexy wardrobe tips?"

Acheron growled, exposing his fangs, as he tightened his hold on his grandkids. "I've had it with your smart mouth." Before Nick could comment, he shouted. "Xirena!"

Ash had barely finished the name before a huge Charonte demon appeared in front of them.

Nick's jaw went slack. How was this possible? Savitar had told him that there weren't any Charonte in this realm. He started to say something about that then decided to wait. This probably wasn't a good time to go into it. And this Charonte appeared even more surly than the Simi Nick was used to whenever Simi ran out of barbecue sauce, early in her meal.

Taller than Acheron, Xirena had blond hair and red eyes. And while Nick's Simi was always cute and a little scary, this one was beautiful and terrifying.

If that was what a full-grown Charonte looked like, Nick would take Simi's adorable Gothness any day.

Xirena's sudden appearance made him wonder if Acheron was going to hand her a bottle of barbecue sauce, point to Nick, and say, "Bon appétit."

"You summoned me, my lord?"

Scary Acheron released his grandkids and nudged them toward her. "Protect them with your life. Call me if *anything* comes near them."

She inclined her head to him.

"Grandpa—" Simi vanished with her brother and Xirena before she could utter another sound.

Acheron turned his full attention to Nick, who suddenly felt like a mosquito in a science lab jar. "Now, you and I are going to chat."

"I thought that was what we'd been doing."

"No . . . and if you don't tell me everything about yourself, I'm going to feed you to my Aamon. But not before I rip out your guts just enough to leave you living in utter agony. Understood?"

Nick wasn't afraid of that threat, just very apprehensive. Mostly because he knew the ancient being could definitely carry it out. "Got it. But first, you have to promise that you won't hand me over to my enemies or cause anyone I care about to be harmed."

Acheron scoffed. "Are you out of your mind to try and make a deal with me?"

"No." Nick kept his emotions under control and a lid on his sarcasm. "If I'm going to die, it's on my own terms and alone. It won't be after I've told you some-thing that could get a lot of people I love hurt. Do *you* understand?"

The ancient immortal considered it before he fi-nally acquiesced. "Very well."

Screwing his face up, Nick hesitated. "You didn't say the magic words."

"Please?"

"No. That you promise not to hand me over to my enemies or see the people I love get hurt."

The expression on Acheron's face telegraphed his anger and irritation. But luckily, he didn't act on ei-ther. "Fine," he said at last. "I promise not to hand you over to your enemies or allow the ones you love to be harmed because of what you say. Now tell me every-thing."

"That still binds you in this realm, right? You once told me that you can't go back on a promise without dying."

Acheron stiffened. "I didn't tell you any such thing."

Nick held his hands up to calm the rising anger that caused Acheron's eyes to turn as red as Xirena's. "True or false. You can't break a promise?"

Again, Acheron hesitated before he answered. "True."

"Okay." Nick took a deep breath and braced himself for the worst, because he didn't think Ash would handle this news well. "I really am the Mala-chai."

Bingo. Acheron mind-gripped him and shoved him against the wall with enough force to make it count.

"It's the truth!" Nick ground out from his constricted throat.

"Don't lie! You're human!"

"Separated from my body."

"Yes, you're about to be."

Nick shook his head. "Seriously, dude? I tell you the truth and *this* is how you do me?"

The grip left his neck so fast that he almost fell.

Acheron's eyes returned to silver as he paced a small area in front of Nick. "Very well. Explain."

Rubbing his neck, Nick put some distance between them. Not that it really mattered, but it made him feel a little more in control. "Somehow, someone separated me from my body and sent me here, into your realm."

"The body you're in now? Are you telling me it's not yours?"

Nick held his arms out. "Definitely not mine. Trust me. I'm much goofier in my real body. This belongs to some human kid I never knew existed until I woke up as him. I think he was sent into the past to live in my body and I was yanked here to this realm to be inside his. But he does have the better wardrobe. Props to *his* mom."

Acheron cursed. "And the Arelim are after you and have attacked me to get to you. Care to tell me why?"

"I'm the Malachai?"

The red returned to Acheron's eyes.

"Dude, look, I don't know. Okay? I don't know what they are so I can't even begin to guess why they're here for me. The most common answer whenever something wants to eat or capture me is that I'm my father's son. If you have another suggestion, I'm all ears. Personally, I'd like to be wanted for something else, like my sexy, studly appeal, once in a while."

Acheron began pacing again. "That does explain Thorn's interest."

"He's into my nerdy, sexy, studly appeal?"

Ash completely ignored his comment. "As the Mal-achai, you have the ability to command him in this dimension."

"Really? 'Cause I told him to leave me alone and he definitely played Beethoven."

Pausing, Ash had an expression on his face of confusion mixed with severe intestinal woe. "The composer? Why would he play *his* music?"

Wow, for an ancient beast who'd probably had dinner with the man, Acheron could be remarkably obtuse. "No. Thorn played deaf. Like Beethoven."

Snorting, Acheron shook his head. "Where are your powers?"

"Wish I knew. Wish I had them. They were bound up tight when my father died."

Acheron curled his lip as if he was standing knee-deep in a sewer. "Why?"

"For my safety. I was having a hard enough time learning my own powers and not killing someone while I did so. Last thing any of us wanted was for me to have even more psychic crap I couldn't control. I could've put my eye out or lost another body part or something . . . Maybe even added one or two."

That only seemed to confuse Ash more. "You haven't had your powers from birth?"

"No. I had no idea I was a Malachai's son until a few months back, really."

"Fascinating." Ash paused to scowl at him. "And what demon class is your mother?"

"Not. She's human."

Ash gaped at the news. "Why?"

"Why what?"

"Why would a Malachai procreate with a human?"

Nick shrugged. "Pretty sure he didn't mean to. He definitely didn't think much of me. Other than the male fruit of his loins was a keen disappointment."

His scowl deepening, Ash renewed his pacing. "In your realm, you were raised alone? An orphan?"

"No. I live with my mother."

"Who hates you."

Nick sneered at the assumption. Which actually wasn't that farfetched. The Malachai was supposed to be hated by his maternal unit. But it ticked him off that anyone would assume anything bad about his saintly mother. "Hardly. I'm all she's got and she loves me more than anything."

Acheron shook his head. "You are a total freak of nature."

"*Excusez, pischouette!* Have you looked in a mirror lately? You wouldn't exactly win any normal awards yourself. Rather, you look like you done got dragged through the whole freak forest, and went back in for a second row."

Incredulous, Acheron arched his brow. "Did you just call me a little girl?"

"That's all you got out of what I just said?"

"No. I heard every word, I'm only stunned you dared insult me so."

"Yeah, well, in case you haven't noticed, fear ain't exactly my friend. I don't invite it into my house or sit with it at lunch, so it leaves me alone."

Ash rubbed at his brow. "And yet you're half human. . . ."

"Meaning?"

"You should never have survived with Malachai blood. Humans are weak. I've never even heard of a Malachai touching one before."

"If you met my mother, you'd understand. She's beautiful and loving. An angel in human form. There's no one else like her."

"She'd have to be someone special to love a child conceived like you had to have been."

That would have stung more had it not been the truth. It was a guilt that hung heavy in Nick's heart. "She never even told me. I knew she had no love of my father, but I assumed it was because he was a felon. She's never once given any indication that I was different from any other wanted baby born to parents who dated each other." Tears choked him as he thought back to all the times his mother had sacrificed her life and dignity to give him things so that he wouldn't know how poor they really were.

All the times she'd held him as if he was the most valuable thing in the world to her.

"You really do love your mother," Acheron breathed in disbelief.

"I told you that."

Ash continued to stare at him as if he smelled like Mark in his "special" ghillie suit. "A Malachai capable of love . . ."

"Yeah, nobody's perfect."

Acheron laughed. "You've no idea."

"Actually, I do."

The Atlantean fell silent as he continued to pace. Awkward with the sudden intensity of Ash's thinking, Nick debated the sanity of interrupting him. He really wanted to, but there was an air about Ash that said he needed a few minutes to get a handle on everything. And that was something Nick understood better than anyone. There was nothing about his life that was simple or easy, and especially normal. Many days, he had a hard time wrapping his own head around his reality.

Finally, Acheron spoke again. "Why did you save Simi after what I did to you?"

"It was the right thing to do. *She* never hurt me. Not her fault her granddad's a jerk."

"And my Aamon? You held him off you, but you never fought him."

Nick shrugged. "He didn't insult my mama. I had no real discord with him." He glanced down at the wounds on his forearm. "A few bites ain't nothing witch hazel won't fix. Didn't feel like kicking Lassie for his idiocy. Figured you probably do that enough for the both of us. No need to add to his misery. But, dude, really, you should buy him a toothbrush or Altoids, 'cause, man, his breath is nasty."

"And *you're* the Malachai." His tone said that Ash couldn't reconcile any kind of compassion with Nick's DNA. Made sense. As a Malachai, he wasn't supposed to have any whatsoever.

For anyone.

But that had never been him. Nick Gautier was a different kind of beast. Unique to himself.

Nick grinned at the confused Atlantean. "That's what everything that has attacked me has told me. I assume they can't *all* be lying."

Hands on hips, Acheron let out a tired breath. "I'm going to be honest. My first inclination is to murder you where you stand."

"Option B?"

Ash snorted at his sarcasm. "You helped my granddaughter. For that alone, I grant you a reprieve."

"Gracias."

"Da nada." Ash paused before he spoke again. "Ac-

tually, it is something. You are a threat to my family, therefore I only have one choice."

The deadly tone of his voice sent a chill down Nick's spine. "And that is?"

"I have to get rid of you immediately." And by the severe tone of his voice, Nick knew Acheron didn't mean he'd take him home.

Ash was most likely going to kill him.

CHAPTER 12

O ne second, they were in Ash's study, and in the next, they were in the middle of a massive and impressive war zone. Beautiful winged soldiers battled Aamons in wolf form and hell-monkeys. Axes and fire blasts mixed with snarls, hisses, and curses.

But as soon as the winged soldiers saw Nick, they pulled back from the fighting to stare at him. Everything came to a sudden stop.

Yeah, *that* was disturbing. It felt the same as standing naked in the gym in the middle of a pep rally.

A tall winged soldier who was dressed in reddish-gold armor approached them slowly. His pale blond hair fell from under his helm to his shoulders. More than that, the soldier was pretty enough to make even the hottest swimsuit model turn green with envy. "So, Acheron, you've come to your senses." He stopped abruptly, just like Kody had done when they'd tried to leave Karma's house. Touching the invisible force-field, he glared at Ash. "What is this?"

Ash answered his question with one of his own. "Why do you want this boy?"

"That is not *your* concern, Atlantean. Now hand him over or we'll tear this house down."

With a grim gleam in his eyes, Ash held his ground. "You're willing to go to war over a human?"

A slow smile spread across the soldier's face. "Are you?"

Nick held his breath as his life hung in the balance of this conversation. He had no idea why the winged soldiers wanted him, but he was pretty sure it wasn't to send him home with puppies, roses, and rainbows.

The soldier glanced over his shoulder to the rest of his army and said something Nick couldn't translate. All of a sudden, they threw their arms out in unison and sent a sonic blast toward Ash and Nick.

Nick expected it to rebound off the force field.

It didn't.

Rather, it sent both him and Ash reeling. Nick slammed against a wall with enough force to knock the air from his lungs. His back burned as his vision dimmed. Now, *that* stung.

The leader stepped over Ash's body and grabbed Nick by his arm and hauled him to his feet.

"What are you?" Nick breathed.

"Death."

Nick snorted at the arrogant tone. "No offense, I've met the man and he's a lot more badass than you . . . prettier, too."

Laughing, the soldier grabbed him by the throat and choked him.

"Ameretat!" Acheron snarled as he rose slowly to his feet. "Let him go!"

The soldier blasted Ash away while he increased the pressure on Nick's neck.

Unable to breathe, Nick did his best to break Ameretat's hold, but there was nothing he could do. His face turned hot. His ears rang fiercely.

Just as he started to black out, Ameretat went flying. An instant later, Acheron tossed Nick over his shoulder and teleported them out.

Coughing and wheezing, Nick tried to focus his gaze as he found himself back in Acheron's study. Ash set him down on his feet then stepped away. He gave a shaky laugh as he met Acheron's gaze. "Admit it, Ash. I'm too fluffy and adorable to kill." He batted his eyelashes.

For a second, he was sure Ash would take over where Ameretat had left off and choke the rest of the life out of him. Finally, Ash rolled his eyes and scoffed derisively. "When we get you back to your mother, you better hug her close and thank her."

"Not that I don't always do that, but for what in specific?"

"The fact that I can't break her heart by doing what I'm sure would be the best thing for everyone. Handing you over to them."

Nick drew a ragged breath through his sore throat. "We both thank you for your restraint."

Ash ignored the comment. "I've never tried to send someone into an alternate universe before. Never mind send them in and pull someone else out. But—"

"Wait," Nick dodged Acheron's hand.

"What?"

"My girlfriend's here, too."

Ash gaped in disbelief. "How do you mean?"

"When Thorn attacked me, somehow I pulled her here. Kind of like saving Simi. No idea how it happened. It just did."

Cursing under his breath, Ash glared at Nick. "Where is she?"

"She was at the convent where your hell-monkeys found me. Pretty sure she's not there now. But that's just a guess."

The expression on Ash's face said that he was about to follow through with his threat and return Nick to his enemies. "Is she human?"

"Kind of."

Ash cursed again. "I know I don't want to ask this, but the compulsion's more than I can bear. What's *kind of* human?"

Debating the sanity of answering, Nick decided that he owed some kind of explanation to Acheron for not allowing him to die at Ameretat's hand. But he had a bad feeling Ash wasn't going to like it. "She's a ghost."

Acheron scowled at him. "A ghost?"

He nodded. "Weird, right? But true nonetheless."

"Can't I send you back and then you call her?"

"I'd rather you not . . . just in case I can't. No offense, but the whole girlfriend designation means I'm kind of attached to her and would be very put out if she didn't make it back and I did."

"What kind of idiot dates a ghost?" The expression on Ash's face said that he was about to send Nick back anyway. Until his phone rang. He pulled it out of his pocket and checked the ID. After hesitating a few more seconds, he made a sound of supreme irritation before he finally answered it. "Savitar . . . it's been a while."

Grateful for the reprieve, Nick said a quiet prayer of thanks for Savitar's timing.

And that new look Ash cast in his direction told him that he was the prime subject of their conversation. A conversation that was worsening whatever intestinal woe had besieged Acheron.

SHERRILYN KENYON

Nick cupped his hands around his mouth. "Tell Sav I said hi."

Acheron narrowed his eyes in warning. "Yeah, I'll bring him to you." He turned off the phone and grabbed Nick's arm. Before Nick could blink, they were back in the Burdette mansion. His mom and Bubba were sitting on the couch not far from Savitar while Kody stood in one corner, chewing her thumbnail. A tall blond man Nick assumed to be Mark was next to her.

The moment Kody saw him, she dropped her hand and gave him a smile that set fire to every male hormone in his body. "Oh thank the gods!" She ran to him and hugged him close. "We've been worried sick."

Nick closed his eyes and inhaled the sweet scent of her hair. Yeah, okay, he'd take a beating and then some for this. There really were no words for what he felt anytime Kody was with him.

"Girlfriend?" Acheron asked sarcastically.

Nick grinned. "You don't think I'd let just anyone molest me like this, do you?"

"Now I get it," Ash mumbled as he and Savitar locked gazes. Something dark passed between them that said they had a bad history with each other. But what Nick didn't miss was the way Kody reacted as she realized Acheron was with him. It was subtle. Just a tensing of her body. A flash of pained recognition in her eyes. Most people wouldn't have caught it at all, but Nick was attuned to every nuance of her.

She knew Acheron. Well.

Gently, Nick tilted her chin until she met his gaze. "What is it?" he whispered.

Refusing to answer, she shook her head. "Nothing."

Yet he knew better. It was another secret she refused to share. Had she dated Acheron or something?

Gah, he hoped not. That would mess up his head even worse than Bubba dating his mama. Never mind the fact that the two of them were married in this realm.

It was sick all the way around.

"Well," Ash said to Nick. "Now that you're reunited, let's get rid of you both."

Savitar snorted. "Won't work."

Acheron glared at Savitar. "What do you mean?"

Savitar jerked his chin toward Nick. "He's been split. You can't send him home and bring the other kid back."

"How do *you* know?"

"How do you *not* know?" Savitar challenged Ash.

Rolling his eyes, Acheron scoffed. "When was the last time you were right about anything?"

"That's a cold, low blow."

When Ash started for Savitar, Kody broke them apart.

The scowl returned to Ash's face as he stared down at her. "Do I know you?"

Kody swallowed hard before she shook her head. "Please don't fight."

"Are you sure we don't know each other?"

Nick held his breath, waiting for her to answer Ash's question.

Clearing her throat, Kody glanced at Nick. "We've never met."

His lip curled, Savitar moved to stand by a wall. He crossed his arms over his chest before he sneered at Acheron. "A double transmutation through dimensions . . . Not even *you* can do that."

Ash gestured toward Nick. "If it's been done, it can be undone."

"And we're not talking about turning iron into

gold, oh great alchemist Acheron," Savitar countered. "We're transmuting two living creatures across dimensions simultaneously. I've never even heard of this being done. Have you?"

Acheron didn't answer.

"Well?" Savitar prompted.

"Yes." Ash gestured at Nick and Kody. "How else did he get here?"

Savitar let out an extremely rude noise that was followed by an even ruder gesture.

"Would Arelim have that power?"

Every eye in the room turned to Nick with an intensity so disturbing, he felt a sudden need to make sure his deodorant was still working.

Kody frowned at him. "How do you know that term?"

That intense look made him squirm even more. "Um . . . we ran into them earlier."

"What?" she gasped. Her face went white.

"They attacked my home and stabbed my granddaughter."

Kody gasped at Acheron's news and she paled even more. "Mia was hurt? Is she all right?"

Acheron slid a scowl toward Savitar that questioned Kody's sanity. "Who's Mia?"

"Your granddaughter."

"I thought you didn't know Ash?" Nick asked, interrupting them.

Kody stepped away from him.

"My granddaughter is Simi."

Kody pressed her hands to her face. "Sorry. I keep forgetting that everything's so different here." She glanced back at Acheron. "Is she all right?"

Ash jerked his chin at Nick. "He saved her . . . healed her somehow."

Nick held his hands up as Kody turned to him for an explanation. "Don't ask. Don't know. Still have no known powers here. But there is something that I learned even more interesting than my would-not-be powers. Ash has a living Charonte."

Now it was Acheron's turn to squirm under their scrutiny.

Incredulous, Savitar pushed himself away from the wall. "I thought they were all dead."

A tic started in Ash's jaw before he spoke. "I still have Xirena."

Savitar's expression darkened. "Why didn't you tell me?"

"I never intended for anyone to know she survived. I swore to protect her and I will. She and my grandchildren are in a location where no one can reach them. Not even you." Ash turned back toward Nick and Kody. "But one Charonte is nothing against an entire Arelim battalion."

"Who led them?" Kody asked.

"Ameretat."

Pressing the back of her hand to her lips, Kody moved away from them. Now *there* was an expression Nick was more than familiar with.

"You know him," Nick said as a statement and not a question.

To his complete shock, she nodded. Wow, she *could* actually answer a question without hedging. That was a miracle. "Or rather, I know the one in *our* time. He's brutal, but under the command of others. Ours wouldn't have attacked on his own. But this one . . ." She met Acheron's gaze. "What did he want?"

Ash pointed to Nick. "Your boyfriend. Hog-tied and delivered."

"And they attacked you in your home and assaulted an innocent . . ." Her voice was scarcely more than a whisper. "This is so bad."

Nick closed the distance between them. "What?"

Biting her lip, she looked up at him. The fear in her eyes made his gut tighten. He couldn't stand for her to be hurt or afraid of anything, especially not of him. "I think I know what happened. When I failed to kill you, Sraosha and the others must have banded together to split you in half in your time period. Even as a fledgling Malachai, you were too powerful for them to take on. It's why they sent me to *your* predecessors first. They were hoping to prevent your birth." She laid her hand against his cheek. "You truly have no idea just how powerful you will be in only a handful of years. How deadly and cruel the Ambrose Malachai is. And when we bound your powers to prevent that, they must have used the opportunity to do this."

Savitar gestured at Nick. "But *how*?"

Shrugging, she dropped her hand from his face. "They're the keepers of Time and Order. I'm assuming that as they've sent me from time period to time period to battle his forefathers, they could have moved

Nick's soul to this one without his body. It's the only thing that makes sense."

"So how do we get them to undo this?" Nick asked.

"They won't." Kody pressed her lips together. "But let me contact them and see if I can find out anything more. If I can learn how they did it, we should be able to undo it."

Nick inclined his head to her.

Kody went to Ash. "Can you take me to your house so that I can teleport from there?"

Nick didn't like the sound of that. Why did she want to be alone with Acheron? "Why not here?"

She glanced back at him. "They want you, Nick. Apparently at any cost. I don't want them to use me as a locator and then attack all of you here. Let me go where I know they can't use me to trace you." She turned to Ash. "I'm assuming your house is shielded?"

"Yeah. I still haven't figured out how they got in to attack us."

Kody knew, but it was a secret she had no intention of sharing with anyone. Even her uncle. She was in enough trouble with her people already. No need in worsening it.

When she started to leave, Nick stopped her. "Be careful."

"You, too." She kissed his cheek then allowed Acheron to teleport them to his home.

As soon as they were in the grand foyer, Ash pinned her with a gimlet stare that was so similar to the one her father used whenever he was angry. Pain flooded her with that memory.

And Ash gave her no reprieve. "You were lying earlier. You do know me, don't you?"

Against her will, tears filled her eyes and tightened her throat. "I do . . . and I don't."

"What do you mean?"

A sad smile toyed at the edges of her lips as she ached to hug him. He looked so much like her father that it was hard to be with him and deal with the savage grief that wanted to send her to her knees. She would give anything to have one minute with her father again. Just one.

"You're my uncle, Acheron, but I never really met you in my mortal lifetime."

Acheron stepped back with a curse. "You're lying."

"No. Truth. My father is your twin brother, Styxx."

One stray tear fell and she quickly wiped it away. "In my world, you and my father went out to fight together, and you never returned from battle."

"I was killed?"

She shook her head. "Frozen with *ypsni* and carried off so that no one could reach you. My father spent the rest of his life searching, trying his best to set you free."

He scowled at her. "Styxx?" he asked incredulously. "My brother fought for me and tried to free me?"

"My father loved you dearly. Always." In her world, she would never dare tell this to Acheron, where it might change the future. But here . . .

Everything was so different. His knowledge or lack thereof couldn't change anything in her world. Not to mention, Acheron knew the dangers of changing anything. He would die before he altered time in any dimension.

"I don't know if you and my father are enemies here or not, but in my dimension, my father would still be held on the Vanishing Isle in Hades's domain by Artemis. Eventually, the two of you become friends again and forge an unbreakable bond of brotherhood. Before my birth, you two are best friends."

He shook his head as if he couldn't believe her story. "That's not possible. My wife killed my brother centuries ago."

Kody scowled at the impossible. "No, she couldn't have. So long as you live, my father lives. Your life forces were bonded together by your mother. He can only die if you do. It's how the Malachai finally kills my father and breaks his army. Once the Malachai realizes the truth of your bond, he reanimates you and kills you both."

"The Malachai kills us?"

She nodded. "But that's the history of my world. Not the one here. Maybe here, Apollymi failed to combine your life forces?"

He paused to think about it before he answered. "No. We were bound at birth to protect me from harm." He winced as if a bad memory went through him. "Maybe Artemis didn't kill him, after all. I can see her imprisoning him and then calling it death to protect me. She was always precious that way."

Now it was her turn to be stunned. "Aunt Artie is your wife?"

"Was. Yes."

Still, she couldn't grasp it. Not given what she knew of their past. "Aunt Artie?"

"Why do you keep saying it like that? We loved each other more than anything. I can't imagine we could be different in your world."

Oh, she could. But that was her dimension and time. No need in ruining his memories of her aunt here. "Never mind. It doesn't matter."

Kody offered him a bittersweet smile even while she ached inside. What she really wanted to do was have him hold her like her father had once done. Have him tell her that everything would be okay. But that would never happen again.

I want you back, Daddy.

But Acheron wasn't her father. And this would be infinitely easier if he wore his hair black in this universe as he did in hers.

Blond Acheron . . . that hit too close to home.

Not wanting to hurt anymore over memories she couldn't change, she needed to put distance between them before she said or did something even more stupid. "I'll be right back with information." Closing her eyes, she summoned her powers and used them to teleport to the realm where the Arelim had built their fortress and homes long ago.

Existing outside of human time and space so that it didn't matter what dimension she accessed it from, theirs was a sterile and austere place. The Arelim as a rule were very circumspect and puritanical. They never met a rule they didn't embrace wholeheartedly. Because of that, she rarely ever came here to check in.

Usually her contact found her on the mortal plane where she worked to thwart the Malachai bloodline. And mostly at the worst possible times.

With a deep breath for courage, she walked to the grand hall where their commanders often gathered to exchange information or socialize.

Today, it was eerily empty. Only the lights from the winged torchieres that lined the walls burned. The fire made a light hissing noise and left a scent of cinnamon in the air.

She moved to the center of the vibrant white room and braced herself for the worst news. "Sraosha?" she called, summoning the Arel who was her direct contact.

He appeared instantly, dressed in his battle armor. Extremely tall, blond, and beautiful, he dwarfed her with his massive girth and height. "So, you finally remembered your station and duties. I have to say I never expected to see you again."

The accusation and anger in his tone surprised her. While she'd known he wouldn't be pleased that she hadn't killed Nick yet, she hadn't anticipated this much hostility. "What do you mean?"

"You failed to complete your mission. Again." He spat those words at her as if they left a bitter taste in his mouth. "I do believe that I instructed you to destroy the Ambrose Malachai."

"No. You ordered me to murder Nick Gautier. He isn't Ambrose." At least not yet.

He rolled his eyes at her. "You disgust me—you and that bleeding heart that sees lies instead of truth. You were given a direct order. You failed and now . . ." His scowl deepened as if he had another thought. "Why are you here?"

Something wasn't right about this.

For that matter, something wasn't right about him.

Everything was off and every sense she possessed rang out with warning.

Kody glanced around to see faint burn marks on the wall. Several of the chairs were missing and one window had been broken. Even though it was forbidden by their ancient laws, it was obvious someone had fought in here. Fiercely. "What happened?"

"That doesn't concern you."

She looked over her shoulder as she felt someone approaching her from behind. It was Ameretat and another Arel whose name she didn't know. When they reached for her, she twirled away from them.

"What's going on?" she demanded.

Sraosha curled his lip. "You're being decommissioned, Nekoda."

Her eyes widened at his declaration. What he meant was executed. "Why?"

"Insubordination. Refusal of orders. You have put our enemy's life above that of the entire world."

She shook her head in denial. He couldn't issue that order alone. Not even *he* had that kind of power among their ranks. At least five Arelim had to agree for a death warrant to be issued on their own kind. "Where's Adidiron or Suriyel?"

"They won't save you. They can't." He jerked his chin at Ameretat. "Take her and show her how we treat traitors."

CHAPTER 13

Kody dodged Ameretat's arms. She tried to
teleport out, but couldn't. With no other
course of action, she ran for the doors. They
threw fireballs to stop her retreat, some of which came
so close, they singed her arm. She dodged them as
best she could and summoned her armor for protection. Thankfully, that part of her powers still worked.

If only the power to teleport out would operate, too.
That would be just tasty perfect. But no matter how
hard she tried, she couldn't escape here.

Twisting and dodging, she made it across the room
and headed for the main doors. With no clear-cut plan
or destination, she'd almost reached them when someone grabbed her from behind, threw her through them,

and held her in his muscular arms as he dragged her into a small hidden alcove in the marble foyer.

Her scream and squirms were cut short as the one holding her put his hand over her mouth and whispered in her ear while Sraosha and Ameretat continued to hunt her.

"Sh!" It was Suriyel. "Stop struggling. I'm here to help. I swear." He loosened his hold.

Still, her heart pounded so hard that she was surprised it remained in her chest. Relaxing a small bit, she allowed him to carry her away from the ones who searched for her.

She expected him to take her to one of their modest-sized homes that had been placed on the hill, around the hall. Instead, he took her to a dark underground shelter where Adidiron and a small handful of others waited. Everyone was dressed for battle and some of them were bleeding from fresh wounds. That explained the damage in the room she'd just left. They must have fought each other mercilessly.

Suriyel released her and stepped back to give her a little space.

Turning around to scan each Arel there, Kody

frowned at the group. Ragged defeat and daunted determination burned in their eyes as they watched her warily—as if she'd turn on them, too.

"What is this?" she asked.

His gaze even more troubled than the others', Suriyel sighed. "Sadly, the small number of Arelim who oppose tyranny and stupidity."

That made no sense to her whatsoever. "What?"

With his blond hair braided down his back—something he only did for battle—Adidiron stepped forward, out of the shadows. His beautiful face now had a fresh, healing scar running down the left side, from hairline to chin. "After the senior Malachai was killed last night and his powers drained, Ameretat and Sraosha took it upon themselves to stop the Malachai bloodline. Forever."

Suriyel gave a solemn nod in accordance. "They think that if they kill the younger Malachai, they can reset Order and bring about the Sada."

Kody's frown deepened at his words. The Sada was said to be the time of innocence and purity. A utopian world where all evil was vanquished and only good survived.

In theory, it was a great thought.

But in reality . . .

"It's a myth," she said. "Sada upsets the necessary balance. If you do that, it will destroy the entire universe." A universe that hinged on an ever-shifting balance and harmony with all things.

Even good and evil.

Adidiron snorted. "You know that and we know that, but *they* don't believe it. Or worse, some of them do, but since they know the world will end by the fledgling Malachai's hand, they're willing to cut the deadline short and let it perish under *their* kinder, gentler destruction now."

But that made no sense. Her jaw went slack. "You're kidding me . . ." Even as the words left her mouth, she knew she was being rhetorical. She'd seen the madness in Sraosha's eyes herself. For whatever reason, he wanted Nick's throat and he wasn't going to let anything, even world destruction, stop him from getting it. "Why have they done this?"

A ferocious tic started in Suriyel's sculpted jaw. "Simple. When you bound Nick's powers, you provided them the perfect opportunity to kill him while he's too weak to stop them. Or protect himself. Right now, they don't need you to do it. They're more than capable and willing to end him."

Sick to her stomach, she struggled to breathe. "What have I done?"

By trying to save Nick, she'd handed his head to his enemies on a platter.

Adidiron put his hand on her shoulder to steady her. "Your job." He tightened his grip. "You've done nothing wrong, little sister. This sin is on their heads. They are the ones seeking salvation through destruction."

As so many do . . . Kody squeezed her eyes shut as the horror of it all racked her and she tried to come to terms with her own part in this wretched play. "We can't let them destroy everything. What do we do now? This is awful."

Adidiron patted her shoulder before he stepped away to pace among their small group. "No, Nekoda. It's prophecy. We've always known this day would come. We just didn't know when or how."

She arched a brow at something no one had told her. "How do you mean?"

Suriyel picked up the explanation. "In the Mashuan, it was written that the last Malachai would bring about the downfall of the Arelim."

Adidiron inclined his head to Suriyel. "We always assumed the Malachai would defeat us in battle at the End Time."

"Now we know better." Suriyel folded his hands behind his back as he paced in an opposite direction. "For the first time since the Primus Bellum, we're divided against ourselves. Our order is split and in chaos. Our brethren have become our enemies."

"Because of the Mashuani," Kody breathed as she finally understood what they were telling her.

The Mashuan was the tablet of fated destiny while the Mashuani was the tablet of prophecy. Twin documents that had been written by the original gods, aeons ago when the world was brand new.

The Mashuan told what was destined to happen, the other foretold ways to accomplish or divert the Mashuan. It was the tablet of what-could-be.

And it had been written on the Mashuani tablet that a Malachai would be born who could turn

SHERRILYN KENYON

against his dark nature and become an instrument for good. One who could restore balance and make sure that the world didn't end. That he held it in tandem with his brother. And so long as they stood united, nothing could destroy the world or universe.

Because Nick's father, Adarian, had seemed more vulnerable and human than any Malachai before him, Kody had thought he was the one it'd spoken of. It was part of the reason she hadn't killed him when she'd had the chance. Why she'd hesitated.

But one look in Adarian's eyes as he mercilessly stabbed her while she'd been helpless before him, and she'd known better. Even though he could cleverly mimic compassion, Adarian had lacked all humanity. All decency.

It wasn't until after that, she'd learned Adarian Malachai had been the same soulless monster who had betrayed her uncle Seth and had left him in the hands of their enemy to be brutally tortured for centuries. Even though Seth had risked his life to free Adarian from their master, Adarian had gleefully sacrificed Seth for his own selfish gain.

For that reason alone, she'd held no hope for Nick's

humanity. Surely, the son would be even worse than the father.

Yet Nick had surprised her in every way. *He* was the one the tablet had predicted. She was even more sure of that now. No Malachai before him had been born of a human mother. None had known love. None had been capable of love.

Not until Nick. He was nothing like the others.

He, alone, could save them. . . .

If he didn't kill them first.

Terrified to think about the fact that Nick would most likely stab and kill her in the future, she faced Suriyel. In the past, he had adamantly refused to hear anything good about Nick. Like Sraosha, he'd wanted the boy slaughtered before he ascended to his Malachai role. "So you believe me now?"

Biting his lip, he glanced away. "I never would have had I not seen it with my own eyes."

"Seen what?"

"Adarian Malachai sacrifice himself to save Cherise Gautier and their son. Against everything, that rabid animal did love her. Right to the end. Even more than himself."

Yes, but he hadn't known how to show it. Adarian had single-handedly ruined Cherise's life and traumatized her. Instead of cherishing what he'd loved, he'd been abusive and mean. And that was no way to have a relationship with anyone. Marriage and friendship were built on trust and loyalty. Not deceit and lies.

Love could only be given. It could never be demanded.

But in the end, Adarian had given every bit of his power to his son so that Nick could protect his mother at all costs. As Suriyel had said, Adarian had loved Cherise completely. No Malachai before Adarian had ever placed the needs or welfare of anyone above himself. They were creatures of ultimate hatred and violence.

Of betrayal.

Yet something in Adarian had changed when he met Cherise. And while Cherise hadn't been able to completely alter or tame the demonic beast that was Adarian, she had nurtured their son from Nick's very beginning. Her love and kindness, her personal sacrifice for him, kept Nick anchored to her. It overrode the innate congenital need in him to be cruel and violent. To lash out in hatred and destroy everyone near him.

Including himself.

So long as Cherise remained alive, there was hope for Nick. He would do nothing to shame or harm his mother.

But when she died . . .

That would be the first step toward Nick's devolution into the Malachai. It was a path Kody intended to change, no matter the cost. Given Nick's heart and compassion, surely it could be done.

No destiny is set by any birth, no matter how lowly or how high. All creatures have the right and ability to choose who and what they become. . . .

Be it good or evil.

She met Suriyel's gaze. "So you finally accept that Nick is the one the prophecy speaks of?"

He nodded. "No."

She scowled at his contradiction.

Laughing, he let out a tired breath. "I want to believe it. I do. But you yourself faced him centuries from now. You have seen firsthand what Nick will do if he's not stopped."

"And I have seen a boy who is more than capable of defending himself, who had the powers of a Malachai at his command, allow a mere human to beat him to the brink of death because he made a promise to his mother to never fight again. What Malachai would ever do such?"

He glanced toward Adidiron.

Kody looked at the others. Her lips trembled from the weight of her painful emotions and memories. "I know what it is that I'm asking of you. I do. And all of you know what I have lost in this battle already." And that included her sanity, most days. "What I stand to lose in the future if he's not stopped." Tears of grief filled her eyes as she relived the deaths of her family and friends at the hands of the Malachai and his demonic army. She had seen too many ripped apart and murdered. Too many brutally slaughtered.

"It is not easy for me to find anything other than sheer hatred and contempt for the monster who will one day rob me of all I hold dear. There's not a being here who hates the Ambrose Malachai more than I do. Believe me, it's not possible. Yet . . ." She broke off as her agony overwhelmed her.

Angrily, she brushed away her tears and forced herself to continue. Her voice shook with the weight of her grim determination. "Nick is *not* that beast. He is not a monster. Not yet. The boy he is deserves a chance to be saved."

"And if you can't save him?" Vahista asked.

"No one will suffer more than I, I assure you." Kody held her breath as they exchanged looks with each other and she waited for them to decide Nick's fate. "Nick Gautier is worth it. I promise."

After a long, nerve-racking minute, Suriyel stepped forward to face the other Arelim. "We all know what is at stake. If we allow the others to kill Nick now, the Sada will definitely destroy the balance and end the universe for all creatures. There is nothing to stop that from happening. The balance can shift from one side to the other, but one side can never be fully destroyed. All of us have sworn to maintain the Order and to observe that balance, in all its incarnations. If there is a single chance of saving the universe, we have to fight for it. United. That is the oath we're sworn to, and we will die upholding it."

Kody swallowed hard. "I hope it doesn't come to that."

"So do we," Adidiron said under his breath.

Suriyel ignored him. "Are we in accord?"

One by one, they inclined their heads to him and reswore their oaths of loyalty.

Relieved that she wouldn't have to fight alone after all, Kody relaxed.

Adidiron crossed his arms over his chest. "Tell us what you need, little sister."

A miracle. But she didn't say that out loud. They knew that one as much as she did. So she focused on the more immediate concern. "I need Nick returned to his own body and his own time period."

Each of them looked away, shame-faced.

That was not a comforting reaction and it most definitely wasn't one she wanted to see. Dread hugged her close to its heart. "What?"

Suriyel cleared his throat. "We'll need the Magus Stone to do that."

She'd never heard of such before. "What is the Magus Stone?"

"A very special piece of Libyan desert glass. It was formed when the first primal gods were at war. While fighting, Rezar hurled a piece of the sun at Braith. She deflected it and it landed in the desert and made a stone that was as bright a yellow as the sun itself. Perfectly smooth and round, it radiated the sun's brilliance. When the war was finally over, Rezar retrieved it from the desert—his domain—and had it set into a sun medallion that he gave to Braith as a peace offering."

Kody's jaw went slack as she realized something that had never occurred to her before. "Is that why her symbol is a yellow sun and he's considered its protector?"

He nodded. "And while Rezar fashioned the necklace for her, he cut himself and bled into the stone. That imbued it with some of Rezar's powers, including his ability to create chaos and split the dimensions . . . and remove the soul from a body."

Kody winced. While she loved and adored her grandfather, she could choke him for that gift to his own enemy. Little had he known then that when he gave that power to Apollymi, she would one day use it against the human race to create the Daimons who preyed on them. "Where is it now?"

They all looked to Adidiron. She turned to face him.

He shrugged helplessly. "The last person who had it was your mother. The goddess Apollymi gave it to her to celebrate your birth."

Scowling, Kody searched her memory for such a piece. Her mother had worn very little jewelry. Only the necklace that bore her father's emblem and the sapphire wedding ring he'd given her in ancient Greece. "I've never seen it. Are you sure about that?"

"Positive. I saw it on her myself, on several occasions."

How weird that she had no recollection of this particular necklace at all. Especially since it had passed through the hands of three people she knew extremely well.

Suriyel growled angrily. "Sraosha or one of the others must have found it somehow or stolen it, and used it on the weakened Malachai. It's the only thing that makes sense."

A weird chill skipped down her back as a thought struck her. "Would it have worked had Nick been at full strength?"

Adidiron laughed aloud. "Uh, no. At full strength, it would have been like throwing a grenade into a gas plant. As a descendant of Apollymi, the Malachai would have absorbed her powers and Rezar's out of it.

But because his powers were bound to the point he was human . . ."

"It allowed them to pull him apart," she finished for him.

"Exactly."

She really wanted to beat herself for the stupidity of her actions. It'd seemed so logical to bind Nick's powers so that those hunting him wouldn't be able to use his powers to locate him. To keep him from using them and accidentally harming himself or others.

But in the end, it'd been the worst solution.

Let it go. It was useless to continue reliving the event and beating herself up over it. There was no way to change what had already been done. She needed her full attention on finding another solution. One that might actually work.

"How do I locate the stone?" she asked them.

Adidiron shook his head. "No idea."

Sighing, she patted Adidiron's cheek. "You really don't believe in making my job easy, do you?"

"Where's the fun in that?"

She laughed bitterly. "Can I ask one favor?"

"Feel free to ask, but the answer might be no."

Of course it might. There were times when they really made her want to throw her hands up and cower in a corner. "Can you get Simi into this dimension to help us?"

"Simi? The Charonte?" He scowled. "Why?"

"Because if the stone belonged to Apollymi, my little horned cousin will know it and she'll be able to sniff it out like a blood-demon. It's a sparkly yum-yum, after all." And there was nothing Simi loved more than sparkly yum-yums.

Suriyel and Adidiron exchanged a look she couldn't quite discern.

"We will try," Suriyel said after a pause. "But Simi has to agree to do it. We can't cross dimensions with her if she fights us."

That was a major understatement. No one, other than Acheron, made Simi do anything she didn't want to do.

Well, except for Simi's husband. For some reason, he'd always had more control over her than Acheron did. Something her father had told her had both irritated *and* amused Acheron.

Kody had always found it charming, and that made her miss her aunt and uncle all the more.

Please let Simi come here. Simi would make this task much easier. At least for Kody. For the ones sent to ask Simi to join her for the fight . . .

"Word of advice," Kody said to the men. "If Simi breaks out her barbecue sauce, run."

Suriyel snorted. "Thanks."

"Any time, sport." Kody bit her lip as she scanned the faces of her coconspirators. By going against Sraosha and saving her from the guillotine, they had all committed treason against their brethren. If she failed, they would pay a steep price for it.

Adidiron gently took her arm. "Remember, Sraosha and the others will be searching for both of you. Every time you use your powers outside of this shelter, they will know it. We do have several spies among his army, but don't count on them to be able to rescue you if you're found again."

"I understand." She was used to being on her own. In both lifetimes.

Suriyel inclined his head to her. "Keep Nick alive."

"I'll do my best, but we have only two days to finish this before the ušumgallu unites and they march on the world. With or without their general."

"Yeah, we know. Thorn is already gathering his forces here."

Kody shivered. "Is Cadegan with him?"

"Who?" Suriyel asked.

"Cadegan. He was once Thorn's right hand. At least in my world."

One by one, they all shook their heads. "We don't know that name."

Strange, but she would go with it. Though it didn't happen often, there were a number of supernatural beings she knew that they didn't. Mostly ones who didn't interact with the human world any more than they had to.

And that definitely described the two of them. Thorn and Cadegan together had been an invincible team. Honestly, she was more than happy to not face their united strength in a fight here. She and Nick had enough against them already.

"Good luck with Simi," she breathed to them, then teleported back to Acheron's house.

Kody had barely appeared in his office before she saw Acheron staring at an old photo with a longing in his eyes that was heart-wrenching. She knew that aching loss firsthand and it reeked.

The woman in the photo was his daughter, Katra, who was holding two children Kody assumed to be the Simi and Ash Nick had spoken about. But the man in that photo was definitely not the same as the Sumerian god Katra had married in Kody's world. The love Acheron bore for his daughter and grandchildren, though, was every bit as potent.

"Acheron?"

Clearing his throat, he turned slightly toward her and put the photo out of sight. "Did you learn anything helpful?"

"Yes and no. It's as I suspected. My boss wants Nick dead."

Acheron snorted. "Having spent time with him, I can well understand his motivation."

Kody tsked at him, but didn't comment on that. "They told me about a Magus Stone. Have you ever heard of it?"

He put his hands in his jacket pocket. "Vaguely.

It's a legend about the first war of the gods and one of them threw down a bit of the sun at another one. Or something like that. Honestly, I never paid those stories much attention."

"Does the stone exist in this realm?"

He shrugged. "If it did, it went missing a long time ago."

Of course it did. Because nothing could ever go easy for her. It never had. As her father so often said, there were those who were born to be great and those who were determined to be great. And those who were determined were the ones life challenged the hardest.

Rise to the occasion, my daughter. Never let anyone tell you that you lack courage or conviction to see your tasks done. The only opinion that really matters is your own, and you are a creature of absolute beauty and strength, through and through.

Never, ever forget that.

So in the midst of the storm, stand proud against it, lift up your middle finger, and defy the fates with everything you have. If they want to fight, bring it. You have more than enough intelligence and skill to battle them until they beg you for mercy.

Gods, how she missed her father. The fire and spirit in his eyes that nothing could daunt. It was infectious.

Just like Ari's . . .

Knowing better than to let her thoughts linger on her family, especially when she stood this close to her father's identical twin, Kody cleared her throat. "Shall we rejoin the others?"

Before she could answer, something hard slammed against the walls. It reminded her of a battering ram. She covered her ears to shield them from the noise. "What is that?"

Acheron's face paled. "In short . . . our deaths."

CHAPTER 14

While all calamity broke loose on New Orleans, Nick strapped on a Kevlar vest. Across the room from him, Mark and Bubba armed themselves with crossbows and throwing knives. And other things Nick was sure he didn't want to know about. In the event he was arrested for being with them, he wanted plausible deniability.

His mom watched him in awe. "You look like you've done this a few times."

Nick smiled as he finished up. "Just a few. At home, Caleb's always terrified I'll get eaten and he'll have to face my mother's wrath over it."

She wrinkled her nose at him. "Am I *that* different there?"

Nick hesitated as he thought it over. "Not really. You just dress in more expensive clothes here than the mom I'm used to. And I'm way too close to your height here."

"Hey, Mike? You there?"

Scowling, Nick turned toward Mark and Bubba, who both groaned at the thick Tennessee drawl over their radio. "Who's that?" he asked his mom.

She growled low in the back of her throat. "Someone *I* hope gets eaten by the demons." She winked playfully at Nick.

With a painful sound of resignation, Bubba picked up the radio and answered the call. "Yeah, Toph, what can I do you for?"

"You and Mark anywhere near a TV?"

Mark went to turn it on.

"What channel?" Bubba asked into the radio.

"Don't think it's going to matter much. Sure it's on all stations by now." No sooner had the unknown Toph spoken than the TV screen showed a horrific scene in the city.

Nick's jaw dropped as he stepped closer to the screen. It looked just like something out of his recent nightmares or from the Great New Orleans Fire of

1788 that had destroyed almost every structure in town. Buildings were ablaze all over the Quarter while winged demons and Daimons openly preyed on the hapless humans who'd made the mistake of not taking shelter. National Guard soldiers and police had been mobilized, but it made little difference.

The innocent humans in uniform only became more targets for the nonhuman predators.

Savitar entered the room and cursed as he saw it, too. He cut his eyes toward Nick. "Looks like Thorn is seething that you got away, kid."

Nick was even more aghast. "Are you saying all that's because of me?"

Savitar nodded.

Sick to his stomach, Nick turned away from the TV. "I can't let this happen."

"What are you going to do?" Savitar asked sarcastically. "Spill your guts on their shoes? Hate to break it to you, kid, but that really is all you *can* do without your powers to fight them."

Mark agreed. "You go out there and there won't be anything left of you but a stain in the cracks of the pavement."

Nick wanted to growl a denial at them both, but he knew it was the truth. In this incarnation, he was as useful as tears to a warthog.

I've never been more worthless. And that was saying something.

His gaze went to the photos that his mom had placed all over the bookshelves in front of him. They showed a boy Nick didn't know and it wasn't just because the two of them didn't favor physically. The boy in those photos had never been forced to swallow air in an attempt to make his stomach feel full because he had nothing to eat. That boy had never walked his mom home from work at three in the morning on a school night, trying to keep her safe from predators— human and otherwise. He'd never been forced to use Bubba's duct tape to hold his shoes together because he couldn't afford another pair.

And he'd never had to fight for his life against those who wanted to end it.

A part of Nick envied that boy that normality. That innocence and happiness. He couldn't imagine growing up in a world with a pantry stocked full of food and snacks. Having parents to check his homework, go to games he played in, or make sure he'd had a good dinner at a reasonable hour.

But all that being said, he strangely missed his real life. And he definitely missed the people in it.

Even Mark's duck-urine cologne.

Savitar waved his hand in front of Nick's face. "Are you in a coma?"

Nick shook his head. "Just thinking."

"You think any harder and your head might explode."

He snorted at Savitar's teasing and ignored it. Zarelda had told him that he still had his Malachai powers. That no one could take them from him.

So how could he activate them?

The believing part hadn't been real conducive to getting them back. And it was so frustrating to know that he'd had those powers at one time and now . . .

He flinched at the live feed of a patrol car being blasted so hard by a demon that it caused the car to launch into the air, roll, and then land upside down in the middle of the street, right in front of Jax Brewery.

A red fortified pickup with black roll bars and hunting lights went streaking by the overturned patrol car as someone from inside it launched Molotov cocktails into the air, at the demons.

"Topher!" Bubba snapped. "Is that your ignorant hide I'm looking at on TV?"

"Am I on TV? Ha! Daddy, hear that! I'm famous!" All of a sudden, a man, who reminded Nick a lot of the Bubba he knew from home, stuck his head out of the truck and waved at the news helicopter that was now trailing after them.

Bubba growled in the back of his throat. "Son, stick your head back in before you lose it, and tell Big Topher to take his belt to you for being stupid."

"Big Topher?" Nick repeated to Mark.

A pained expression lined Mark's face. "Big Topher is Michael's uncle. Little Topher is his cousin"—he gestured toward the television—"that special moron who's still waving at the camera."

Nick rubbed his head in agony of that man's particular level of idiocy. "Do I want to know what kind of person names their child Little Topher?"

Mark laughed. "Probably not, but . . . Christopher was great-granddaddy. He went by Chris until he had a son who was named after him. So he was Big Chris, son was Little Chris. When Little Chris had a son, he named him after his daddy, but to keep from getting everyone confused, he called him Topher. Then Topher found someone desperate enough to marry him. My vote still says he must have hit her too hard on the head before he dragged her into his cave . . . but anyway, he named his son after his father and so Little Topher entered the world."

"And was promptly dropped on his head by his mother who was horrified she had to name him that," his mother said under her breath. "I can just imagine the day Topher the Fifth is born."

More horrified over that than the sight of the demons, Nick shook his head. "Oh. My. God."

Mark clapped him on the back. "My thoughts exactly."

"Hey Mark, get Cherise into the shelter." Bubba turned the television off.

Without asking why, Mark obeyed. At least he tried.

"What's going on?" his mom asked Bubba, refusing to leave without an explanation.

Bubba sighed in irritation. "Baby, please. Just go. Quick."

She reached for Nick.

Bubba held Nick by his side. "He needs to stay with me."

Biting her lip, she hesitated. "Why?"

"Baby . . ."

"C'mon, Cherise." Mark placed a gentle hand on her shoulder. "You know Mike isn't going to let anything happen to him."

"He better not." She kissed Nick on the cheek before she followed Mark into the basement—something that was exceedingly rare in New Orleans, where the city was built below sea level and flooded often. But then Bubba had installed a sump pump system that was more than impressive. One that had a generator on it that would see them through a month or more even if all the power went out.

As soon as they were gone, Bubba motioned Nick over.

"What is it?" Nick asked in a low tone.

"We're about to be under siege. That mass you saw

following Topher is heading toward us and I didn't want Mom to see it and panic."

Nick looked back at Savitar. "Is there anything you can do to stop them?"

Before he could answer, a loud siren sounded through the house. Cringing, Nick held his hands over his ears to shield them from the godforsaken noise. "What is that?"

Bubba pointed to the monitor he had on the gate where the demons were wrenching it off its hinges. "Looks like they figured out you're here."

Nick wasn't sure what he found more disturbing. The demons or the fact that Tabitha, Amanda, and Selena were with them.

Savitar rubbed at his chin. "To answer your earlier question, kid, all I can do is fight with you to the end."

There was an odd note in Savitar's tone that made Nick curious. "Why are you so willing to bleed for me?"

Savitar refused to meet his gaze. "Because what was done to your line was wrong."

Again, that note . . . Savitar knew a lot more about

Nick's ancestors than he was willing to freely admit. "Were you there?"

Savitar shook his head. "Long time before I was born. But I know what it's like to lose everything you love and not be able to stop it. To see the one thing you love most be cursed over blind stupidity and fear. And it's an awful place to live." He shifted his gaze to Bubba. "I'll lead as many away as I can."

Before Nick could say another word, Savitar was gone. He appeared a few seconds later on the monitors, out in the yard between the gate and the house. With a reckless disregard for his own life, Savitar tackled the first demon he reached and kneed him to the ground. After that, it was on in true Roman gladiatorial style.

Unable to stomach it, Nick turned away from the gore and lifted one hand up to shield his eyes from the monitors. *"Nos morituri te salutamus."*

Bubba arched a brow. "Pardon?"

"We who are about to die salute you."

Snorting, Bubba grabbed a crossbow and pushed Nick toward the stairs. "Yeah, but if you die, I won't see my kid again. And I love my son. So you are not to do anything stupid. You hear me?"

"I hear, master. But I never obey." Nick clapped him on the arm. "See, that's where your kid and I differ."

"And here's where your ma and I differ." Bubba lifted him up and tossed him over his shoulder.

Nick did his best to break free, but Bubba was worse than an octopus on steroids. "Hey!"

"Hay's for horses, boy." Bubba held fast until he had Nick locked into a small fortified room.

Anger darkened his vision. Nick pounded against the steel door. But as expected, Bubba ignored him completely. His fury mounted. He'd never particularly liked tight spaces, and this one seriously pissed him off. "Let me out!" Nick shouted.

No one responded.

Nick bared his teeth and then grinned as he re-membered something *his* Bubba had taught him. No matter how fortified a door was, there was always one vulnerability that couldn't be helped. . . .

Hinges.

They were always *inside* the room. Even a closet. "Lock me in . . . I'll show *you* something, *boy*," he mut-tered as he toed off one shoe and reached for a coat hanger. Stretching it out of shape, he bent the neck into a makeshift spike that he held underneath the top hinge. Then he used his shoe to hammer at the hanger.

At first nothing happened, but after a few minutes more, the hinge began to lift. Once it was an inch up, Nick moved to the middle hinge.

While he worked, he heard the sound of fighting outside. And it was coming closer. He had no idea who was winning. But it was going bad for someone he prayed wasn't Bubba.

Just as he moved to the bottom hinge, the door was ripped open and slung back. On his knees with one shoe in his hand, Nick looked up to meet Thorn's furious glower. Without a word, Thorn grabbed Nick by the arm and wrenched him to his feet.

For once, Nick held his smart mouth at bay as he saw Mark, his mom, and Bubba in the custody of demons. Bubba held his mother against his chest while she sobbed uncontrollably. Another group came forward and dumped an either dead or unconscious Savitar into the foyer.

"I told you, you wouldn't escape me."

Nick still didn't speak even though Thorn's taunt

set fire to every piece of Cajun in him. He was too busy skimming every enemy around him, looking for an opening.

Thorn grabbed his arm again. "Now, we're—"

"Don't touch me!" Nick snarled, wrenching his biceps away from Thorn. "You want me, fine. Let my mom go. And Bubba and Mark."

Thorn laughed. "You have no power here."

"There you be wrong, boy." Nick dug down deep for every piece of courage he'd ever had and stood strong in front of his enemies. "I *am* the Malachai."

Granted, that might have been a little more impressive had he been wearing both shoes and not holding one in his hand, but looking like an idiot had never stopped him from being brave before. It certainly wouldn't stop his stupidity today.

Nick dropped the shoe to the floor and stood up to his full less-than-impressive height, which barely reached the middle of Thorn's chest. Even so, he refused to be intimidated. Or rather refused to let Thorn know he was intimidated by the much larger and more powerful being.

Thorn seized him by the throat. "You're a Malachai with no powers. Do you know what that makes you?"

Dead was the most obvious answer. But Nick never went with the first answer to anything. That made life too easy.

"Seriously pissed off. I got me one bad bad case of short man syndrome, buddy. Just letting you know."

Ignoring that, Thorn leaned down to whisper in Nick's ear. "No, little friend. It makes you bait."

Nick snorted. "Trust me. You don't want to catch the things that want to make me their lunch. Met a few. They're guaranteed to give you even more indigestion than I am."

"Oh, I don't know about that, Akri-Nick. The Simi thinks nothing can be harder on the digestive track than them blue-eyed Cajun people. They's so hard to go down. Kick the whole way. Scream a lot, too."

A slow smile broke across Nick's face as he heard the most wondrous singsongy accent imaginable. A blessed accent that belonged to only one person he knew.

"Simi! Welcome to the *fais do-do, cher.* So glad to

see you. You are truly a sight for these mighty sore eyes."

The look of confusion on Thorn's face was comical as he turned his head to take in the exceptionally tall teenage demon. Dressed in a black fishnet shirt that was covered with a modest purple corset, Simi had black hair streaked with green. She wore a frou-frou short black skirt over purple and black leggings, and the tall Goth biker boots Nick was used to. At first glance, there was nothing to mark her as supernatural. But only an absolute moron would make that mistake.

Unfortunately, Thorn wasn't an idiot. "Get her!" he roared.

Simi let loose a stream of fire at them as her wings unfurled and she took flight. Thorn went to grab Nick.

Twisting away, Nick headed toward Simi. She seemed his safest bet. But as he reached her, someone grabbed him from behind. He swung with intent, until he realized it was Kody.

Nick barely caught himself before his fist made contact with her beautiful face. *"Ma bele,"* he breathed before he kissed her cheek. "Did you bring Simi?"

"No. But I'm glad she's here."

He nodded in agreement. "Where's Ash?"

"Covering my retreat. He said he'd join us as soon as he could."

For a moment, Nick almost felt like himself again. Until he went to blast the demon after Simi and couldn't throw a fireball for anything. Luckily, Kody could, and she nailed it, but as she did so something strange happened. Nick staggered back as he felt that weird sensation he'd had at school. Glancing down, he saw his hand was translucent again.

"Nick?"

He heard Kody's voice, but he couldn't respond. She seemed to be falling away from him. Or maybe he was falling away from her. It was hard to tell for certain.

Why is this happening again?

What was happening to him?

"Nick!"

Kody's scream echoed in his head. He tried to make his way back to her. To will it so. Nothing listened. Not his head or pounding heart. And definitely not his fading skin.

Instead, he drifted faster away from her.

Give me your name! It was the voice again. The one

he'd heard when he'd been yanked out from Selena and them.

Why did it keep asking him that?

"Don't you know?"

Name! Now!

Suddenly, he slammed into something hard and unyielding. At first he thought it was a wall, until he realized the wall radiated warmth.

And was covered with hard muscles. Ew!

"Barely one day a Malachai and you've already screwed it all up. You are even more worthless than *I* thought."

Nick's eyes widened as he recognized his father's angry growl in his ear. No. It wasn't possible. It wasn't.

"You're dead."

Adarian snorted. "Not as dead as you're about to be, boy."

CHAPTER 15

Nick struggled even harder against his father's hold.

"Stop!" Adarian snarled in Nick's ear. "I'm not the one who's going to kill you. Though in retrospect, I should have slit your throat the first time I heard your mewling cries at birth. Why did I ever think something as pathetic as you could protect Cherise?" He literally tossed Nick away from him.

Nick caught his balance and swung around to face his father. Adarian's skin had a sick, grayish-white pallor to it and his eyes were sunken and black. There were no visible eyes at all. Just scary darkness that seemed to see right through him and judge him lacking. "What are you?"

SHERRILYN KENYON

"Dead, you lickspittle. Did you miss the memo? You were there when it happened. Or did you think you dreamed it all?"

"Then how—"

"How do you think?" His father grabbed Nick's hair and snatched him forward.

Grimacing in pain, Nick tried to fight, but even dead, his father was way too strong for him. It was like going against a tank. Dang, did the man have to be so strong? Of course, Nick had no body, either. That kind of put him at a serious disadvantage.

"You are not human," his father growled in Nick's ear as he tightened his grip to hold him completely immobile. "Stop thinking of yourself as such. You have *never* been fully human. Nothing can contain or constrain you without your implicit consent. Do you understand? *That* was my most hard-won lesson and it's the only thing I'm giving to you for free, boy." Adarian loosened his hold. "We are unlike any other species ever created in this universe. Because of that, your soul keeps slipping out of that frail human body they've forced it into. It knows it doesn't belong there and it's trying to get home despite the spell they've used against you."

"They who?"

"Laguerre." He spat out the name as if every syllable was a swallow of poison. "That vicious *pute* is working with your enemies. She is one of your generals. In theory. One we have never been able to trust. She would sell her own mother to the devil for a used bottle of stagnant fingernail polish."

That was harsh. "How do you know this?"

Adarian spun Nick around in the darkness. "Open your senses and listen, boy. Feel. Smell. This is the ether you've been trying to tap into for so long. It is everything in the universe. In all universes. With it, there's nothing you can't see or know. The past. The present. The future. Every heartbeat of every creature is recorded here. All at your fingertips, once you learn how to use it."

Fine, I'll try it again. That seemed like a good idea until he actually did it. Nick staggered and had to put his hand on his father to steady himself as a trillion things hit him at once. It was so loud and overwhelming that he couldn't breathe. He couldn't think. His stomach plummeted as bile rose in his throat. But the absolute worst was all the emotions he felt from other people and sentient beings throughout the entire universe. The sadness, grief, and anguish. It was debilitating.

And extremely painful. Like being stomped in the stones and then rolled over hot coals while naked and basted in accelerant.

His father tightened his grip again as if another wave of anger had seized him. "And *that* will always be your greatest weakness."

Nick gasped for breath as he tried to understand. "What? Having nerve endings? You're right. It stinks. Especially when I slam my toes into something when I'm not looking."

His father viciously growled at him—Nick had that effect on a lot of people. "Your bleeding heart, boy. By choosing a human mother for you, I weakened you."

"Then why did you—"

Adarian grabbed him by the neck again and cut him off, thus proving his point about nerve endings. Even in a noncorporeal form, it hurt. "I loved her." Those words left his father's throat as if they'd been torn out. When he spoke again, his voice trembled with raw emotion and agony. "I knew something so pure and precious as she would never be able to love something fouled and damned like me. No matter what I tried, her affections went to others. I was the most powerful being in existence, and the best I could compel from her was time spent with me because *she* pitied my loneliness." He laughed bitterly. "I fought for her honor and instead of being grateful, she took me to task for beating an apology out of the one who'd insulted her. After that, she wouldn't even hold my hand. She'd barely look at me, and when she did, her eyes showed a disappointment that cut me soul-deep."

Yeah, that sounded like his mom. And Nick knew that look a lot better than he wanted to. It, like the closet monster he now knew was real, was one of those things that seriously disturbed his mental peace. Cherise Gautier really deplored violence for any reason. It chafed his butt, too, whenever she fussed at him for not turning the other cheek. Yet in his world, the meek only inherited earth six feet deep.

"And *you*," his father sneered. "I hate you for having the part of her I could never claim."

Sympathetic pain racked him as Nick finally understood the true tragedy of his father's heritage. To forever crave the very thing he could never have.

Love. Acceptance.

The gods' final punishment for the Malachai bloodline over a treaty they'd had no part in, and a war they'd been ordered to fight. As punishment, the firstborn Malachai had been forced to see his pregnant wife die. To endure centuries alone.

None of them were to know happiness. Ever. Nor were they to live to see their heir grown. As soon as their son was old enough to come into his full powers, the elder Malachai was doomed to die by his son's hand.

For all eternity.

His father increased the pressure of his hold. "I should have killed you when you were born." Growling again, he moved away as if he was planning to give in to that urge unless he put more space between them. "But I'd harmed Cherise enough." He winced in pain. "You were still wet from your whelping when she cradled you against her breast and swore no one would ever harm you. Not without going through her. As much as I wanted to take your life, I never wanted her to cry. Not because of something I did to her. I owed her that much."

Roaring, Adarian spun on him and seized him again. "You, pathetic waste that you are, mean more to her than anything else. You, she cherishes, and you were given one task—to make sure nothing harms her."

Nick tried to speak, but his father held him too tightly now. He couldn't even let out a squeak.

"If you don't fix this and subdue our generals, she will die in all worlds. Do you understand? Hers is the first life they will take . . . because of *you*!"

Coughing and wheezing, Nick nodded.

His father loosened his grip enough so that Nick could breathe again.

"Believe me, no one wants me out of here more than I do. So, please, Demon Master Overlord"—Nick deepened his voice to duplicate his father's rumbling sinister tone—"Mr. I-have-all-power-and-you-suck"—he returned to speaking normally—"tell me how do I get back? Please, enlighten me, oh great father mine." He glared at him. "I already tried clicking my heels together. Not much luck there. Should I sneeze when I do it or just fart in your general direction?"

His father shoved at him. "You are the Malachai. You are the son of the Destroyer of Worlds. Your name is Conquest. Pain. Suffering. Betrayal. No one can defeat you unless *you* allow it."

"Oh, okay," Nick said sarcastically. "Let's just all be happy and shiny then. No sweat that." He beat his fist against his chest in an ancient salute then barked out his orders. "I will win this for you, Father."

His father raked him a withering glower. "I am not one of your putrid humans to suffer your backtalk, boy."

Nick snorted. "You're dead, right? What can you do? Shake the chandelier. Ooo, I'm so terrified. Please don't rock the chair in the corner or slam a door in my face. I don't think I could mentally take that. You might send me into therapy for the rest of my life. Oh, the humanity!"

His father grabbed his hair again. Yeah, okay, that did hurt. "Don't test me."

Grinding his teeth, Nick tried to extricate himself. "Mom says I get that better irritating quality from *you*."

To his complete shock, Adarian laughed and released him. "You do, actually. And to answer your earlier question, Laguerre is working with our enemy. They are the ones who divided you."

"That's all well and good. Nice to know I have yet another ancient, omnipotent power trying to eat my gizzard with onions, but what I really need is info on unification. Put me back together again. Now how do I do that?"

"Unlock your powers."

"Give me the key." Nick spoke in the same aggravated tone. "Or at least a friggin' clue. Hey, Pat. Can I buy a flippin' vowel? Please?"

His father clenched his teeth so hard, Nick could hear them grinding. Not the first time he'd reduced an elder to that. Probably wouldn't be the last. Though he should score some bonus points for the fact that he was causing an inhuman ghost to do so and he wasn't even really trying to annoy him.

Give me your name. . . .

Nick flinched at the intrusion of that voice inside

his skull again. Someone needed to turn the decibel level down a few hundred notches. "Is that you?"

His father turned around slowly. "Don't answer them."

"Wasn't planning to. Why?"

Adarian swung back toward Nick. "Do you know how to command and own a demon?"

"Tell it I'm the Malachai . . . Oh wait, no. They usually burst out laughing when I do that. Really nuclear devastation for my ego, I have to say."

His father made a sound that was disturbing enough to make Nick take two steps away from him. "No, imbecile. You tell it your true demonic name that is written in the Damonicon the moment we're spawned. With that, any demon can be summoned, regardless of our wills. And with it, we can all be enslaved . . . even the Malachai. It's why we never use our Summoning names. Not for anything."

But that didn't make sense. Everyone knew Nick's full name. He'd never kept it a secret. And even if he'd ever tried, all anyone had to do was be within an eighty-mile radius whenever his mother blew a gasket and shouted out the whole thing to get his attention for God and all His saints to hear. Nick was quite sure a number of people in Mississippi, Alabama, and Florida knew his name better than most of his teachers.

"I don't follow."

His father mumbled something—no doubt it was insulting and degrading—before he spoke up. "Whenever we're asked, our kind uses 'Malachai.' It's our classification or basic significator. It's a meaningless designation that can't harm us."

"Ah," Nick said as he got it finally. "So you wouldn't tell anyone you're Adarian."

"No, fool. Adarian Malachai is my common name to differentiate me from my father and from *you*." Man, that was an impressive lip curl and told Nick just how much his father loved him . . . never. "My summoning name is Adrius. No one, not even your mother, was ever given it."

"Then why are you telling me?"

"What does it matter at this point, if I'm summoned or not? I'm dead and have no powers left to use. Everything I had, I handed over to *you*." Bitterness echoed in his tone. "And since you've inherited Malphas, you should know his real name in case he ever refuses to come when you call."

Nick bit back a laugh. Yeah, that power could come in handy. Caleb was the only being Nick knew who made him look like a poser in the arena of grand sarcasm. Testy little booger had an attitude that knew no limits or boundaries.

"Well, I know it's not Caleb 'cause I shout that name out all the time and he blatantly ignores me . . . even when I'm on fire. Literally."

Adarian gave the impression that he was rolling his missing eyes at him. "Cabal."

Nick's jaw went slack. "Cabal?"

His father nodded. "Speak that name out loud three times and he can be summoned to you. Anywhere. Anytime. It is the name of owning."

Awesome opossum. Pwn one for me. At least that was the thought until it dawned on him that both his father's and Caleb's summoning names were eerily similar to their mundane ones.

Ah, crap . . . Nick cringed at the implication and likelihood of what that would mean for him. Yeah, his luck was never kind. "Please, Lord, please. Tell me that mine isn't Dickless Nicholas."

His father screwed his face up. "What?"

"It's what the troglodytes at school call me whenever they want to send me to the office for assaulting them."

Adarian bellowed in agony. "It's like talking to an ape, I swear," his father mumbled. Then louder and sharper, he barked at Nick. "Would you be serious?"

Nick pressed his lips together. "Sorry. Serious-face time . . . but that *is* a major concern." He cleared his throat and braced himself so that he didn't upset his father any more.

Until another unsettling thought went through his mind and sped out of his mouth before he could stop it. "It's not Nick the Dick, either, right?"

His father reached for his throat, but he dodged and twirled to a distance of relative safety. Something greatly helped by the fact that his father no longer had telekinesis.

"Hey! Not my fault Mom pegged me with a name so easy to mock it ought to be banned from children for eternity. You would be amazed at the cruel creativity of people when it comes to mocking someone. . . ." Nick paused as he realized who he was talking to. "Then again, you were probably the ringleader of said tormenting."

"Perhaps I should geld you. It might settle you down."

"Yeah . . . no. Besides, pink isn't my color. Clashes with my complexion."

What is your name!

Nick let out an aggravated sigh at that insistent demand in his head. An expulsion that lasted for three seconds until he realized what his summoning name had to be. Oh. No wonder his older self was so cranky. "It's—"

His father clapped his hand over Nick's lips to keep him from speaking it. Then he bent and whispered in a low tone in Nick's ear. "Not Ambrose. It's your Confirmation name."

A creepy chill went down Nick's spine at the coincidence. He'd chosen Aloysius because it'd sounded cool and was semi-close to his middle name, Ambrosius. Not to mention, St. Aloysius was the patron saint of youth and students. As a kid who'd been trying to get into St. Richard's at the time he was going through Confirmation, Nick had thought it an intelligent idea to get on the good side of a saint who might be able to pull some celestial academic strings.

At least that had been the thought back then. Now . . .

Nick lowered his father's hand away from his lips so that he could whisper back. "Are you telling me that I picked my own downfall?"

His father snorted. "Trust me, boy. We always do. Every step we take is one inch closer to our salvation and one foot closer to our doom."

That strangely made sense to him. And how weird that he'd instinctively never told anyone his Confirmation name, other than his mother, who never used it. More than that, a mistake had been made on his Sacramental Record and his Confirmation name hadn't been registered. Because his middle name was so unusual, especially given how common his first name was, the secretary who'd done the paperwork had assumed Ambrosius was the name he'd picked, and that was all the church had officially on file for him. When he'd told his mom about the error, she'd started to correct it then stopped herself.

The Lord moves in mysterious ways, Nicky. If He didn't want it recorded, I think we should leave it and trust Him to know what's best for us. Besides, I like the names I gave you, just fine. You already got two great saint names. Why would you need a third one?

Yeah, that was seriously disturbing in retrospect.

Which begged another question . . . "How do *you* know what my Confirmation name is?"

His father laughed evilly. "It's the name I gave you the first time I saw you."

Nick scowled. Aloysius? Really? "Why?"

"It's a name that means fame and war. What better name for my heir to hold?" His father cupped the back of Nick's head in his massive paw of a hand and pulled Nick against his shoulder so that he could whisper in his ear and not be overheard. "You are Conquest, boy. *That* is your destiny. You are the one who leads the others, and without you, they cannot win. You are the head of the ušumgallu, while they are merely the body. Chop off an arm or leg and the creature still walks and fights. But you . . . you are the one piece they must have. You are the only thing that Death and War and Bane and the other three generals cannot defeat. Without *you*, there can be no victory in their endeavors. Ever. *That* is why the only one who can kill a Malachai is the very son he sires."

Nick's scowl deepened as he tried to understand. "But what of the last Sephiroth?" In the first war of the gods, the Malachai army and the Sephirii had been mortal enemies who had slaughtered each other until only one Malachai and one Sephiroth had been left. Kody had told him that the surviving Sephiroth *could* kill him.

His father laughed deep in his throat and tightened his arm into something that almost felt like a hug. "Trust me, boy, Jared is no match for you and he knows it. Our blood boils with fury. If he were to attack you, it would be for *you* to kill him and put him out of his misery."

And if Nick were to do that, it would end his life, too. He and the last Sephiroth were tied together. The ultimate evil and the ultimate good. Yin and yang.

His father patted him hard on his cheek. "*That* is the only way Jared could possibly kill you. As you said, you pick your own destruction."

"Malachai!"

That feral shout startled Nick.

His father moved away from him. "See how hard your enemies are calling for you? They are desperate to capture you and use you against your own will."

Crouched and ready to battle, Nick turned around slowly, trying to locate whatever was hunting him. "Where is he?"

"Have no fear. He can't reach you here."

Nick straightened up. "Why? Where are we?"

"Nowhere."

Nick scoffed. "Ah, gee, Dad. Thanks so much for that. Like I didn't know that already."

Adarian shook his head. "You misunderstand. This is the nothingness between everything. That minuscule flicker that you can sometimes glimpse right before the dark becomes light. It's the lost place where souls go when they can't find their way home. And this is where you'll be stranded if you don't return to your real body before the ušumgallu rides."

That was definitely not comforting, and somewhat confusing for him. "Why ride if they can't win without me?"

He snorted. "War doesn't care if she wins or not. It's about the slaughter. The same is true for Death. Grim wins even when he loses. And while it is nice for them to be on the winning side, it's not necessary. They don't have the same drive to be victorious that you do, because they don't have the same goals. Since we are Conquest, it is not in us to lie down and lose. Not for anything. So long as we breathe, we will fight to win."

Anything worth doing was worth overdoing. One of Bubba's mottos that Nick subscribed to.

It was true. Never give up. Never give in. Never surrender. Toe-to-toe to the bitterest end.

That was the true strength of the Malachai. It was never about the size of the dog in a fight, but rather it was all about the size of the fight in the dog.

And Nick was done running and hiding. He wanted his body back and he was more than willing to battle. Right here. Right now.

"Hey!" he shouted at the voice in his head. "You want my name, boy? Come get some."

His father gaped. "What are you doing?"

He flashed a taunting grin at the older spirit. "I am my best at my worst."

"Meaning what?"

"Meaning I'm about to flaunt my stupidity. You might want to take a few steps back, Dad, 'cause I'm pretty sure you're standing in the splash zone, and some of my bodily fluids might spray out on you when he clobbers me."

CHAPTER 16

C losing his eyes, Nick took a deep breath and reached down deep inside himself to tap the powers he barely understood. It was time for this to stop.

Sooner rather than later.

His heart pounded a fierce rhythm. *Come on . . . work.* Surely if he could set Stone on fire in class without trying, he could weasel some modicum of power out of himself with this herculean effort born of stringent Cajun stubbornness and all-out desperation.

Right?

Right!

And despite everything, nothing happened.

Arthritic minutes dragged by as he struggled for

the most minuscule ability. *Move a hair . . . bust a seam. Have a thought.* Anything. But the harder he tried, the less he achieved. Like him, it was useless.

Just as he was about to give up, he heard a piercing drone inside his head. Suddenly, the darkness around them seemed to expand and then contract like a rubber band snapping back on him. And in that one moment, his senses sharpened and he saw . . .

Everything.

Literally. The entire universe was laid out before him. The Nick he'd replaced in this realm was destined for law school. He'd graduate at the top of his Harvard class and end up in Congress, an advocate for real change that helped everyone. Best of all, he'd marry his college sweetheart and have a huge family that adored him and their grandparents. In the flashing images, he saw Kyrian's death in ancient Greece. Saw Kyrian's resurrection at Artemis's hands, and his centuries of guardianship where Kyrian stood strong. Until the day a kidnapped Kyrian awoke with Amanda Devereaux by his side, and the two of them were forced to run from an enemy out to kill them both.

Unable to control the visions that came at him like a supersonic strobe, Nick swung toward his father.

Only he didn't see the fierce beast he knew the man to be. He saw his father much younger, in the hands of their enemy gods. Beaten and branded. Bleeding and chained. Trembling from the weight of his physical agony, his father knelt at the feet of a creature who held no compassion or mercy. *"You were born to serve us, Malachai. Never forget who owns your life. Who you answer to."*

Noir—the god Nick couldn't even mention by name without feeding his powers—savored his control over the Malachai. And he was aptly named. His hair was blacker than Caleb's and his eyes were so dark it was hard to see where the iris stopped and the pupil began. Laughing, Noir fed from Adarian, draining his powers until the Malachai could no longer support his weight even on his knees. He hit the ground and lay in a defeated lump with tears streaming from the corners of his eyes while he begged silently for death. It was how all Malachai had been kept since the dawn of time, and it was what had made them so lethal and brutal. A weapon of ultimate massacre.

Instead of being treated like people, they'd been kept as animals and trained to kill on command. The more feral and afraid of their masters they were, the better. That was why Nick's Thorn and Caleb had been so determined to keep Nick from Noir's grasp. They knew exactly what the primal god would reduce him to before he unleashed Nick onto the world to end it.

More and more images came, faster and faster, clearer and clearer, but the most disturbing were the ones of Nick himself, in the future, destroying the very world that had birthed him. The world Kyrian and Acheron fought every night to protect. Lost and abandoned by everyone, Nick, too, had turned on humanity. All he wanted was to end his own pain.

The only way to achieve that was nuclear-level devastation of the entire planet.

I am the Malachai. The end of all things. Spawned for no other purpose than to bring down the primal light gods and serve Noir, Azura, and Braith—the originators of darkness and death—in any way they demanded. All of his species were born to suffer. And there could be no escape.

Throwing his head back, Nick roared with the weight of a destiny he wanted no part of.

I will not become that monster!

His body began to spasm and seize up, until he no longer had control of it. His teeth chattered so hard, he was amazed they didn't shatter. The darkness slithered over him like a deadly boa constrictor. It wrapped itself around his limbs and climbed up his chest, squeezing him ever tighter.

"You will always be mine," it whispered to him before it licked his cheek.

Adarian pulled back from Nicholas as he realized what was happening. Each of the primal gods had an element they controlled completely.

In all realms.

Somehow Noir had located Nicholas in this one. And he was using the darkness to reach the new Malachai and claim him. To bring him home. If Adarian didn't do something, the boy would be sucked straight into Noir's greedy hands.

A slow smile curved his lips at the thought. It would serve Nicholas right to know the horrors Adarian had survived. The little punk had no idea what real humiliation and pain were. He thought his pampered life was hard. . . .

He had no concept.

Nicholas had never tasted true brutality. Degradation. He had no idea what it was like to be surrounded by creatures who lived to break you. Creatures who could only feel pleasure while they drove pain into every molecule of your body.

It's what you deserve. Suffer and choke on Noir's kindness, just as I had to.

But as those words wrung smug satisfaction from him, he saw in his mind the first time Cherise had brought Nicholas to meet him. After what he'd done to her, he'd voluntarily returned himself to human prison so that he would never again be tempted to harm her. He'd been convinced that she would rather die than ever stand for his presence in her company.

Until he'd been told he had a female visitor. Assuming it was Laguerre—his primary general—with some kind of mischief she wanted to start, he hadn't thought much about it.

Bored and irritated, he'd gone into the common

room and scanned the rough occupants. At first, his gaze had swept over the crowd as he sought the dark-haired demon who lived to torment anyone unlucky enough to stumble upon her. Moving fast, he'd barely registered the terrified blonde in a very sedate, over-large blue sweater and jeans.

Then his brain had kicked in with recognition. He'd snapped his attention back to Cherise, who sat at a table in the back, looking tiny, delicate, and petrified. When her gaze had met his, it froze him to the spot. For a full minute, he'd been unable to breathe. Somehow in the last two years, he'd forgotten how beautiful she was. How very precious.

As she'd done on the day they met, she'd stolen his heart. That hesitant, sweet glance had gone straight inside him and gutted him where he stood. A part of him had wanted to run to her and kiss her. But he knew she wouldn't welcome his touch. Not after the nightmare he'd put her through.

For the first time in his entire existence, he'd been unsure of himself. Scared even. His hands had actually trembled as he made his way over to her.

He'd been almost on top of her before he realized

she wasn't alone. Asleep in her lap was a small human child. Completely baffled by that, Adarian couldn't imagine why she'd have brought a toddler to such a place. That wasn't like her.

Swallowing hard, he'd pulled out the chair across from her and taken a seat. For several awkward minutes, neither of them had spoken. Instead of looking at him, she'd kept her gaze on the sleeping toddler to the point he'd been ready to kill it for distracting her.

Then those blue eyes had glanced up and held him spellbound again. When she'd parted her lips to speak, he'd wanted her to declare her undying love for him.

Yet before she could do so, that puny, wretched creature awakened and started bawling.

"Shh, Nicky," she'd breathed in that dulcet tone that had never failed to weaken him. "*C'est si bon, Boo.*" And just like Adarian, the boy had been soothed instantly. With a bright, dimpled smile, the small creature had pulled himself up to stand in her lap. Kissing the boy's chubby cheek, Cherise had attempted to tame the riotous dark brown curls that were rumpled from his nap. The toddler had laid his head down on her shoulder and buried his hand deep in her blond hair while he bounced on his chubby legs and laughed. Adarian had sneered at the child, who seemed to mock him with the fact that he could hold Cherise while Adarian was forbidden to touch her at all.

After kissing his cheek again, she'd wrapped her arms around the child protectively, holding him tight to her as she bravely locked gazes with Adarian and expelled a heavy breath. "Adarian . . . meet your son, Nicholas Ambrosius."

Those unexpected words sucker-punched him. In all his wildest imaginings, the thought that they could have had a child together that would survive past its infancy had never dawned on him. He'd assumed the infant she'd carried was long dead and buried. But this . . .

"My son?"

She'd nodded as tears glistened in her eyes. "He was born just over a year ago . . . but don't worry, I expect nothing from you. And neither of us expects you to be a dad to him. I just didn't feel right not telling you that he was here. I'm sure one day, he'll have questions about you, and I don't want to lie to him."

The Malachai anger inside him had boiled, wanting

the innocent blood of the boy in her arms. He'd started to call her a liar until he realized that his powers had done the impossible.

They'd waned.

Something that inside a human prison filled with absolute evil should never happen to him. The only way for him to lose any power at all was for his son to be near him.

No, not his son.

His heir.

It wasn't unusual for Malachai to have children. That had happened throughout history. But the children never survived for very long. A week or two. Maybe a month. Not unless they were to be the new Malachai. The one who would kill the father and take his place.

Unbeknownst to her, Cherise had birthed his doom.

Horrified by his obvious future, he'd watched the way she'd cuddled her child and he'd hated Nicholas for that love she bore him. For the gentle way she soothed him while Nicholas had buried his mouth against her chin and blew bubbles.

When the boy had turned to him and reached out, Adarian had recoiled from him. He had no intention of touching that creature. Not unless it was to end its life.

Now that tiny, putrid beast had almost grown into manhood. In their realm, Nicholas stood eye-to-eye with him.

And while Adarian still hated Nicholas with every part of his being, he knew that Cherise loved this child, this putrid part of him, with all her heart. His loss would devastate her.

That was something Adarian couldn't allow.

Growling, he knelt on the ground and reached to save the brat. "Boy!"

Nick couldn't respond as something choked him even harder than before. Was his father still trying to kill him and regain his place as the single Malachai?

His vision dimmed more. Just as he started to black out, he was jerked from the floor and slammed against granite. Someone slapped at his cheeks.

"Nicholas? Can you hear me?"

What was crushing him? Nick blinked slowly as the

pain and pressure receded. Coldness brushed his cheek with a tender caress.

"Speak to me, boy!" It was only then that Nick realized that the granite crushing him was his father's muscles. The elder Malachai was holding him and it was his father's hand he felt stroking his face.

Yeah, right. The devil was eating ice cream from his own hand and sitting on icicles. That was the only way for his father to be this nice to him. It just wasn't possible. Not unless pigs were flying around the moon, and cats were building homes for dogs.

"Am I dead?"

That familiar sneer twisted his father's lips, but still he held Nick against his chest. "I should kill you."

Now *that* sounded right. Murder. Maim. Slap. Skin. That was what his father was into. Not playing nice and being cuddly. His father would rather throw him through a wall than toss a ball at him.

Groaning, Nick pressed his hand to his eye, where he discovered something warm and wet. He pulled back to see the blood on his fingers.

"It's all right." His father wiped the blood from his

hand before he cleaned Nick's face with a tenderness Nick would have never thought him capable of.

And that terrified him more than anything. "Who are you and what have you done with my father?"

Adarian paused his rough cleaning to stare down at him with a fierce, frightening scowl. "You have your mother's eyes."

Nick duplicated his father's frown. "Yeah. I know."

His features softening, Adarian cupped Nick's face with his cold, dry hand. "I never noticed that before. All I ever saw in you was me, and I hated you for it." He took Nick's hand in his and studied it as if it were an alien object. "How can she love you like she does when you look so much like me . . . after what I did to her?"

"I wonder that same thing every day." Nick swallowed hard as he stared up at his father. "She tells me that she hated you with everything she had until the moment I was born. And from then on, she couldn't hate you ever again."

"I don't understand."

"Yeah, me either. Some reason, she's delusional and

thinks that my sorry butt is the best thing that's happened to her. It's why she's tolerated you ever since and
why she used to take me to visit you in prison, even
though she's terrified of you. Without you, she wouldn't
have me. And for that, she says she's eternally grateful
to you. Go figure, right?"

Adarian shook his head. "But for you, I would have
never seen her again, would I?"

"Doubtful. Like I said, you scare the bejesus out of
her. I can't even raise my voice in happiness that she
doesn't jump back in fear. It was bad when I was a kid.
Now that I dwarf her, I have to be careful to make no
sudden moves, 'less it startles her."

Adarian winced in pain as he gentled the tight hold
he had on Nick. "I'm sorry I tried to kill you."

Nick had no idea how to respond to that. *Gee,
thanks?* Yeah, that didn't quite cover the mixed emotions at war inside him. They had never been father
and son.

Or even friendly.

But even so, Nick had always wanted to have a dad
like other kids did. He'd wondered countless times
what it would be like to hold his head up with pride at

school functions and proudly introduce his progenitor to his friends and teachers. He had no idea what that felt like. Only the sick cringing dread in his stomach whenever someone asked him what his father did for a living. He would dodge the question as best he could, and when he couldn't, he'd tell them that his father worked in the prison system.

Not really a lie. Just not the whole truth.

It wasn't something anyone wanted to admit to, especially not a kid who feared other people thinking he'd grow up and be a criminal, just like his father.

Now, Adarian held him as if he actually cared. As if Nick mattered to him. But he knew better. He was nothing to his father. He never had been.

Despising that truth, Nick started to pull away from his father, yet Adarian refused to let go.

"You have seen the future, Nicholas. Noir will not rest until he has you in custody. And as strong as you think you are, he will break you. When you rise to subdue your generals in your world, he will know you as the Malachai. No one can spare you that. And he will send everything he has after you."

"Can't wait," Nick said, his voice dripping with

sarcasm. "Been needing a good party to attend. Nice to know I won't have to pay for it myself."

Adarian snorted. "I was arrogant like you once. After I killed my father, I thought nothing could touch me. That I was without equal. The strongest, most powerful Malachai ever conceived." He laughed bitterly. "There's a reason I spent the last two hundred years in and out of human prisons. Why I spent centuries in hiding. While we are the most powerful of all demonkyn, we are not gods. And we cannot kill the ones who created us. The best we could hope is to imprison them, and that is impossible for us. They made sure of it."

"But I've seen the future where I've—"

"No," Adarian snapped, interrupting him. "You've seen your rampage against the gods who hold your leash. Every year we live, we lose more sanity. The hatred inside us grows exponentially. Because of your mother, yours has been tied down and mitigated. Without her . . . nothing will stop it from taking you over, and it will accelerate. In ways you can't even begin to conceive. You will turn on everyone near you and especially those who are close to you. You won't be able to stop yourself. And you will learn the lesson that was spoon-fed to me by my own whore mother."

Nick so loved the rosy landscape his father painted. "And that was?"

"We came into this world alone and that's exactly how we'll leave it. Don't expect the years in between to be any different. No one can be trusted. You only have friends until you look the other way. That is the truth of all species. But never more true than it is for our kind. Every Malachai born has been betrayed . . . starting with his own mother. And the one thing I learned at the business end of Noir's whip is that fear, pain, and intimidation will ensure your safety and make sure that nothing and no one ever goes for your throat. They won't dare so long as they fear the fact that you will get back up and come for them the way they went for you."

Nick didn't believe that. Not for a minute. He'd never had an enemy yet whose jugular he wouldn't go for if exposed. It didn't matter how much they beat or bullied him. He would not be intimidated by them and he refused to give them his fear. To the devil with that. No one would ever hold that kind of power over his mind and soul.

No one.

But his mother, Caleb, Acheron, Kyrian, Kody . . . there was nothing he would do to hurt them. Ever. He would die to protect their lives. And they had all proven the same loyalty where he was concerned. It was love that bound them together much tighter than hatred and fear ever could. As Kody so often said to him—*into all gardens rain will fall. But the heart and the love it's capable of will give us shelter from even the worst storms.*

Love and respect kept someone in check a lot more than fear and hatred. He would explain it, yet he knew better than to waste the breath. His father had no concept of those emotions. He never would.

Suddenly, Nick's head started spinning. He felt like he was falling again.

His father tightened the grip he had on him. "You're fading back to the false body. It won't hold you. It can't. But the spell that separated you is strong. You have to unlock your powers, son. Protect your mother. Be the man for her that I should have been. Not the beast that hurt her. I deserve no mercy and she deserves no sadness. Whatever you do, Nicholas, don't become me." And then his father did the most unbelievable thing of all.

He kissed Nick's cheek.

As he pulled back, his father's black, inhuman gaze bored into him. "The Ambrose Malachai will never be forgotten. But it's up to you as to how he'll always be remembered."

Nick wanted to speak. Nothing would leave his throat. He reached out for his father.

It was too late. One heartbeat he was in the land of dark nothing and in the next he was back with Kody, who held him just like his father had. Worry creased her brow as her green eyes warmed him.

Had it all been a delusion? Had his mind transposed Kody's actions into his subconscious and made him think that his father held him while in reality it'd never happened?

Was it a dream?

"See, Akra-Kody, the Simi done told you that he'd be alive and licking again."

Nick grimaced at Simi's messed-up syntax. "You mean alive and kicking."

It was Simi's turn to make a disgruntled expression. "No. Why you want to kick something when you can put barbecue sauce on it and lick it? You human-like people make no sense to the Simi's demon mind."

Nick grinned at her. "That's okay. You make none to me, either." He shook his head as he tried to clear his blurry vision. "Are we still under fire from Thorn?"

"No." Kody brushed his hair back from his face to feel for a fever. "Ash and Savitar, along with Simi, routed them."

Simi made a sound similar to a horse. "Bah! Akra-Kody helped us a lot, too. She a good helper in a fight."

Those words of praise brought a slight blush to Kody's cheeks. "Savitar and Ash are still out, making sure our enemies don't come back any sooner than necessary." She stood up, then helped him to his feet. "So what happened to you? You were saying all kinds of crazy things while you were out."

He could just imagine. "At least tell me I didn't snore."

Kody laughed. "You didn't snore, but you did call me by your father's name. I hope that's not some weird psycho thing you have where you subliminally want to date your father."

Nick choked and shuddered. "Hardly. Besides, I look so much like him, that'd be narcissism to the extreme. And while I occasionally like myself, I definitely don't *love* myself. In *any* sense of that word."

Taking a deep breath, he surveyed the damage around him, which wasn't as bad as it could have been. Bubba and Mark were tending wounds not far away and restocking weapons. Nick had to say that they'd looked better. 'Course, they'd also looked a lot worse.

"Where's my mom?" he asked them.

Bubba set his Neosporin aside and jerked his chin toward the fortified door. "She's in the shelter with Topher looking out for her, under severe death threats. I don't know how long Acheron and Savitar can hold Thorn and them off. Thorn promised he'd be back and I'm pretty sure the psycho meant it. Hell-monkeys be danged. I don't think anything is going to stop him for long. Not even your friends."

Nick bit his lip as he considered the best course of

action. Bubba was right. Thorn would return as soon as he could. They had to move fast.

"Kode? If we had Caleb here, could the two of you reverse whatever it was you did to my powers?"

"Maybe. But we don't have Caleb."

"Or do we?"

She arched a brow at him. "Did you hit your head again, sweetie? I've warned you about the dangers of concussions."

He grinned. "Kind of, but I did learn something that I hope isn't a lie."

"And that is?"

Praying his father wasn't setting him up for slaughter or a ton of therapy-inducing humiliation, Nick took a deep breath then called out. "Cabal. Cabal. Cabal. I summon you to me. Now."

Simi and Kody exchanged a look that said he was as crazy as he suddenly felt when nothing happened.

Great, Dad. I can look stupid on my own. Didn't really need you to help out on that front.

That was his thought until he heard a curse and something slammed into him, knocking him against the wall. Nick shoved his attacker away, then froze as he looked into a pair of familiar, startled brown eyes. Now *this* was the giant, badass-tough demon that Nick was used to.

"Malphas?"

Tense and braced to fight, Caleb turned around slowly, surveying every aspect of his new surroundings. He paused as he faced Kody and Simi. "Where the heck am I? And how did I get here?"

Kody pointed to Nick. "Apparently, Nick summoned you."

"Nick?" Caleb glanced right past Nick and kept searching the room with his gaze. "*Our* Nick? Where is the little booger?"

She gestured even more exaggeratedly at Nick's position. "Right there."

Caleb's jaw went slack as he faced him. "Nick?"

"Caleb?"

The word had barely left his lips before Caleb grabbed him into a bear hug and held him tight. Which was extremely awkward and gross. Completely weirded out by it, Nick tried to disentangle himself from the demon. It wasn't like Caleb to show any emotion toward him other than irritation or frustration. Sometimes anger.

Okay, a lot of times anger.

Still, affection toward anything other than food . . .

Completely unnatural.

"Stop, C! If you're going to hug me like this, you got to buy me dinner first, boy. And it's got to be someplace nice, like Antoine's or Brennan's. I ain't easy or cheap."

Laughing, Caleb stepped back and narrowed his eyes on Nick as he held him by his arms. "Dude . . . did you lose a bet with a sorcerer or something?"

Nick gave him a droll smirk. "Don't taunt me now that I know your real name. I'm told I can do some damage to you with that. Make you fetch my slippers and stuff."

Now it was Kody's turn to gape as she understood. "Cabal? His summoning name is Cabal? Really?"

Caleb visibly cringed. "Don't, Nekoda. Just don't. I can wreck your day, too, you know?"

She held her hands up in surrender. "Yes, you can. Please don't. I've already forgotten I ever heard it."

"Good woman."

Nick tilted his head as he took in Caleb's bruised face. "What got ahold of you?"

"A lot of things that were trying to snatch your body from my custody. And we can't leave Zavid alone with it. He's extremely likely to throw it out the door and let the others have you to save his own hide. Unlike me, he's not real attached to you, and I don't like or trust untested loyalty."

Neither did Nick. "I have been told by countless dead people today that you and Kody have to free my powers first."

"Countless dead people?" Caleb asked.

"Long story." Nick inclined his head to Kody. "Can you two fix me?"

She met Caleb's gaze. "I was told we needed the Magus Stone to restore his powers. It's what they used to do this to him."

Caleb choked on that. "Apollymi's necklace? Are you nuts?"

"Ooo," Simi breathed. "The sparkly, shiny one. I know that necklace. Akra used to pacify the Simi with it when she was a very little simi. It's why the Simi loves her sparklies so."

Kody sucked her breath in sharply. "Do you think you could borrow it?"

Simi burst out laughing, then sobered. "Oh. You were actually serious with the Simi and not making a joke. . . . Um, no. Akra need it to feed her Daimons and she'd pull the Simi's wings off if I tried to take it. That mean old Stryker would probably help, too. He bad that way. And no offense, but the Simi done like her wings. They make traveling very nice and very easy. Much faster than walking. And I know you know what I mean."

Caleb crossed his arms over his chest. "It wouldn't matter if we had it. Nick would still need his powers. It's worthless to us without those."

"How so?" Kody asked. "I have the blood of Set in me. Shouldn't it work if I used it?"

"Want to bet our lives on it?"

"Uh, not really, and especially not with our combined luck." Kody sighed. "Fine. Let's try to unlock his powers and see where it gets us."

"Hopefully not the hospital," Nick mumbled under his breath.

Bubba cleared his throat to get their attention. "Whatever you have planned, you might want to step it up a notch and be quick about it. We have bad guys heading in again and they're moving double-time."

Nick moaned out loud. "Can't we catch a break?"

Caleb snorted. "Pretty sure one of them would be willing to break a knee or any other bone they can reach."

"Ha, ha."

Kody held her hand out to Caleb. "Let's do this."

While Caleb took it, Nick glanced over to the monitor that Bubba and Mark were watching via webcams stationed down the street. His eyes bugged at the sight of their impending doom. Bubba wasn't exaggerating even a little bit. Thorn was back with a lot of reinforcements. Reinforcements that were dragging, bound in chains, a number of Acheron's hell-monkeys in their wake.

And then he realized what else they were carrying.

No . . . it couldn't be.

"Is that—"

"Our former allies?" Mark asked, confirming Nick's worst fear. "Yes, it is."

Horrified by the sight of Savitar and Acheron in Thorn's custody, Nick barely heard the words Caleb and Kody chanted behind him. He was too transfixed by the fact that they were all about to die a painful and grotesque death.

Rising up from the others, Thorn flew at the house and threw a fireball that slammed against the fortified front door. It was so powerful that it shook the entire structure. Mark and Bubba went pale. Without a word, Mark hurriedly finished arming himself. Bubba continued to sit in his chair as if unable to cope with what was coming for them now.

Simi started for the door, but Nick stopped her. "It's me they want. Maybe I should just hand myself over and stop this."

The Goth demon tsked at him. "Akri-Nicky, on the grand scale of stupid, that would be epic. And lethal." She patted his shoulder. "Trust the Simi, you don't want to do that. It'd ruin your clothes and you look very nice out of your ugly shirts."

He smiled at her, until he felt the hot stab of something going through him. For a second, he thought he'd been shot. He felt his stomach for blood.

Nothing was there.

Apprehensive, he glanced over to Caleb and Kody. And as he did so, he felt that light-headed sensation again. His hands turned translucent.

The Malachai power resides with your spirit and soul. It can never be separated from that. He looked around for his father, but he saw nothing. Just the voice in his head.

Suddenly, that familiar warmth filled his entire body. That indescribable je ne sais quoi he had whenever he tapped into his demonic inheritance. Leaning his head back, he closed his eyes and let it wash over him. The ether roared in his ears as he heard a million voices at once.

Someone grabbed him from behind. Instead of fighting, Nick leaned against them and allowed them to hold him while he swayed with the weight and pain of everything.

"Just breathe, baby. Just breathe." He felt Kody's gentle hand on his cheek as she whispered in his ear.

"I have you and I'm not letting go. Don't fight it. Remember that your powers are a part of you. Like breathing."

He tried to do what she suggested and not tense or fight the flow of power inside him. At first he thought he was settling down and returning to normal. Until his stomach heaved. Nick staggered away from Kody and ran to the bathroom. He'd barely made it to the toilet before his stomach unloaded itself with a violence that would make the girl in *The Exorcist* movie proud. Over and over, his stomach spasmed with no mercy given to his dignity.

To his complete shock, Kody knelt by his side and stroked his back until he was finally finished. With a shaking hand, he flushed the toilet.

She gave him a small damp towel that he pressed to his lips. "Better?"

His breathing ragged, he nodded, then shook his head. "You have an iron constitution, you know that?"

Laughing, she brushed the hair back from his forehead. "Compared to what you see in battle, vomit's not so bad."

He heard the pain in her voice that belied her light tone. Honestly, he didn't want to know what horrors she'd been through that this was preferable to them.

And all because of him and what he'd do to her and her family in the future.

Not wanting to think about that, he looked down at his hand that had finally returned to normal. He balled it into a fist. "Are my powers back?"

"Not sure. Care to try them and see?"

Nick cupped his hand and concentrated so that he could manifest a fireball. Instantly, fire engulfed his hand. Now it was his turn to laugh as he repeated it with his other arm.

Oh yeah . . .

He was back and he was ready to battle.

Extinguishing his arms, he rose to his feet and headed for the door with a deadly intent.

"Nick?" Kody chided. "What are you doing?"

"Going to ruin Thorn's day."

"Do you think that's wise?"

"Not at all." He kept going.

She tried to stop him, but he gently shrugged her

hold off. He was too set on payback. Nothing, not even Kody, was going to get in his way. Determined, he headed straight for the front door and ignored Mark and Bubba, who were armed to their teeth as they gaped at him and his apparent intentions.

Without a word, Simi and Caleb fell in behind him as his escorts.

Nick opened the door with his telekinesis and stood on the front porch. Caleb took position just behind Nick's left side while Simi squared off on his right.

Arching a brow, Thorn froze a few feet from the bottom step. "Well, well . . . how stupid and brave of you, little boy. But it'll take something more than two demons and elementary parlor tricks to scare or stop us."

Nick glanced to Simi and Caleb, then looked over to where Thorn's soldiers were dragging what he hoped was only an unconscious Acheron and Savitar onto the front lawn so that they could dump them by the driveway. He wanted to go to them and make sure they were alive. But that would be all kinds of dumb.

And while stupid was his better friend most days, this wasn't the time to court it.

Forcing that urge down, Nick locked gazes with Thorn and gave him a slow, taunting smile meant to irritate the other being into performing his own kind of idiocy. For further effect, he rolled out his thickest Cajun drawl. "Oh now, why you want to go and insult me, eh, Boo? What'd I ever do to you?"

Thorn stepped forward.

Nick rubbed at his jaw. "I would advise against doing that."

Another step. "I don't take orders."

"That's where you're wrong, *bon homme*. Last I heard, you are *my* general . . . and you take orders from me."

Thorn scoffed with a mocking laugh.

Nick tsked. "Last chance."

"Or what?"

Nick unfurled his wings and let the fire roll down both his arms until it pooled into his hands where it flamed in pulses that matched his rapid heartbeat. "I'm gonna barbecue me some Thorny meat and let the Simi here break out her hottest sauce and say, *bon appétit, cher.*"

Simi sucked her breath in sharply. "Don't go teasing me, Akri-Nick. Don't say something you don't mean. That's just wrong."

"I mean it, Simi." He glanced back at Thorn. "So what's it to be? You ready to make Simi's day or you want to back down and leave with all limbs attached?"

Thorn paused as he considered his answer.

"He's bluffing," Tabitha said as she walked through the demons to reach Thorn's side. "He doesn't have his powers. They're trying to trick us. I saw what he looks like as the Malachai and that's not it."

Thorn swept a speculative glance over Nick's body. "My girl's calling you a liar."

"If my girl was here, she'd be calling you an idiot."

Thorn growled.

Nick growled back.

Caleb laughed at them both. "Simi, we should be filming this. We could make a killing on it."

"Already recorded, akri-demon. Just let the Simi know whenever you want the full-color playback."

"Good." Caleb turned back to Nick. "This is probably where I ought to inform you that the way you sub-due the ušumgallu is you have to confront each general in your army, and prove yourself worthy of leading them."

The fire went out on his arms immediately. Nick held his hand up to Thorn. "Hang on a minute." He glared at Caleb. "Clarify that last statement."

"You. Malachai." Caleb stepped forward to clap him on the back. "Must sally forth unto each šarru and proclaim yourself the Uma-Šarru. For lack of a better term, head badass. Then when they laugh in your face, you throw them on the ground and make them cry uncle. Clear enough for you?"

A little too clear, honestly. His stomach pitching again, Nick nodded. "You know, Cale. This informa-tion would have been a lot more useful to me *before* I walked out the door."

"Yeah, well, you got that whole bad habit of leaping over a crack while not noticing that it's right in front of a cliff with no guardrail. Maybe you should look a little farther ahead than the tip of your nose from time to time. Just saying."

Thorn laughed out loud. "Seems Tabitha was correct then. You belong to us."

This time when Thorn moved forward, Nick set him on fire and forced him and Tabitha backward, into the yard. "Did I say you could move, Alpo? Pretty sure I told you to stay put. Think you, I didn't mean it?"

"Nice work," Caleb congratulated in an amused tone.

"Thank you. Now back to what we were talking about."

"Uh, not to interrupt, but . . ." Caleb pointed to the demonic army that was now attacking them.

Nick let out a sound of fierce irritation before he sent a wave across the yard that knocked them down and sent them skidding toward the street.

When they rose back to their feet and ran at them again, he passed a droll stare to Caleb. "They ride the short bus, don't they?"

"Pretty sure that big demon in back *is* the short bus."

Kody grimaced at them both as she joined them on the porch. "Gentlemen, this isn't a video game. Those

caught Thorn's shoulder. Yelping, Thorn manifested a sword and lunged forward.

With his powers, Nick created a staff and deflected it, then parried with a blow that caught Thorn across his spine.

Kody gaped as she watched Nick and Thorn spar. She met Caleb's equally stunned expression. "When did he learn to do all that?"

"Not one hundred percent sure. But remind me the next time I say something snarky that he's come a long way with his battle skills."

Yes, he had. In the past, Nick could always take a punch. Now, he was able to give them.

He fought like a boss.

Until Thorn turned it on him. Kody started forward, but Caleb stopped her. "He has to defeat Thorn on his own. Without help. Otherwise, he won't be able to subjugate the ušumgallu."

She glanced around the yard where Simi had already routed the other demons. Selena and Amanda had vanished into the crowd. Tabitha was heading for Nick and Thorn. *I might not be able to help with Thorn, but* . . . She could definitely take that witch down. No one was going after Nick while she was around.

Kody headed for her.

Nick saw Kody from the corner of his eye. That distraction cost him as Thorn moved in and caught him a significant blow to his jaw that sent his head spinning. He staggered back. Thorn kicked him hard in the solar plexus.

Everything darkened. And for a second, he honestly thought he was going to black out. Until he saw the darkness slithering again. It was like a living, breathing creature.

I'm hallucinating.

What if he wasn't? Given all the other weirdness in his world that wasn't crazy, what if . . .

Nick held his hand out to pet it. The dark rose up to caress his arm and lick it. Before he could rethink it, Nick slung his hand out and sent the darkness for Thorn. With his thoughts, he commanded it.

One second Thorn was about to stab him, and in the next, the darkness jerked him out of reach. It was only then that Nick saw it for what it really was. Not one single creature, but an amalgam of night. Lifting his hands, he orchestrated it to go after the others, including Tabitha.

Holy crap . . . it was working. He could actually do this and the power wasn't malfunctioning on him. At least not yet.

Kody froze as Tabitha was pulled back from their fight and held immobile by nothing. No, not nothing.

By the element of night.

Terror filled her as she realized what was happening. Nick had embraced the darkness. He was commanding it. Something he shouldn't be able to do for decades yet. And for him to do that now boded the worst kind of evil for them.

Biting her lip, she watched breathless as Nick started to transform from a human into a demon. He stalked toward Thorn with eyes so red they glowed and snapped like a living fire. The Malachai powers were alive and they had possession of him. Completely.

What have we done?

Once tapped, Noir's powers were seductive and all-consuming. Irresistible. Worse, they allowed the primal god to locate his property. So long as Nick used them, Noir could hone in and attack him.

She met Caleb's concerned gaze and saw the same horror mirrored on his face.

"Nick!" he cried.

But it was too late. Nick was transforming in front of them. And he was about to kill Thorn and absorb his powers, too.

CHAPTER 17

*Y*ou command the power of the universe. Life, itself, is in the palm of your hand. There is nothing that can stop you. No rules that apply to you. You *are the only one who matters in this existence. The rest are pawns and tools to be used and destroyed as you see fit.*

Embrace your fate, Malachai. Become what you were born to be.

Nick let the truth ring in his ears as he effortlessly pinned Thorn to the lawn with one hand. The demon lord wasn't so powerful now that he squirmed like a worm caught on drying pavement by the heat of a sun he couldn't fight. He was every bit as pathetic and helpless as those insignificant creatures that crawled up from the belly of the earth and were used as nothing more than bait for and by their betters.

Kill him and you'll be even stronger than what you are now. You'll have powers the likes of which you cannot imagine.

Nick scoffed. *I don't know, disembodied voice in my head. I have one heck of an active imagination. You'd do well not to underestimate it.*

In his mind, Nick saw himself as he wanted to be. Confident. Suave. Sophisticated. Tough. Like Kyrian, Talon, Caleb, and Acheron. The epitome of badass respectability. Not the pathetic loser dork who banged his arms and feet into everything he passed. One who bumped his head anytime he neared low-hanging signs or plants.

Just once, he wanted to walk into a room, without tripping over nothing, and not have someone snicker or comment about his clumsy awkwardness or foul clothing.

Kill him and it's all yours. Everything you want. You will be the very top of the food chain. No one will ever dare to mock you again.

Nick tightened his hold on Thorn's throat. It was *so* tempting. All he'd ever wanted in his entire life was respect.

And the voice was correct. Right now, he saw terror in Thorn's green eyes as he struggled against Nick's iron grip that would not be broken. Gone was any hint of condescension or contempt. Thorn definitely wasn't smirking now as he began turning blue and his eyes bulged.

I could kill him and no one would care. Who would miss a creature like Thorn?

No one. It would be easy. . . .

So *very* easy.

But as Nick felt Thorn's weakening grip on his hand, he loosened his hold. *I am the Malachai.* The baddest beast in the land. What would killing Thorn really prove?

A truth he already knew? That he was stronger? Better?

What was the point? He didn't need blood on his hands to show the world who and what he was. Nick already knew, and so did the people who mattered to him.

The devil take the rest. He didn't owe them anything. And they weren't worth his life.

Definitely not worth his soul.

Nick Gautier had nothing to prove to anyone in this, or any, realm.

But he still had people to protect. People he cared about and loved.

With that in mind, he slackened his hold to give Thorn some breathing space. "Do you yield to me?"

Thorn growled at him.

"That's not an answer." Nick traded hands and increased the pressure on Thorn's throat again. "Do I really have to kill you on the front lawn of Bubba's house? Is that truly what you want? Because, no offense, killing you is not the way to get my girl to kiss me at the end of the night. And I'd much rather snuggle with her than step over your dead body and tick her off. Pretty sure you'd rather I not kill you, too. Or am I wrong? Are you suicidal? Do we both go home happy or will I later be defacing your corpse because you got me in the doghouse?"

Thorn's eyes glowed red in the darkness. "I will follow no one ever again. And that includes *you*."

"Good. 'Cause I'm not leading. There will be no battle and you're not being summoned to my army or to any kind of fight on my behalf. The only war I want is the solo one against my own stupidity—which seems a losing battle most days. And while I'd like to defeat that, I don't want to end the world or you or anything other than this ridonkulous standoff. . . . However, I will kill you if I have to, to stop this, but I hope it don't come to that. Honestly, all I expect is for you to crawl back to your hole and stay there like a nice demon lord. Because the next time I confront you, boy, I won't show mercy. You will bleed and I will be in the perpetual doghouse with both the women in my life. Got it?"

Kody started for Nick, but Caleb caught her arm. She glared at the demon. Did he not understand what was going on? If they didn't do something fast, it would be over for all of them. "Nick's metamorphosing."

A slow smile broke across Caleb's handsome face. "Yes, he is."

How could he be so nonchalant? So happy? Did he want Nick to become a bloodthirsty monster? If Nick gave in to his dark powers, Caleb would suffer as much, if not more, than she would. Especially now that Nick knew his real name.

Terrified, she glanced to Nick, who was about to finish Thorn off, then back to Caleb. "We have to stop it! If he becomes the Malachai—"

"Kody," Caleb said in an even tone, breaking her words off. "Can you not understand what they're saying?"

She shook her head. "It's demonkyn. I only know a handful of words."

"Yeah, well, I know a few more."

All of a sudden, Nick stood and backed away from Thorn. With a glower of fury at him, Thorn slowly pushed himself to his feet. She expected him to attack Nick again.

Instead, he saluted him, then gathered his demon minions and Tabitha and her sisters, and left.

Completely confused, she stared at Nick as he went to check on Savitar and Acheron, who were still lying as lumps on the lawn. By the relieved expression on his face while he felt for a pulse, she knew they were okay.

And while that thrilled her, it didn't take away her shock at Nick's actions. She gaped at Caleb. "He's in control of himself?"

Caleb nodded. "Completely. Somehow he pushed the darkness out and resisted it."

How? It was unheard of. No one turned down Noir. And they definitely didn't do it like this.

As Nick headed toward her, he gave her that devilish grin that never failed to speed up her heartbeat. But as fast as that smile came, it vanished with a curse. Clutching his chest, Nick fell to his knees on the lawn. Then he collapsed.

Petrified, she ran to him. "Nick?"

Arching his back, Nick screamed out. He shook all over. She met Caleb's and Simi's wide-eyed stares as they joined her by his side.

"What is this?"

They shook their heads in unison.

Kody knelt and placed her hand to Nick's cheek. "Sweetie? Can you hear me?"

He bit his lip and cursed again. "It burns like fire."

"What?"

He pulled his shirt down so that he could blow across his chest. And as he did so, an ancient symbol formed over his left pectoral. It was a circle that held Noir's emblem on top and Azura's on the bottom. The mark of their ownership.

But why was it appearing on his temporary body? That made no sense at all.

Swallowing hard, she met Caleb's wide gaze. He paled instantly. "What is this, Caleb?"

"He's marked."

She understood that part. The demon was being evasive and she wanted to beat him for it. "Elaborate."

Caleb shook his head slowly. "You really don't want me to."

"Oh, I really do."

Caleb grimaced and continued to hedge. "Why ruin all our days?"

"Caleb!" she snapped simultaneously with Nick.

Nick reached up and grabbed the front of Caleb's shirt. "What is happening to me?"

"Your parents want their baby home, son. And

this—" Caleb touched his mark. "Is their Tactical Trunk Monkey."

Scowling at the term, Nick dreaded the answer in the worst sort of way. "What's a Tactical Trunk Monkey?"

Caleb made another grimace. "In a couple of years, you'll know exactly what I mean. For now, think of it like a homing beacon from hell."

Nick stifled the fear in him that was trying to take over. Not a good time for that. He really needed his levelheaded sanity. Although honestly, he couldn't think of anything better than to panic right now. For that matter, his sanity hadn't proven all that beneficial, either.

Maybe freaking out would help?

Nick ground his teeth against the agony that continued to pierce him. "How do we get rid of it?"

"The Simi could barbecue your skin. That would take it off. Might take some muscles and other things, too. Should we try?"

Nick made a high-pitched noise of disagreement. "No!"

SHERRILYN KENYON

Simi bared her fangs at him. "The Simi don't like that word, Akri-Nick. It a bad bad thing."

"And I don't like being burned by flaming demon breath, either, Simi."

She blew him a raspberry. "You big demon baby."

"Dang right." He tightened his hold on Caleb's shirt. "What do I do?"

"Run."

Nick scoffed. Caleb made it sound so easy. But if he knew anything, it was that his life never had a simple answer to his problems, and he couldn't breathe or stand, never mind get up and sprint across the lawn. "Won't they find me if I run?"

Caleb didn't hesitate with his response. "Yeah."

"Then what's the good in running?"

"You'll feel like you at least tried?"

He gaped at his friend, hating Caleb's sarcasm. "Not comforting, Caleb. Not comforting."

Kody cupped his face in her hands and forced him to look at her. "You have your powers. Can you take us home? If you're back in your own body, they won't be able to track you. Right?"

Caleb shrugged.

Kody popped him on the arm.

"Ow!" He rubbed the spot where she struck him. "I don't know, woman. Sounds good to me. It's worth a try, I guess."

Ignoring them, Nick glanced around the yard to where Savitar and Ash were still unconscious. Bubba, Mark, the two Tophers, and Cherise were cautiously leaving the house. He met Simi's gaze then Caleb's and finally he returned to Kody, and all the while the pain in his chest burned deeper and more ferocious. He had to do something. Fast. "I can try."

She leaned down to place a chaste kiss on his lips. "You will succeed."

Like Caleb, Kody made it all sound so easy. But Nick lacked her optimism. At this point, they'd been told so many differing things on what he needed to do to get home and be safe that nothing made sense anymore. He felt as though he'd been stuck here forever.

Stop complaining. At least you have your powers back.

That was true. Not to mention, his father had told him that this body couldn't contain his real spirit. If he could bypass that realm his father had been in, then maybe, just maybe, he might make it back to where he came from and no one would be able to track him there. All he had to do then was kick the other Nick out of his skin and hope for another miracle.

Yeah, he felt like laughing at the ridiculousness of that, too.

Closing his eyes, he tried to focus.

"You can do this, Nick," Kody whispered in his ear as she clutched his hand in hers. "I have complete faith in you. Think of your mom and Aunt Mennie and Liza and Kyrian. All the people who love you. The ones who need you."

Her voice was so hypnotic. It lulled him into a sense of complete peace while she continued to remind him of the things he valued at home. The people who were his family, even without blood ties.

Instead of helping him, though, it felt more like she was putting him to sleep. In spite of the pain, his eyes became heavy. His limbs weak. Before he knew what was happening, he went completely limp and fell into a black hole.

Panicking, Nick tried to grab hold in the darkness.

Nothing was there. He couldn't even hear Kody's voice anymore.

Was he dead?

Dying? He had no way of knowing. This was an absolute cessation of sensory input. He could no longer hear, see, taste, smell, or feel anything. His eyes rolled back in his head.

And still he fell.

Angry and scared, he summoned his powers with everything he had and did his best to stop the free fall.

Suddenly, the darkness began to cradle him. It slithered around his limbs and wound itself tightly over his chest just as it'd done earlier. He heard the sound of a thousand hooves running far away like a powerful thrumming heartbeat.

Then he saw the Ambrose Malachai in all its glory. Tall, evil, and unstoppable. Covered in armor, the beast was terrifying. Caleb stood to his right, with a sick look on his face. Dressed in his own battle armor and with his wings extended, Caleb brushed his hand over the blood that covered him. "Your enemies have been routed, my lord. They are down to only a tiny handful who've taken refuge in the church."

Nick, as the Ambrose Malachai, arched a brow at Caleb's tone while he gave his report. He turned his red gaze to his once trusted friend who no longer meant anything to him. "You dare condemn me?"

"No, my lord. It's not my place." What had he done to Caleb to make him so subservient? Never had he known the demon to be so obsequious.

Nick hated seeing him like that.

Fear was not respect. It was only a cold substitution. He would rather have Caleb's biting sarcasm than this shell of a boot-licking sycophant, trying to placate him. But the Ambrose Malachai didn't seem to care or to notice the difference. He merely walked all over everyone around him.

Disgusted by the sight, Nick shook his head to clear it and forced his thoughts to his mother and his home. He had to return to her. Without him, she was defenseless.

"Talk to me, Kody. Guide me back to my New Orleans."

Oppressive silence answered him. It rang in his ears until it overrode the sound of his own heartbeat.

I'm lost.

No. He couldn't think that way. If he did, he really would be lost and he'd never return to the world he knew. The world he loved.

I must stay focused. Keep his eye on the target. The landscape was home. Back to the world that made sense to him. To the place where Madaug was his nerdy friend and Stone was the one who slammed him into lockers.

Natural order.

Positive. Negative.

Abnormal normality.

"Come to me, Nicholas. I can make it all better."

Nick hesitated at the beckoning voice that filled him with an inexplicable joy. It was like a mother's caress. Soft. Gentle. Soothing. Alluring.

He almost gave in, until he remembered one fact he'd learned the hard way—*beware the easy path. It's never as simple as it seems.* Even Zavid had warned him of that, and he knew it for fact. *Don't sell your soul for a lifetime of slavery to avoid a brief time of misery. This, too, shall pass.*

If he was going to go down in flames, it'd be to the tune he picked. Not something forced on him by someone else.

"You want me, lady. Come get some. But I'm not going to you." And he dang sure wasn't going to make it easy on her.

Nick concentrated as hard as he could on the home he wanted to return to. He imagined himself in his room, grounded for life by his mother. The darkness spun faster as if trying to drag him away from that image.

In true Gautier form, he dug his heels in and refused to let it sway him. "I am not your pawn or your tool!" he growled. "You will not own me. You will *not* control me."

As if offended, the darkness let go and he fell fast enough that his eyesight blurred.

He slammed into a wall so hard, it shattered around him like glass. His spine felt busted. Fragments showered him as he finally came to a rest, flat on his back. His breathing labored, he groaned out loud in utter agony. Afraid yet determined, Nick opened his eyes to meet his newest threat.

It came in the form of a slobbering, growling wolf with bared fangs.

Nick started to attack until he realized where he was. He knew that elaborate crown molding. That ornate French mural that was painted across the ceiling.

This was Caleb's house.

That would mean the wolf was . . .

"Zavid?"

The wolf pulled back to glare suspiciously at him.

Nick pushed himself up. "Dude, we need to get you some serious breath mints. Stop panting on me, I'm not your Saturday night girl."

Backing away, Zavid returned to his human form. He narrowed his eyes suspiciously. "Gautier? That really you?" He reached out and his hand passed straight through Nick's body.

Nick let out a sound of disgust. He didn't even want to know what he looked like right now. "That's not a good sign, is it?"

"Depends. Are you alive or dead?"

"I'm going with alive because it beats the alternative."

Zavid rolled his eyes. "Where's Malphas?"

"Cabal!" Nick shouted, hoping it would work. He glanced to Zavid. "Do I really have to call a demon in triplicate every time I want to summon it?"

Before the wolf could answer, Caleb appeared by his side.

"Guess not," Nick answered. This was getting better. His powers were holding and doing what they were supposed to. At least for the time being. "How do I get S—"

As if sensing the question, Simi appeared instantly on his six. "Akri-Nick! You made it. Good for you." She slapped Caleb playfully on his arm. "See, the Simi done told you that that mean ole darkness wouldn't eat his head like you said it would. You didn't believe me. Next time the Simi tells you something, you'll listen. Mmm, and speaking of, all this inner dimensional travel done made the Simi hungry again. What you gots to eat in this place?"

Caleb pointed to Zavid. "I hear barbecued wolf is a delicacy on most continents."

Offended, Zavid glared at him. "Excuse me?"

"I would, Z, but you keep doing stupid crap. And there's just no excuse for that."

Nick ignored them while he waited on Kody to join their group.

After a couple of minutes, he glanced back at the two demons, who were still arguing while Simi was rooting through Caleb's kitchen pantry. Lightning flashed outside before the sound of thunder rattled the windows.

"Hey, guys! Can I have your attention for a sec?" He counted his concerns off on his fingers. "One, where's the alternate me so I can repo my bod and get back to normal? Kind of miss it, and I don't want to stay like a ghost. And two, where's my girl? I miss her more than my body."

Zavid grimaced in distaste. "Since I don't hear the screeching whine of a child that makes my ears bleed, I'm assuming Nick Two is still unconscious inside the closet I locked him in."

Caleb rolled his eyes. "Are you serious?"

"You told me not to let him get eaten or kill him until you got back. He's not eaten and I didn't kill him. Really, you should congratulate my restraint . . . which was seriously hard won."

"Congratulations. I'm not going to kill you."

And still, neither answered the most pertinent question. "Where's Kody? Do I have to summon her by name, too?"

"She's not a demon," Caleb reminded him. "That only works on us."

"Then where is she?"

Zavid shrugged while Caleb scratched uncomfortably at his neck. That was never a good thing where Caleb was concerned.

An awful feeling went through Nick. "What?" he asked Caleb.

He refused to answer.

Oh yeah, this was going to suck. . . .

With a box of Ding Dongs in hand, Simi drifted back into the foyer where they stood. "Man up, demon. Tell the boy what he's asking about."

Still, Caleb hedged.

"What?" Nick repeated, this time to Simi. "What's happening? Why isn't Kody here?"

Simi sighed heavily then swallowed her mouthful of cupcake. "You know Miss Akra-Kody not human, right?"

"Yeah, I'm not that oblivious."

Simi dug out another package from the box. "Well, see, there's a little problem. Akra-Kody be a ghost and they can't travel like we does and Caleb couldn't bring her back like he did me, 'cause she got no real living body. She gots one of them borrowed bodies that are . . . different. Once they leaves a dimension, they can't really get back to it."

The knot in his stomach tightened to the point he thought he'd be sick. "I don't understand."

Caleb groaned under his breath before he picked up the explanation. "You know the old joke about the dead, don't go into the light?"

"Yeah."

"We went into the light. Kody won't be able to cross back . . . ever."

Rage erupted inside him. Before he could stop himself, he grabbed Caleb and slammed him into the wall. He wasn't sure how he could do that while Caleb still couldn't touch him, but he was too angry to question it right now. Not while he had more pressing concerns. "You're lying to me!"

Caleb shook his head. "I wouldn't do that. And you know Simi could never."

Releasing Caleb, Nick didn't want to believe it. Tears made his vision swim as an unbelievable agony tore through him.

Kody gone? How could that be true?

"Why didn't she say something?"

"She knew you wouldn't come back without her and we didn't have time to waste. We still don't. You have to merge back into your body, kick down your army, and seal them out before the next new moon. Which is roughly sixteen hours from now, give or take."

A loud, piercing screech erupted from somewhere Nick couldn't locate. It sounded like the air itself made it. The storm outside increased its intensity. If he didn't know better, he'd think they were in the middle of a hurricane.

Zavid flinched as if something had struck him. "Definitely less. That's the cry from another šarru. Something just broke its seal and released it into this world. We have to move fast." He rushed for the stairs.

"Nick?" Caleb said in an earnest tone when Nick didn't rush after Zavid. "What are you thinking?"

He was thinking that he wanted to go back and get Kody. Right now. He was thinking that he had no desire to be here without her. To live in a world where she didn't exist.

She'd given up everything for them, without hesitation.

And that made him even angrier. Did she not love him at all? How could she just let him go without saying anything, knowing she'd never see him again?

Did she not care?

I meant nothing to her.

She hadn't even put up a fight about it. She'd just kicked him out of her life as if he was nothing but an unwanted nuisance.

Caleb snapped his fingers in his face. "Nick! Stop!"

He glared at the demon. "Stop what?"

"I can tell by the fire in your eyes what you're thinking. Kody loves you. More than you understand. What she did, she did for *you* and you alone. Had you not left, Thorn *would* have returned and enslaved you, and the others would have killed you. Don't you dare let that Malachai hate build up inside you and take away from her selfless act. I was there after you left. I saw her break down and weep like you can't imagine. And now she's trapped there, completely alone. With no one at all. So don't you dare hate her for what she did to save *you*."

Even so, it was hard. The Malachai wanted to hate, and keeping that at bay was a constant struggle for him. Hatred was quickly becoming his go-to happy place.

But the thought of Kody in tears . . . that hit him hard. He couldn't stand the thought of her in pain. Especially not because of him. "I have to go back for her."

Caleb shook his head. "Without the Magus Stone, you can't. And right now, the most important thing is to reunite you and your body and put down your army before they get together and party. Not to mention, we don't know what your spirit will do here in this realm if it's not grounded in your body, and with the two of you existing in the same time and space . . . that's never supposed to happen. And I don't know the full ramifications if you exist together for long. So let's take care of one catastrophe at a time. Okay?"

A human scream sounded from upstairs.

Zavid growled low in his throat. "Speaking of catastrophes, wanna bet that's Nick Two getting eaten by something?"

Without hesitation, Nick teleported to Caleb's room. Ready to battle to the death, he froze at the sight of the true terror that awaited him.

No, Lord, anything but *this.*

Demons, vampires, werewolves, brain-hungry zombies, cruel jocks—Nick could handle anything, *anything* . . . except this—this was way beyond cruel, and far beyond his ability to cope.

Truly, truly horrified, he gaped at the boy in his body who was standing on a chair, squealing and pointing at the floor, where the most terrifying thing in the world looked up in horror, too.

Disgust overwhelmed Nick as he glared at the stranger in his body. "What are you doing?"

"It's a spider!" Nick Two screamed as he continued to gesture toward the tiny creature on the floor.

A spider? Really? Thank God it wasn't a rat. That would have probably sent him into an epileptic seizure.

Nick sighed wearily. "You screamed like that over a bug? Seriously, dude? We live in New Orleans. Ground zero for insects. And here I thought something was about to kill you."

Something other than him.

"It is! That's a brown recluse! They're poisonous."

Nick scoffed at his unwarranted hysteria. Thank goodness this hadn't happened at school—he'd never live it down. And rightfully so. Anyone this big a baby over something so ridiculous needed to be mocked. It was a moral imperative. "It's a granddaddy longlegs and he's laughing his butt off at the human idiot he chased up a chair. Dude, have some dignity, especially while you're wearing my skin. Last thing I want is for someone to think I got treed by a harmless spider. It'd kill my rep forever."

Trying not to roll his eyes or say something really mean about it all, Nick stepped forward to pick up the spider and remove it from the room. But the moment he touched it, an electric shock went through him.

One second it was a tiny, harmless spider, and in the next, it was a beautiful woman with a vampiric dental problem. An evil smile curled her lips as she reached for Nick. Jerking him into her arms, she sank her fangs into his neck.

"You are mine, Malachai . . . All mine."

CHAPTER 18

Nick's head swam as he appeared in a large living room with antique furniture. He wasn't sure if he was still in a human realm or in an alternate one. There was no way to get any real bearings here. It might be New Orleans.

Heck, it might all be a dream or hallucination. There was no telling. Especially when it came to his extremely screwed-up life.

The woman holding him let go and stepped back to give him a hot once-over he might have found seductive had she not just taken a chunk out of his neck. He glared at her as he rubbed at the nasty wound that held a perfect impression of her serrated teeth. "For the record, nibbling on a guy's skin is nice. Taking a bite out of his flesh, not the way to get a second date. Just letting you know, you need to update whatever whacked out guy manual you're using."

Tall, raven-haired, and pale-skinned, she licked his blood from her lips as she smiled and playfully ruffled his hair. "You're much sweeter-tasting than Adarian. I think I like you better already."

Yeah, okay . . . There was so much about this that made him uncomfortable, he had no idea where to start listing things. But the primary concern he had was simple—"How can you bite me and make me bleed when I don't have a physical body here?"

She laughed. "You're very real to me, and no matter where you are, I will always be able to find and touch you."

Had that come from Kody, he'd be thrilled with it. From this woman . . . that ranked up there with a Freddy Kreuger threat. "Who are you?" More importantly, *what* was she?

Laughing again, she nipped at his chin with enough pressure to make it hurt. "I'm your Šarru-Ninim, Livia.

As soon as I awoke, I followed the scent of your blood to you. Or so I thought. I knew the real Malachai couldn't be that sniveling coward who feared my lesser form so. While many things have changed about the world while I endured my stygian nightmare, some things will always be. And a strong, fearless Malachai is one of them." She ran her hand down his chest toward an area of his body that made him jump away from her reach.

Nick caught her hand and pulled it away. "Babe, I don't know you and my *no zone* has a very short guest list. Consider my belt the velvet rope no one crosses without an express invitation."

She fisted her hands in his shirt and pulled him against her for another kiss.

He dodged her lips then twisted out of her arms. "Demon, please. You don't just bite a guy, make him bleed, and expect him to fall all over you. Don't know where you're from, but here, that's considered rude."

She scoffed at him. "You need to feed from me, Malachai. I am the one who will always give you the most power. I'm the one šakkan you have on your team that no one is immune to."

He removed her hand from his arm. "I still don't understand how you can touch me when I have no body."

"Like you, there is only one of me, and we are bound by the blood of your ancestors. Corporeal or not, makes no difference. Now come, kiss my lips and feast on the nectar you need to take your rightful place to unite and lead us into battle."

Nick shook his head. "No offense, I don't want to feast on anyone's nectar." Mostly 'cause it didn't sound all that sanitary or healthy, especially given how free and nonchalant she was with handing it out. But he didn't want to hurt her feelings, either, so he quickly added, "Not until I have my body back. Until then I don't need to be partaking of anything other than working on an eviction notice for an arachnophobe who's currently humiliating my real body."

She stared at him as if he made no sense to her what-soever.

"Malachai!"

Startled, Nick turned around to find Zarelda behind him. "What's wrong?"

"They're coming."

"They?"

"The ones who want you dead. They've tracked you down." She passed her hand through both him and Livia. "I can't stop them. Not even *she* can see me. Only *you*, Nick. But you need to know. They're about to attack my brother. Please help him."

"What is wrong with you?"

Nick glanced over his shoulder at Livia. "You really can't see her?"

"See who?"

Nick shook his head as Zarelda ran for a wall and vanished into it. "Never mind. You have to put me back together."

"I don't understand."

"I'm your commander, right?"

She nodded.

"Then that's my first round of orders. I need to get back to the others. Now. Take me to where you found me."

Her eyes turned deep, dark red. Resistance burned bright inside them as if she was fighting against some inner force so that she could disobey him.

Finally, she let out a frustrated sound. She threw her head back, wrinkled her nose, and stomped her foot. Then she sighed and looked at him as if nothing had just happened. "Fine." It came out like an insult the way she said it.

But before she could make good on his order, another flash blinded him to the point he saw stars from it. He held his hand up to shield his eyes from the intense light source. A loud, enraged hiss rang out, followed by a blast that exploded so close to Nick, he could feel the heat of it.

Livia returned the attack with a blast of her own. "Xevikan! Down!"

"I'm not your dog, Livia. Mind your place."

It took Nick a second to understand the creature's words through his thick, heavy accent. Man, it made Kyrian's and Talon's sound mild by comparison. Not an easy feat by any stretch of the imagination.

Dressed in black pants and a long leather coat of an archaic style with a hood that concealed his features completely, the newcomer seemed humongous. Until he stepped closer to Livia and Nick realized he was probably only an inch or two taller than Nick was in his normal body. Their build was about the same, too. Only this guy had an aura about him that would rival Acheron's for sheer lethal grace. He definitely had a high body count on something other than *Castlevania*.

For that matter, Nick held no doubt that the guy's heavy combat boots were probably laced with some victim's intestines.

Rigid from head to toe, Livia stood up to him without flinching. She raked him with a sneer that said she was unimpressed by his grand entrance. "Oh little boy, do I have to school you on your manners? I know you were thrown out by your mother just minutes after she spawned you, but trust me, I hold even less love of you than she did."

He stepped closer to her as if trying to intimidate her with his much larger frame. And he did dwarf her. Even so, she didn't flinch or back off a bit.

"Why do you protect something so weak and ineffectual, Liv? The only place this one can lead us is straight into defeat."

Laughing, she stepped back and held her hand out toward Nick. "Fine. If you really believe that, take him . . . if you can."

Nick gaped at the way she just casually threw him to the . . . whatever kind of demon, inhuman nightmare creature this was. "Excuse me? I'm not *pour chien* here, *cher.*"

Livia didn't comment as she stepped back, out of the line of fire.

Great. He really was dog food. With no place to run, Nick braced himself for the fight.

An inhuman growl came out from the bowels of that black hood. He held his hands out and lightning sizzled over the creature's entire body. It intensified and danced around him. Throwing his head back, he let loose a cry of anguished fury. The hood fell down against his shoulders, exposing his perfect features.

Nick held his arms up to defend against whatever attack he planned to unleash. Suddenly, the lightning stopped. For a full minute, nothing moved. No sound came from any of them.

Not even breathing.

Then slowly, the man lowered his arms and raised his head. He curled his lip. "Damn. He really is the Malachai."

Completely confused by the display of power and free light show, Nick arched his brow as a pair of searing hazel eyes met his gaze. They were the strangest he'd ever seen. Like a kaleidoscope of reddish earth browns and greens. The color reminded him of rust nestled in summer leaves.

But that wasn't the most peculiar thing about him and his pretty-boy looks. Oh no . . . This guy not only wrote the book on weird, he printed and owned every copy. Unlike virtually every guy on the planet, his hair wasn't a single color.

It was three.

He parted it on the left side of his head. The bulk and longest strands of his hair that fell from the part were a very vivid and unnatural dyed bloodred. From his part down the shorter right strands, it was a bright unnatural yellow—like anime hair. That being said, his peekaboo roots, and strands that were laced through in places, were jet black—which had to be his real hair color. Cut short in back and longer in the front so that the red draped over his right eye, his hairstyle gave the impression that the guy was targeting whatever he was looking at. Well, that, and the intense hatred that came from the visible left eye. Yet the oddest part of all was his dyed, arctic blue eyebrows.

Nick started for a snarky Toonami refugee comment until he realized something.

Xevikan's unorthodox hair and eye color represented each of the six primal gods.

For that matter, he was as perfectly formed as Acheron. His features would be considered beautiful if not for the rugged line of his jaw and the sheer ferocity of his presence. He stood with his legs planted and his body tense as if ready to go to war with the entire world.

Xevikan ground his teeth so fiercely, it caused his jaw to tic. "I can't believe *this* is what I'm forced to follow." Sneering his obvious contempt, he slid his gaze to Livia. "Where are the others?"

"They're not here yet."

Xevikan cursed. "Of course not." He turned his sullen glare back to Nick. "Let me guess . . . don't get too comfortable here. This one lacks the same stones as his predecessors? Back into the box we all go?"

Nick went rigid at the insult to his manhood. "Let *me* guess. Xevikan isn't the Babylonian term for *happy optimist?*"

"Swap places with me, Malachai. Just for a week. Then see if you're still up to cracking jokes about it."

Biting her lip, Livia sidled up to Nick. "I don't know, Xev. . . . This one might let us ride."

Xevikan scoffed as he lifted his hood and covered his features again. "Get it over with. Send me back." There was no missing the relegated pain behind those words. The raw anger.

As much as Nick hated to admit it, Xevikan's resignation to an existence that sounded deplorable brought out his compassion. When his father and Kody and the others had talked about the ušumgallu, he'd envisioned heartless creatures like the hell-monkeys or Adarian, who lived to brutalize others. Scarred and jaded adults who had no ability to feel for anyone other than themselves. But Livia and Xevikan didn't look any older than his group of friends, or Acheron.

They seemed . . .

Human.

Vulnerable even.

And that made him very curious about them. "So, Xevikan, which member of my merry band are you?"

Sighing heavily, Xevikan crossed his arms over his chest and stood as rigid as a statue. "What difference does it make?"

Livia answered for him. "He's your Šarru-Dara, who reigns over blood and fire."

Suddenly, Xevikan threw off his hood again and cocked his head as if listening to something in the ether. He cut a harsh stare to Livia. "Hear that?"

"What?"

His skin turned as translucent as Nick's had done when he'd been in the future. Lightning appeared to flash all through his body before his skin tone returned to normal. "It's our enemies. They're coming for the Malachai."

"How do you know?" Nick asked.

"Xevikan is the oldest šarru we have. And he was the first. He knows more than any of us."

As Livia spoke, Nick saw something flash in his

mind. It was an image of Xevikan in armor, with wings, fighting alongside Nick's demon form. But he wasn't sure if it was an image from the future or if it belonged to the memory of a previous Malachai.

Xevikan growled before he charged at the wall and vanished through it.

Nick looked to Livia for an explanation.

"He's after the Arelim who have come to claim your human's body."

"Then why are we still here, wasting time? Let's go!"

She shook her head. "You're safer here."

"Yeah, but if they kill my body, I'm screwed. I need that."

"Oh." Her nonchalance might have been amusing if his life didn't depend on her quick action. She took his arm and teleported them back to the bedroom where Nick Two had been treed by her spider form.

Unfortunately, there was no sign of him now. Nick started to ask where he was when he heard a loud crash from the first floor.

He ran for the stairs and tore down them as fast as he could.

As bad as the battle had been in Acheron's house in the alternate future, it was nothing compared to this fight. Nick tried to join his friends against their attackers, only to learn he couldn't. Since he didn't have a body, their enemies couldn't see him at all. And no matter what he tried, he couldn't harm them.

This was so irritating. He couldn't stand not being able to help them.

Caleb fought against two of the armored Arelim while Zavid held three more off the other Nick, who was even more worthless in this battle than he was. At least he wasn't crying and whimpering on the floor.

Xevikan was bleeding badly while he fought a small group with Simi at his back. But not even the Charonte could make much of an impact on the Arelim. They were incredible warriors. Unlike anything Nick had seen before. It was as if they'd been born for nothing but battle.

Without a word, Livia ran to help Zavid protect Nick's body from Ameretat. He was a beast as he tried his best to kill Nick Two.

"Hand over the Malachai and we'll leave."

Nick Two whimpered for mercy and cowered in the corner, behind Zavid.

Caleb scoffed as he kicked back the Arel in front of him and turned to fight another. "Not going to happen, Ameretat. We will defend him to our bitterest ends."

Ameretat raked him with a sneer. "Why?" he asked incredulously. "I know the future, Malphas. He will kill you one day. Brutally."

"There are worse things than dying."

Ameretat arched a brow. "Such as?"

"Living with the knowledge that I betrayed someone who trusted me. I'm not that kind of demon, Arel."

"Then the End Times begin."

Nick rushed past them to his body. He tapped Nick Two on his shoulder. Unlike the Arelim, his double had no problem seeing him.

"Give me back my body."

"If I knew how, I would. Believe me. I don't want to be here. I just want to go home."

Boy, did he know that feeling. Inclining his head to him, Nick summoned everything he could and then tried to walk into his body. For a few heartbeats, he felt an electrical current rush through him as if something was happening.

But as quickly as he felt it, it was gone, and he was still separated. Dang it all!

"Could you at least put up some kind of fight?" he said to himself. "Help out my friends, who are about to be slaughtered while they protect you."

"I don't know how."

Nick was flabbergasted. "Big Bubba Burdette's your father and you don't know how to throw a punch? Seriously?"

"I was never allowed to fight. My mother wouldn't let me."

Rolling his eyes, Nick heard a strange gurgle coming out of Livia. He turned to see her falling to a sword stroke as a group of Arelim brutally attacked her.

They were losing this battle. And there was nothing he could do. He didn't have his grimoire. His dagger.

Kody.

His body.

Nothing.

"Simi!" Caleb snapped. "Behind you!"

She turned and barely ducked a blow that would have beheaded her. Breathing out a stream of fire, she tried to barbecue the Arel, but they were too fast and too well trained. Not even the Charonte could make an impact.

Where's a sawed-off when I need one? As tight as they were fighting, one blast would take out at least three of the Arelim.

For that matter, a stick of dynamite. Heck, he'd settle for a jug of Clorox.

A can of hair spray and a lighter . . .

It just wasn't in his genetic code to go down without a fight. Nick manifested a fireball, but unlike before in the other realm, these wouldn't leave his hand here.

Xevikan disengaged his opponent to help Zavid cover Nick's body. He cast an angry glare at the disembodied Nick that accused him of being as useless as he felt.

Ameretat tsked at Xevikan. "You never could choose a winning side."

Backhanding the Arel in front of him, Xevikan snorted. "Win, lose, or draw, if it's opposite of you, I consider it a definite win."

Ameretat raked him with his distaste. "You think it was painful when they ripped out your wings? You haven't met misery yet."

Xevikan scoffed as he turned to fight his verbal tormentor. "I already kissed that bitch this morning. Trust me, anything your pathetic kind does in comparison is a mother's tender loving touch."

Ameretat head-butted Xevikan and stabbed him through the side. He knocked Zavid away before he grabbed Nick Two and held a dagger to his throat.

Nick and the others froze instantly.

"Stand down," Ameretat ordered them all. He turned his glare to Simi. "And drop your barbecue sauce, demon."

The look in her eyes said that she wanted to send out a blast of fire for him. Just as Nick was sure she would, she knelt down and placed her barbecue sauce bottle on the floor.

Simi tucked her wings down. "You an evil bad

thing. The Simi's going to enjoy the day she gets to eats that big old head of yours."

"Please don't hurt me," Nick Two sobbed as he tried to pull Ameretat's hand away from his throat. "I just want to go home to my parents. I don't understand why I'm here. I can't hurt anyone. I've never hurt anyone."

"Shh!" Ameretat snarled in his ear. "You don't speak!"

Caleb took a slow step forward. "Let him go, Ameretat. That's not the Malachai you're holding."

"You think I don't know that? But it is his body. His blood. His heart."

"Yeah, and his shoes and shirt. What's your point? None of that holds his power. That stays with his soul."

Ameretat stepped back, dragging Nick Two with him. "But we both know his power without his blood is weak at best. And without his heart . . . he's nothing more than a blind pup who can't even find his mother's teat to suckle."

Nick screwed his face up in distaste. So not the

image he wanted in his head. *C'mon, Caleb. Pull out one of your miracles. Blast him through the wall.*

Instead, the daeve kept talking. "You know you can't kill him. It'd destroy the balance."

Ameretat shrugged. "Everything will eventually end by his hand, anyway. What difference does it make if it's now or a thousand years in the future? Either way, we all die."

"Please!" Nick Two cried. "Just let me go. I'm not going to hurt anyone."

"Oh shut up!" Ameretat plunged the dagger straight into Nick's body.

Nick gasped as pain exploded through his chest while he watched the other Nick sink to the floor. It burned and ached so badly that he could barely breathe.

It's over. I'm dying.

And there was nothing he could do.

Ameretat stepped back from his body and smiled at the others. "We've done it. We've ended the reign of the Malachai! Forever!"

"No!" Livia shrieked, crawling toward Nick's body.

Xevikan and Zavid stood motionless as the Arelim withdrew. Simi made her way to Livia and they tried to heal Nick Two.

But there was nothing they could do.

Simi pulled the knife from his heart and tossed it aside. She gathered him into her arms so that she could rock him while he bled out. "Shh, don't cry, little human. You go home soon and everything be okay."

Coughing and wheezing, Nick Two clung to her while he wept.

Nick met Caleb's gaze. At first, it was stone cold. Then, as Nick began to fade away, a slow, insidious smile curved Caleb's lips. Nick couldn't believe it. Caleb was actually happy that he was dying. And here he'd mistakenly thought they were friends. Family even.

Yet in the end, Caleb was thrilled to see him go.

Tears filled Nick's eyes as he realized all the things he'd miss. All the things he'd planned to do that he would never be able to do now. All the things he should have said to the people who mattered in his life that he'd let go unsaid. But the worst was the pain he knew his mother would feel once she found out he was gone.

She'd be alone in the world, with no one to watch over her.

And in that moment, he truly understood the love Kody must have felt for him. It was one thing to have someone say that they loved you, it was another to actually understand the sacrifice they'd made for you.

To know absolute grief and true regret firsthand.

Nick glanced over to Xevikan as his words to Ameretat about misery became crystal. In that moment, the magnitude of their shared pain hit him hard. They were all puppets and pawns who'd been placed into a game none of them really understood. A game with no rules and no boundaries.

Winner take all.

If I could have one more day, I would so make it count.

Death brought clarity. And in that moment, Nick realized that what he missed most was the fact that he'd never see Kody again. Never have a chance to prove to her that he could be more than what he'd been born for.

That even he, Nick Gautier, could defy his cursed destiny and become the man she and his mother thought him to be. Now he would never be able to do better for them.

Game over.

A tear slid from the corner of his eye as the darkness he'd fought so hard against claimed him for the final round.

CHAPTER 19

Nick felt himself falling down another abyss. And with each second that passed, his stomach cramped more. After all his best efforts, he was headed south instead of up to the Pearly Gates. It figured.

Man, would his mom be disappointed after the number of masses she'd dragged him to. The only thing all that Sunday genuflecting had gotten him was really strong leg muscles.

But then he hadn't lived the most perfect of lives. And he only had himself to blame for the decisions that had brought him here. The saints knew, his mom had definitely done her best to keep him on the straight and narrow. As the old saying went, there was a reason why there was only a single stairway to heaven, but an entire highway to hell.

Finally, he stopped his free fall. For once, he didn't slam into anything. It was actually a gentle landing that didn't jar him at all. Well, at least hell wasn't as hot as they'd told him it would be.

Taking a deep breath for courage, he opened his eyes to face the devil on his own turf.

Nick scowled as he stared up into a familiar gaze. "Dog, Satan, you look a lot like a demon friend of mine. Are you related to Caleb Malphas?"

"Simi, fetch that dagger. I'm going to stab him again. Preferably somewhere that'll count."

Simi tsked as she moved to stare down at Nick, too, and rub his cheek in a motherly fashion. "You don't want to do that, Akri-Caleb. You gots a big enough mess to clean up already. Why you want to add more nasty blood to it?"

Stunned and confused, Nick glanced around the room. He was flat on his back, in Caleb's house. "I'm not dead?"

Xevikan shook his head and made a sound of supreme disgust. "*This* is our Malachai?" He scowled at

Livia. "Please, gods, someone tell me this is some kind of sick joke."

"Not a joke." Caleb offered Nick his hand. "C'mon, Cajun. Now that you're whole, we need to get you up and over to holy ground to complete the ritual before we're interrupted again."

"What ritual?"

Xevikan lifted his hood and concealed his face. "Putting us back in our boxes."

Taking Caleb's hand, Nick allowed the demon to pull him to his feet. "I'm behind a level here. Anyone got the cheat code to catch me up?"

Caleb rubbed at his bruised jaw. "It wasn't until Ameretat grabbed your body that it dawned on me that if you died, the foreign soul would leave this realm, and with your essence here, it would naturally return to its vessel. . . . And so it did."

Simi grinned. "When it did, Akri-Caleb healed your body."

Heck of a gamble the demon had taken with his life. "You had no doubt it would work?"

Caleb looked about nervously. "No . . . none whatsoever." Yeah, that robotic tone called him out.

"You're such a liar."

Laughing, Caleb shrugged nonchalantly. "Only an idiot tells a Malachai a truth he doesn't want to hear."

"Yes, but I could learn to love that idiot."

"Sure you could." Caleb narrowed those dark eyes on him. "Seriously. Are you all right?"

Nick cocked his head as he took a moment to savor the fact that he was alive and back to a height he was used to. Yeah, he much preferred this vantage point. He'd even take the scar above his eyebrow and those despised "cute" dimples his mom was always begging him to flash. And though he was a little dizzy, it wasn't so bad.

But there was one thing he definitely wanted to check on.

Holding his hand up, he manifested a fireball in his hand. "Oh yeah. Missed you, baby." He clenched his fist and extinguished the flames then kissed his hand and grinned. "Where's my mom?"

"Bubba, Mark, and Menyara are guarding her at Bubba's store."

Caleb's words stunned him. While his mom loved

him and Menyara, she was no fan of Bubba or Mark. "She's okay with that?"

"Not really. Told she attempted to claw out Mark's eyes when he made the mistake of trying to explain to her why she couldn't see you in the midst of what the weather people are calling Tropical Storm Lacy."

"Beautonius." Nick frowned as he took in the blood covering his defenders. Each one of them had taken a beating for him and he was grateful for their loyalty. Heaven knew, they didn't have to. "Do we need to get y'all to Sanctuary for Carson to look at and patch up?"

"What do you care?" Xevikan snarled from the bowels of his hood.

Caleb stepped between them. "He cares."

Grimacing, Livia pressed her hand against the cut she had across her stomach. "It's nothing. Really. We'll live." She glanced at Xevikan. "We always do."

Nick inclined his head to her. "Thank y'all, by the way. You didn't have to help."

Xevikan scoffed. "Of course we did. It's what we do. Bleed for the Malachai."

Nick looked at Caleb for an explanation. "I thought

411

the ušumgallu were crazed killers who would tear the world apart without me."

"Without you, they would. They're your rabid attack dogs, Nick." Caleb glanced at them in turn. "They require a firm hand on their leashes, otherwise they have a nasty tendency to turn on their masters. It's why the Malachai keeps them contained."

"Yeah, but that's not what they've shown me. They've been really decent . . . to all of us. Heroes, even."

Livia arched her brows as Xevikan lowered his hood to stare at him with an unsettling intensity.

Caleb shook his head. "No, Nick, don't even think what I know you're thinking. Trust me, they're animals who need to be kept caged."

"Careful, daeve," Zavid said in a low tone. "You're treading dangerous ground."

Caleb ignored him. "Nick, I've got history with Xevikan. You cannot trust him. At all. He will betray you. It's why he's marked *and* cursed."

Xevikan had no reaction to those words at all. It was as if he expected nothing else.

Nick met that cold, rusty-green gaze. "One thing

Acheron and Kody have taught me. There's always two sides to every story. What's your version?"

Only then did he look at Caleb. Something odd and painful passed between them. "*I* was the one who was betrayed and given a fate and punishment worse than death." Bitter rage radiated in that thick accent.

Nick didn't know what their history was, but he couldn't punish someone who'd bled for him. Someone who hadn't hesitated to defend them all.

Even Caleb, who seemed to hate him. Surely Xevikan couldn't be that bad? Or else he'd have stayed out of the fight and let the Arelim have them.

"If I keep you here, do you both swear to protect me and mine? And by mine, I mean those I hold dear, including Caleb, Zavid, Kody, Simi, and crew?"

"Nick . . ." Caleb growled in warning.

Ignoring him, Xevikan narrowed his eyes suspiciously. "You would trust us, Malachai?"

Nick touched the St. Nicholas and St. Christopher medallions his mother had given him that he kept around his neck. "I'm willing to go on a little faith."

Livia smiled. "I knew I liked you better than

Adarian. I'm in." She threw herself against Nick then kissed him.

Nick quickly disentangled himself. "No offense, there will be none of that while you're here. I'm spoken for." At least he hoped and prayed he could still say that.

"Oh. Sorry." She sedately straightened herself.

Nick turned his attention to Xevikan, who had yet to commit. "What about you?"

He looked at Nick's outstretched hand as if it offended him. Just when Nick was sure he was going to tell him to stick it in any available orifice, he nodded and shook it.

"Until you betray me, Malachai, you have my loyalty."

Caleb cursed then mumbled under his breath. "I knew I should have killed you when I had a chance. I don't care what your daddy or your test scores say . . . moron."

Nick turned to face his irritable compadre. "C'mon, Caleb. Would you really have done that to them?"

He looked past Nick to lock gazes with Xevikan. "In a heartbeat. And in his case, I'd have sealed the case for eternity so that no one could ever open it again."

Xevikan said something to Caleb in a language Nick couldn't translate.

Caleb snorted. "Pray I don't take your proverbial hatchet and bury it someplace fatal." He indicated Nick with a tilt of his chin. "Can we finish the ritual before any more of your friends show up?"

"Sure. What do we need to do?"

Caleb glanced to Simi. "Sim? Can you do me a favor and watch this crew while I take Nick to the cemetery?"

"Absolutely, Akri-Caleb. We can have an ice-cream and barbecue party while you quality akris take your time and do what's you gots to."

Caleb still looked constipated as he swept his gaze around to Zavid, Livia, and Xevikan. "I weep that I'm going to live to regret this." And with that, he vanished with Nick in tow.

Simi turned to them with a bright, fanged smile. "So who be hungry?"

"Me!" Livia said enthusiastically. "Can we really have food?"

"Oh, she-demon . . . Akri-Caleb like his food almost as much as the Simi. You come on, child, and let the Simi educate you on the best eats in New Orleans!"

Xevikan hung back as the women left.

When Zavid started after them, he pulled him to a stop. "What's the deal with this Malachai?"

"I don't know. I just joined him myself. But he seems level. Decent, even."

He wasn't so sure about that. He didn't believe in decency anymore. From anyone. "He's with a half-daeve turncoat, a Charonte, and an Aamon, and you don't find that off?"

Zavid laughed. "Wait until you meet his Arel girlfriend, lunatic mother, and the two human homicidal maniacs he calls family. Buddy, everything about the Malachai ain't right."

Xevikan screwed his face up as he digested those incomprehensible words. "The Malachai has a mother and he hasn't eaten her?"

"No. He worships the ground she walks on."

That was even more peculiar to him than this house they were in.

Without another word, Zavid headed after the women.

Still baffled, Xevikan took a moment to strengthen the spell shielding Malphas's home. Although why he wasted his own powers to protect someone who hated him, he had no idea.

But then, they were family.

Or at least, they'd been born so.

Nick shivered from the cold rain that poured down on them while they stood in the center of the dark cemetery. The sharp winds tore at them with an almost hurricane force. "So what is it with you and Xevikan?"

Caleb paused to look up while he was anointing the circle with the oils he'd brought. "I was one of the judges who had his powers and wings stripped."

Nick's jaw went south. "What? Why?"

Caleb returned to sanctifying the circle. "He betrayed his oath, his brethren, *and* his family. He should have been put to death. It's what I lobbied for."

Man, that was harsh, and it wasn't like Caleb to be

so heartless. Not without a good cause. "What exactly did he do?"

Caleb's eyes turned to a demonic orange that glowed in the darkness. "He snuck our enemies inside our walls and allowed them to lay waste to everything we held dear."

Nick felt sick as he realized what must have happened. "Is that how your wife died?"

"I don't want to talk about it, Gautier. Suffice it to say, he's not to be trusted. Not for anything. And definitely not with anyone you want to keep alive."

Nick knew he should leave this topic alone, but he couldn't. He wanted to understand what would make someone do something so horrific. "Did he say why he did it?"

Caleb stood up and glared at him in the darkness. "Does it matter? *Really?* Would you put your mother in harm's way for *any* reason?"

No. He doubted he'd even do that for Kody.

"*That* is what Xevikan did. He allowed our innocent families, *his* innocent family, our children, to be slaughtered while they slept. In cold blood. And *you*," he sneered the word, turning it into the vilest of insults, "have embraced him as a brother."

"Because you didn't share any of this earlier."

"Would it have mattered?"

"Probably . . . Maybe . . . Yes. Yes, it would have. Why didn't you tell me this?"

Caleb growled. "I don't know what's worse. Your humanity or your demonkyn. Both are liable to kill you and get the rest of us slaughtered in the process. Would you just listen to me once in a while when I try to tell you something?"

Nick rolled his eyes. "Gah, you sound like my mother."

"And you sound like an idiot."

That went over him like a bucket of ice. For a moment, he almost lashed out at Caleb. Only the fact that he knew the demon was in pain kept him from hitting him. "I don't have to take this from you, Cay. I really don't."

Caleb slung the oils out and threw his head back so that he could let loose a bellow that shook the massive tombs around them even harder than the thunder did. His soaking-wet skin mottled from human into its demon orange. His black wings shot out as he gave in to a rage the likes of which Nick had never seen before. Caleb was always in control. Always calm in any crisis.

But this . . .

This was a terrifying reminder of what Caleb really was.

Deadly.

And it was several more heartbeats before Nick realized the demon wasn't really angry. Caleb was crying. His agony reached out and wrapped itself around Nick like it was his own.

Wanting to comfort his friend, Nick approached him slowly. "I'm sorry, Caleb. I didn't know."

His breathing ragged, Caleb glared at him while the rain poured down over them both, drenching them. "Of all the people in all the worlds, you picked the one being I truly cannot stand. The one whose name makes me sick to hear or to say. And it's one I cannot banish from my nightmares no matter how hard I try."

"And again, I'm sorry. You know I would never hurt you. Not intentionally."

Caleb let out a tired breath as he wiped at the tears on his cheeks that blended in with the rain. "Why are we fighting?"

"Because I did something stupid . . . again."

"No, I'm not talking about that. I'm talking about *this*." He gestured at the ritual he'd started. "Why do we bother, Nick? Really? Ameretat's right. In the end, you will destroy everything anyway. All we're doing is delaying the inevitable. Why not stop our suffering now and just get it over with? Let the dark powers take it all."

Nick was aghast at the mere suggestion. Yes, Caleb was hurting, but you didn't throw everything away over a painful past. You didn't just quit a fight because you got a bloody nose. No matter how bad it stung, you shook your head, got your bearings, and fired back with another punch.

Surely, Caleb of all beings understood that.

"Because this is bigger than just us, Cay. I saw that when I died. This isn't about you and me or even Xevikan. This is about billions and billions of lives. If I don't stop myself from becoming the Ambrose, it's not just this world that will end. It's *all* of them. Everything unravels. *Everything.* And you're right. It's hard to get up every day when you know you're going to be slapped back down. Hard to make yourself go face the people who hate and mock you. It's hard to find dignity in a world that hates you and begrudges you every breath you take. But you know why we do it?"

"We're stupid?"

"No," Nick breathed. "We do it for those tiny moments when the world opens up and we're no longer alone. Those moments when we realize that we aren't the center of the universe, but to one single person, we're their entire existence. We are what they live for and we matter to them more than anything. No matter how hard we get knocked down, we stand back up, and we face the darkness that's inside us and we raise our fist at it and tell it, not today. You won't have me yet. I won't let you take that last bit of my soul."

Caleb shook his head in denial and turned away.

But Nick wouldn't let him. He pulled his arm until their gazes locked. "You still care, Caleb. In spite of everything you've been through. I've seen it. I know it. You're wounded and you're hurt. We all are. But we've made our own screwed-up family of misfits out of the chaos that is our life. You. Me. Kody. Menyara. Simi. Acheron. Bubba. Mark. Kyrian. My mom. We have bled, inside and out, for each other. And yes, all of us will die eventually, but that isn't what matters. What matters is how we live in the interim. We don't fight for ourselves. We fight for who and what we love. And if there's any chance to save them, we have to take it. Because they deserve nothing less than our absolute best, and by all the gods of all the universes that's what I plan to give to you and the others. My absolute best. Always."

For several seconds, Caleb said nothing as the thunder rolled around them. Finally, he glared at Nick. "I really effing hate you, Gautier."

Nick grinned at him. "Yeah, me, too."

Grabbing his hand, Caleb yanked him into a bro-hug. "We will get Kody back, Nick. I swear it."

"I'm going to hold you to that." Nick clapped him on his shoulder then stepped away. He gestured at the mess Caleb had made. "So have we completely ruined this? Do we have to start again?"

Caleb shook his head. "It's done. You just need to stand in the center and assume the rest of your powers."

Nick arched his brows. "*All* of them?"

He nodded. "And try not to set the world on fire. Definitely don't make my head explode."

"Great way to build up my confidence, brother."

"I have faith in you."

Coming from Caleb, that said a lot.

Nick took a deep breath and walked to the center, where Caleb had used the oils to draw the Malachai emblem in the rain. He raised his fist high in the air as lightning lit the sky above them. "By the power of Grayskull . . . I have the power!"

Caleb groaned. "By the power of Grayskull, I'm going to cleave your skull from your shoulders if you don't take this seriously."

Lowering his arm, Nick snorted. "Dude, you've seen my screwed-up life. I take everything seriously." He winked at the demon, then used his powers to transform from human to his Malachai form.

Nick stared down at his marbled black and red skin. He would never get used to seeing that. "Tell me I'm better-looking as a demon than you are."

Caleb rolled his eyes. "You're not my type, Gautier. I think you're uglier than a three-toed warthog, and Mark after a four-day swamp zombie hunt."

"Ah, man. Now that's just plain mean."

Caleb shoved at his shoulder. "Get on with it before I get hit by lightning."

Sobering, Nick cleared his throat before he spoke the words he needed to seal off the rest of the ušumgallu. *"Ahira, ahira, esh'in ay. El ee, el loh door* . . . duh . . . d . . ." Crap, he'd forgotten already.

"Dor ey uh."

He inclined his head to Caleb. *"Dor ey uh. Dash ee Malachai tirre tirre el lan de um."* Honestly, he had no idea what he'd just said, but no sooner had he spoken the last syllable than the storm began to recede. The rain slowed.

"It's working?" he asked Caleb.

"It's working."

Relieved that he hadn't had to attack Xev or Livia, or anyone else, Nick returned to his human form. "Man, I'm so glad I didn't have to bleed this time. It's a miracle."

"Actually . . ." Caleb pulled the hem of Nick's T-shirt up to expose the scar on his chest where Ameretat had stabbed him. "You did bleed. Most of it's still on the floor of my house, I'm sure."

Nick fingered the scar that formed an intricate pattern that eerily reminded him of Noir's and Azura's symbols. "This isn't the trunk monkey, is it?"

Caleb laughed. "No. It's not. It's a memento from your enemies."

"Yeah, well, at least it makes my heart surgery scar look cooler."

"Speaking of, how do you feel?"

Nick took a minute to consider it. Honestly, it was hard to put into words what he felt now. "Stronger. More powerful . . . like a target."

"You are all of those."

Great. Just what he wanted.

But he was done complaining about it. All the bitching did was make Caleb crankier than normal.

"So do you think the other Nick made it back home?"

Caleb picked up the remnants of his oils and packed them away. "You would know before I would."

Nick started to ask him how, but before he could, he knew the answer. Somehow. "Yeah, he did." He frowned at Caleb. "How do I know that?"

"You're the Malachai," he said simply.

The universal target for everything nonhuman in

existence. A walking trophy that all preternatural creatures would kill to defeat, slay, or enslave.

Up until now, that had terrified him. Yet as Caleb handed him the basket of oils to carry while they headed back to his house, Nick realized that it wasn't so bad.

Yeah, okay, it really was. It sucked. It blew. It was a destiny he wouldn't wish on anyone.

But this was his life, and honestly . . .

He liked it. It wasn't perfect, yet it was all his.

And while it was true that he'd had no choice in how he'd entered this world, and he would most likely have no choice in how he left it, he did control the in-between years.

As his father had said, the Ambrose Malachai would never be forgotten. But it was up to Nick, alone, as to how he'd be remembered.

And from this moment forward, he intended to make every single day count. Most of all, he intended to minimize any future regret.

EPILOGUE

All right, Xev," Nick said, just outside the locked door. "Brace yourself. There's no telling what we're about to walk into. It could be bloody bloody."

"I think I can take it, Mal—"

"Nnh! What did I tell you about using that name?"

"Gautier," Xevikan corrected. "Believe me, I've been in much bloodier battles than this."

"Doubtful. But keep up that bravery. We're going to need it."

Holding his arms out to the sides of his body and shaking them, Nick took several deep breaths for courage then loosened up his neck muscles. Man, he was terrified. But he wasn't about to admit that out loud, and he couldn't delay this any longer.

It had to be done.

He inclined his head to Xevikan. "Here we go." He opened the door and stepped inside.

Nick had barely taken a step before the fiercest beast of all latched on to him with a Velcro-tight grip that no amount of strength could break. "Ma! Ma! Please, you're killing me! I can't breathe!"

Instead of loosening her hold, she only tightened it more. "Boo, I've been so worried about you. Are you all right?"

"Until you choked the life out of me, yeah."

Tsking, she finally stepped back and stared up at him with a joyous smile that lit her entire face. Her long blond hair was pulled back into a wavy ponytail that made her look more like his older sister than his mother. Her blue eyes glistened with unshed tears. "You have no idea how scary it is to be trapped with Bubba and Mark in a storm."

"Actually, it's probably the safest place to be in New Orleans."

She scoffed at that. "Did you know—" Her sentence broke off as she realized Nick wasn't alone. A deep frown creased her brow while she took in Xevikan's height and unorthodox appearance.

Both Nick and Zavid had tried their best to mask the boy's multicolor hair, only to learn that part of his curse was that it couldn't be changed. No matter what they did, the colors bled through.

"Are you Ash's little brother?" she asked.

Xevikan raised a curious brow. "Ash?"

"A friend of mine," Nick explained quickly. "No, Ma. This is Xev . . ." His voice trailed off.

Crap, somehow they'd forgotten to give him a last name.

"Daraxerxes."

Wow, props to the Šarru-Dara for thinking fast on his feet. Not that Nick could have repeated that name if his life depended on it. "Um . . . yeah. What he said." He stepped behind his mom to frown and mouth the name at Xevikan.

What kind of freaky moniker *was* that?

His mom smiled. "That's absolutely beautiful, but quite a mouthful . . . says the woman with a last name no one can ever pronounce or spell correctly, including other Cajuns. Please say it again."

Xevikan repeated it slowly. "Dah-rah Zuhr-cees."

"Dara-zur-zur-cees?"

He grinned at her attempt. "Very good, Mrs. Gautier . . . I'm impressed. You did much better than most."

"Thank you. Your accent is quite lovely, too, but I have no idea where it comes from."

"It's, um . . . I forget in English. Khvrvarn?"

His mother actually squirmed. "I've never heard of it."

Now it was Xevikan's turn to be uncomfortable as he looked to Nick for help, as if Nick had a clue where on a map *that* was. Most days, he could barely find New York state. "Um . . . it's Mesopotamia? The land between the rivers?"

"Oh! Well, don't I feel stupid, now. Sorry."

"No, you should never apologize for such, Mrs. Gautier. I'm the one who couldn't translate it correctly. It was my bad."

His mom smiled again at his colloquialism that sounded extra weird through his heavy accent. "It's always nice to meet one of Nick's friends." She took his hand and patted it kindly.

The moment she touched him, an unexpected tear slid down his cheek. Embarrassed, he pulled his hand away and wiped at it. "Forgive me."

His mom frowned in concern. "Are you all right, sweetie?"

Nick wouldn't have believed it, but the ancient being was as cowed by his tiny mother as everyone else.

Nodding, Xevikan looked about nervously. "I never had a mother so I don't know what's appropriate. Nick failed to warn me that you would be . . . warm and gentle."

"Oh, you poor Boo!" His mother pulled him into her arms and held him tight about the waist.

Eyes wide, Xevikan appeared terrified as he held his arms out, away from her, over her shoulders.

Nick bit back a laugh at the sight of his tiny mother who barely reached mid-chest level on the fierce Šarru-Dara. She had absolutely no clue. "Just go with it, Xev. My mom mothers everything. She can't help herself. And whatever you do, don't take her to a pet store, especially not on adoption days."

Making a sound of irritation, his mom pulled back and rubbed Xevikan's arm. "Are you staying for dinner? I have chicken jambalaya almost ready and there's more than plenty."

"About that, Ma . . ."

She turned toward Nick. "What?"

"Xev's place got flooded during the storm. Do you mind if he bunks here a few nights until it's habitable again?" Or more to the point, until they found him someplace to live.

She drew her brows together into a puzzled expression. "Where's your family?"

"I-I don't have any."

"Then how are you here?"

Nick jumped in with an answer before Xevikan accidentally outed them. "He's on a student visa. Don't worry, Mom, he's not a serial killer. If he was, I wouldn't have him near you. I promise I'll keep him locked in my room. You won't even know he's here, and he's not nearly as messy as I am." At least, he hoped that was true.

She shook her head at him. "Of course, it's fine for him to stay. You know I can't stand to see anyone on hard times. Now let me go check on our dinner before it burns. Y'all get cleaned up and I'll see you in a sec."

Xevikan watched her leave with a longing in his eyes that wrenched Nick's gut.

"You all right, buddy?"

Blinking, he nodded. "I now understand."

"What?"

"Why you are who and what you are." He locked gazes with Nick. And there in his eyes was a quiet longing Nick didn't understand until he spoke a single question. "What is it like to be loved?"

"Don't you know?"

He shook his head slowly.

Nick laughed, until he realized it wasn't a joke. "C'mon, seriously. Brother? Father? Pet? You had to have family at some point. Right?"

"Yes, but we didn't have love. We had honor, obligation, and responsibility. Nothing more."

"Nothing? Is that why you betrayed them?"

His eyes turned as red as his hair. "I did not betray them," he ground out between clenched teeth. "*I* was the one who was betrayed . . . by all of them."

Nick held his hands up in surrender and to calm down the older being. "Okay, sorry. I heard a different version of the events. I'm not judging you. I wasn't there. Consider me Switzerland."

"Switzerland?"

Nick patted him on the arm. "We got a long way to go with your education." He jerked his chin toward the hallway. "C'mon, I'll show you to my room."

Xevikan followed even while he kept waiting for something terrible to happen. For Nick to turn on him and lunge for his throat.

Or bury a dagger in his back.

After all, Caleb had welcomed Zavid and Livia in to stay in his home, but he'd mercilessly thrown Xevikan out of his house and told them both that Xevikan would never be allowed there again.

Though to be honest, everything considered, it was a much kinder expulsion than the last one Caleb had given him. He wasn't bleeding nearly as badly this time.

Inside or out.

"And this is the bathroom." Nick opened the door.

Sweeping his gaze over the room, Xevikan had no

idea what anything inside there was. "I assume you bathe in here?"

"Um . . . yeah."

"Then where's the pool?"

Nick grimaced. "Ah man . . ." He sighed heavily. "We don't have a pool. You bathe in the bathtub or shower." He showed him how to use it. "You do your business in the toilet, use some TP and then flush it or my mom will kill us both. Understood?"

"Understood."

"And you wash your hands here." Nick illustrated how the sink worked and where the soap was kept.

"Got it now. Thank you."

"No problem." Nick headed back to his room across the hallway.

Xevikan took a moment to experiment with the wall switch and lights. He had a lot to learn about this human world. He hadn't been free in more centuries than he could count.

And so much had changed. . . . But for his powers, he'd have no way of understanding their language or anything else. Yet for all his abilities, he had a lot of gaps in his knowledge, as Nick was proving repeatedly.

I will make do. He always had. Still, he felt lost. Unsure. Hatred and anger, he was used to.

Kindness . . .

That was scary stuff.

Turning the light off, Xevikan headed back to Nick's room, to find him on the phone.

"Caleb, there has to be some spell or something to bring her back. I don't care what it takes. We can't leave her stranded. I want my girl. I miss her."

"Nick!" his mother shouted suddenly.

He covered the phone with his hand. "Coming, Ma." Glancing at Xevikan, he returned to his call. "I have to go. But we have to find something. Fast. Talk to you later." He hung up.

"Your girl?" Xevikan asked as Nick slid the phone into his pocket.

Nick let out a sad sigh that was nothing compared to the pain in his blue eyes. "Kody was left stranded on the other side when I returned to this realm. She helped me reach home and now there's no one to free her."

He related to that a lot more than he wanted to. It was an awful feeling to be imprisoned in an unknown dimension. Alone. Afraid. Ignorant of its rules and customs. "Is she human?"

Nick shook his head. "A ghost."

That was the last category Xevikan had expected. "Your girl is a ghost?"

"Yeah, I know. My life is really messed up. And so are most of the people in it. But I don't mind." Nick swallowed hard. "I wouldn't have made it back here without Kody, and I can't leave her there alone. I owe her too much to just walk away while she needs me."

"I see."

Nick headed for the hallway, then paused as he realized Xevikan wasn't following after him. "Something wrong?"

"I need a minute. Is that all right?"

"Yeah, sure. We'll be in the kitchen. Don't wait too long or I might scarf up all the jambalaya. No one makes a better batch than my mom."

Xevikan waited until he was alone before he shut the door. As he turned, he caught sight of himself in the dresser mirror and winced. No wonder Mrs. Gautier had reacted to him the way she had. He was hideous like this. His family had left him with nothing.

Not even his dignity.

If only they'd listened. But no, they'd been too angry to hear anything more than their own condemnation. He'd been used and then thrown away as if he was nothing more than useless, unwanted rubbish.

Nick and his mother, alone, had treated him as if he mattered. They had finally given him a modicum of dignity. He wasn't sure how much of his powers were left. His family had stripped the majority of them from him when they cast him out. And the Malachai who'd enslaved him had taken his own toll on them.

But maybe, just maybe, he might be able to repay Nick's kindness.

Closing his eyes, he mustered as much as he could and allowed his conscious spirit to leave his body and traverse through realms he used to travel effortlessly.

It took several minutes before he was able to gain his bearings. He'd forgotten how dizzying it could be. How disconcerting.

"Kody!" he mentally called, trying to find the right spirit.

"I'm Kody. You are?"

He turned toward the demon and shook his head. "You're not the one I seek."

"But I could be."

Shaking his head at her offer, he drifted away from her and kept searching. It seemed to take forever as he retraced Nick's path to the other side.

He was just about to give up when something struck him hard between his shoulders.

Hissing in pain, he turned toward his attacker, ready to battle. Until he saw the small Arel who was glaring at him. Instantly, he remembered what Zavid had told him about Nick's girlfriend, and it all made sense. "Kody?"

"You are not overtaking this world!" She rushed him.

Xevikan ducked and twisted away from her. "I'm not trying to take over."

"Don't lie to me. You're the Šarru-Dara! I can smell it on you."

"And you are Nick's Kody."

She retreated a step. "How do you know that?"

"I've come to return you to him."

Suspicion clouded her green eyes. "You can't do that. I can't go back there. Ever."

"Yes, you can. I have the power to restore you."

"As what? Your blood slave? Forget it!"

He laughed at her assumptions. "I can't enslave a ghost. You have no true blood with which to feed me."

"Oh. There is that." She screwed her face up as she continued to watch him warily. "Then how can you take me back?"

"I can pull your spirit with mine."

"Only a god can do that."

He forced himself not to react to her words. "I can do it, too." He held his hand out to her. "Trust me, Kody."

"Why should I trust the Šarru-Dara?"

"For the same reason you trust the Malachai."

She snorted at him. "You make all kinds of sense, don't you?"

"Only on occasion." Still, he held his hand out in invitation, waiting to see if she'd spit on him like everyone else. Honestly, he couldn't blame her if she did. Trust wasn't something he was familiar with either.

She stared at his proffered limb. "Swear to me that this isn't a trick."

"Are you willing to believe me if I do?"

"Strangely, I think I am."

"Then I swear. It's not a trick, Kody. I will take you home to Nick."

She stepped forward and placed her palm against his. For a full minute, Xevikan couldn't breathe at the warm softness in his hand. It'd been centuries since anyone had touched him for any reason other than to cause him pain.

First Cherise.

Now Kody.

In that moment, he hated Nick for what he took for granted. Unlike all the ones who'd come before him, the Ambrose Malachai had no idea what it was like to exist in solitude. To be truly despised and betrayed by everyone. To have no friends.

No family.

But Xevikan knew. And it hurt to a level unimaginable.

Unable to resist the impulse, he closed his eyes and

pulled her hand to his cheek to savor the sweet scent of her warm, soft skin.

She shifted nervously. "Um . . . excuse me, Mr. Šarru-Dara? What are you doing?"

He wanted to hold her there forever. But she didn't belong to him. Or even with him.

Opening his eyes, he lowered her hand and pulled her back with him, through the darkness. As he returned to his body, she was almost ripped from his grasp, but he refused to let the others take her.

An act of kindness deserved an act of kindness. It didn't deserve to be heartbroken. For Nick, alone, he would defy them all.

Even his parents.

No one would take this woman from the Malachai. Not without a brutal fight.

And once Xevikan was restored, fully, there would be plenty of paybacks to come. But that would have to wait.

First he had this to take care of.

Finally, he got her through in one piece. Unscathed. He released her hand and left her to stand by the bed as he merged his spirit back into his physical bondage.

He gasped out loud the moment his spirit reunited with his body. He'd forgotten how much pain his wounds had left him with. That brief respite from the physical realm cost him now as he struggled to breathe.

"Are you all right?"

Stumbling against the wall, he barely heard Kody. "I just need a moment."

"You're shaking."

His breathing ragged, he doubled over in absolute agony. It hurt so much, his teeth chattered. No matter how hard he tried, he couldn't bring it under control.

"Are you bleeding?"

He must have reopened the wound on his return. "It'll stop." Eventually. At least the external injuries would.

"Let me see." She pulled at his shirt.

"No!" he snarled, but it was too late. She'd already seen his shame that had been branded into his flesh.

"You're cursed."

He glared at her. "Aren't we all?" He pulled away

and sank to the floor so that he could steady his breathing and acclimate to the pain of his wounds.

"What are you?" she breathed. "Really?"

He met her gaze without flinching. "As you said, my lady . . . Cursed." Finally, the pain overwhelmed him. Before he could stop it, it dragged him back to the darkness he hated with every molecule of his being.

"Hey, Xev, what's keep . . ." Nick's voice trailed off as he opened the door and saw the last thing he expected.

Kody, in the middle of his room.

A million emotions ripped him apart and froze him to the spot as their gazes met and locked. But the most overwhelming one was joy at seeing her there.

How was this possible?

"Are you real?" His voice trembled with the fear that this was another illusion. That he'd reach to touch her and she'd vanish.

Tears flooded those beautiful green eyes. "I'm real." She ran to him and hugged him tight.

Nick trembled as he buried his face in her hair and inhaled the most precious scent on the planet. He rubbed his face against the silken strands. "How? Simi said you couldn't come back."

She pulled away to kiss him, then gestured toward Xevikan. "I don't know how, but he rescued me."

Flabbergasted, Nick released her and ran to check on his new friend. "Xev?"

He came awake slugging.

Nick barely had time to duck out of the way.

Snarling, Xevikan rolled into a crouching position, ready to attack. His eyes feral, he glanced around as if looking for something that wanted to eat him.

"Xev! You're safe. It's me, Nick."

Finally, he calmed down and relaxed even while he remained on all fours. "Did I pass out?"

"Yeah. You okay?"

He sat down on the floor. Leaning his head back against the wall, he closed his eyes. "I can't die."

"Not the same thing."

"Sure it is."

Kody pulled the blanket from the foot of Nick's bed and tucked it around Xevikan. "Thank you."

He licked his lips. "Just repaying a debt. We're even now, Malachai."

Nick shook his head in denial. "No, Xev. We're not."

He laced his fingers with Kody. "What you did for me . . . for Kody, I can *never* repay."

"As I said, Malachai, we are even."

But Nick knew better. And though he didn't know how, he was going to make this right for his newfound friend.

"You want me to bring your dinner to you?"

"I don't want to be rude to your mother."

"Dude, you're bleeding. I don't think you should be moving around right now. Just rest and I'll be back in a few minutes with a plate."

Pulling the blanket tighter, he nodded. "Thank you."

Nick hesitated as he brushed the back of his hand against Kody's cheek. "You want me to bring you some, too?"

"Please. I'm starving."

He gave her a light kiss before he left them alone.

Kody bit her lip as she turned back toward the Šarru-Dara and a weird feeling went through her. He had a presence that was unmistakable and it wasn't just the fact that he was a member of the ušumgallu.

This was very different.

And very scary.

"Nick called you Xev?"

He nodded. "I'm Xevikan."

Absolute horror filled her at the name of a creature who was only half a step less deadly to the world's future than a Malachai.

Please, please, let me be wrong.

"Xevikan," she repeatedly slowly. "Or is it Daraxerxes?"

His gaze snapped to hers and held it prisoner. "How do *you* know my title?"

Kody stumbled back, away from the creature on the floor. *Dear gods, Nick, what have you done while I was gone?*

Her boyfriend had not only opened the gates of hell, he'd just unleashed the most dangerous ancient god of all time.